2084

The Dance of Technology

and Consciousness

© Jayana Clerk, 2019

ISBN: 9781091596603

BISACScience Fiction General

Front and back cover art by Jyoti Thakore

Cover and interior design by Anugito, Artline Graphics, Sedona, AZ, USA. www.artline-graphics.com

2084

The Dance of Technology

and Consciousness

Jayana Clerk PhD

TA

TULS Associates

For

Essence Energy

TattvaShakti

Acknowledgments

Burgeoning technological advances evoked, for me, insights into a human evolutionary march that's connecting all of creation – humans, animals, trees, plants, minerals – inwardly and outwardly – through a convergence of science and spirituality that's moving us through change into our inevitable future. I am grateful to visionary scientists, AI technologists, space researchers, astronauts, and aquanauts for extraordinary creations, and above all, to humanists, philosophers, and all of us fumbling denizens of Earth, for all the patience and compassion we can muster.

On a personal level, I am grateful to Cat Anderson for helping find a way through the maze of the *2084* manuscript, leading the reader, and me, to a clearer vision of the future dance of technology and consciousness. Without her insights and enthusiasm in the sci-tech side of sci-fi, *2084* would have remained fuzzy.

Jan Teegardin, a long-time yoga connection, surprised me with her email-relays on current tech-strides ranging from medical robotics to buying boats with Bitcoins. "Can't wait to read your book! Look what is happening now – your fictional *2084* could become a fact, girl!" She was a powerful voice supporting me with her excitement and forwarded facts during the creation of this work.

My deep gratitude also goes to long-time friend and always cousin Jyoti Thakore for the cover-art design that captures space for the dance floor of *2084*. She had gifted me a beautiful ceramic wall plate (back cover) with these images years ago, saying "I know not why, I made this for you, connecting two pieces in one art work. Never did it before."

Jean Ford, a former nun and current student of Advaita Vedanta, held me when I got dizzy dancing into the future, and would ask, "What if I don't *want* to dance with technology, with AI?"
"No option," I would say.

Now and foreseeably, I am grateful to all who dance consciously with AI, in all its unfolding forms.

Table of Contents

Preface

It is Here. The Future is.

It's still wrapped in a cocoon, though.

I see through its intricate, convoluted maze, each strand of the cocoon vibrant.

A panoply of scenes roam around, some magically improbable or contradictory, but all carry the constant "hum" of a living, breathing, ever-expanding universe.

These are vignettes randomly connected, or not.

But nothing is isolated. The connectors often are invisible.

They take us from Here to There, from Now into the Future.

Let's enjoy the ride.

1 The Lost Wayfarer

The ocean looked sleepy this morning, caressed by low-hanging foggy clouds. Birds too were taking a longer nap, sensing the Sun was "not yet here." Even dog Marlow seemed lazy, opening one eye to look at the sky and promptly shutting it. A comfortable house, nestled in five acres of foliage, stood alone. The nearest house was at least half a mile away in all directions. That did not make it exceptional.

All houses all over the Earth stood in lonesome glory of varying degrees. In those with three stories – the tallest allowed – people were in closer physical proximity. But regardless of the height or distance of their dwellings, nobody felt isolated. A friendly community of humans, nature, and all living creatures was the new global norm now.

The year was 2084.

A noiseless drone glided out of the garage, programmed by Ella the previous night. This was the first day of school for Anton, her second son. He was three (going on thirteen). When Samir, Anton's father, had given him a Superman cape the day before, as a gift for the first day of school, Anton's imagination flared: "Dada, do you think I'm going to go backward in school and become Superman? It is so *yesterday!*"

Both Ella and her older son, Kumar, the real thirteen-year-old, cracked up laughing. Kumar quipped, "Ho ho ho, what were you thinking, Dada?"

Ella, a pro in genetic engineering, thus aware of the reasons Anton would consider Superman "backward," also wondered aloud. "Really, Samir? Why? You're working on an intergalactic venture. Why the ancient Superman?" Knowing her husband's astute, creative perceptions, she listened for a good answer.

"It's a blessing," said astrophysicist Samir, defending his choice. "The old Superman was the first ancestor of our current dream to reach the outermost reaches of Space. Even the innermost reaches, into consciousness. It is my fatherly blessing for Anton on his first day of school to be the "Superman" for *our time.*"

"You always were original, Samir," said Ella, looking at him with a mischievous twinkle (a little bit of admiration, too).

"Stay Awake." The usual energy call floated in the air around them.

"There you go," said Kumar, still laughing. "The Awake call is backing your blessing, Dada. Let's go, buddy. Can't be late." He picked up Anton's backpack, which was stuffed with the Superman cape, a tablet, and a water bottle.

Anton immediately objected. "I will carry it myself, thank you, bro." Ella and Samir, wondering where Anton had picked up the archaic "bro," shrugged their shoulders. Kumar and Anton walked to the drone that was waiting for them. As soon as they were buckled in, the self-propelled drone launched and followed the pre-set command button "To School."

―᠃ᵛᵗ―

The drone landed in the middle of Central Town Square. All educational centers were in the middle of town, giving easy access to all neighborhoods. Centers for business were in the northeast sector, and those for administration in the southwest.

A stranger, dressed in an unusual outfit, approached Kumar and Anton as they walked from the drone parking area to the main building of the school. The very old man looked lost, from another world, even another time. "Excuse me," he said to the boys, "could you tell me where the nearest café is?"

"No wrist implant?" Kumar asked. The man looked so disoriented, he probably didn't have the latest technology. Everyone, all over the world, had implants in their wrists, with surface displays. Where did this old man come from? Kumar looked at him intrigued, a little cautious.

"I've been walking for hours," the stranger said, in an unrecognizable accent. Was he from another planet? Maybe! Kumar's mind was racing.

Anton, still gaping at the stranger, said, "We'll take you to my teacher, sir. Why don't you come with us?"

The three of them walked together toward the school building.

Kumar was tightlipped, annoyed at his tiny brother's ever-alert, daring attitude. Why could he not keep quiet? Anton observed the strange old man with curiosity. He had never seen anyone so wrinkled, so uncertain. He wondered, as Kumar had, if the stranger had landed from another planet, another time.

~·'·~

"It was in 2020. There was a lot of confusion," the stranger explained intently to John Sargent, the counselor at the school, who'd agreed to talk with the disoriented visitor. "I was nineteen, almost twenty, in Mongolia with my archeology professor and research colleagues. There was an earthquake in California. I lost my entire family – my parents, my brother Jack, and Miriam, my sister. As you can imagine, I was devastated by grief and shock. It made me lose my mind, I guess. I was hospitalized in Mongolia. I refused to return home."

The old man kept shifting his gaze between the counselor's face and the odd glass wall of the room where they were meeting. Indigo-gray shading suffused into the glass kept shifting in intensity, apparently reacting to the sun and clouds outside. Inside the room, with the other three walls painted a pale blue-gray like the sky, the undulating shade made the old man feel he was underwater – a sense that matched his mood.

"So, what about your professor, your research team?" John asked.

"Frankly, I don't recall much about that time." The old man shrugged, paused, and continued. "When I woke up from what I suppose was a long sleep, of sorts, I was with a local family in Mongolia. They took care of me, a herder family with two young girls, ages five and three."

"And then?" John Sargent had been trained to be gently inquisitive, yet was genuinely curious as well. This was a vaguely bizarre situation.

"I lived with the family, helping them, for a couple of years, I guess. But then I *needed* to leave. I was like one of those ancient nomads, roaming around. For some reason I couldn't stop searching for the ancient Deer Stones, also called "reindeer stone" relics, which I'd gone to Mongolia to find. There are plenty of them in the Gobi and Mongolian deserts. In fact, that was our original research project. But by myself, I can still remember I was roaming around, pretty much aimlessly, in some kind of rocky terrain. I found little animals, roots, bushes, underground streams. I survived. Local families helped. I worked in their fields or tended their animals. No complaints. Lost track of time, I guess." The old man still seemed confused, but had begun to have a contented look on his face, remembering.

"How did you communicate with the locals? You had your Idiom?" John asked.

"Yes. That certainly helped in the beginning. Then I didn't have the charger to reboot it. And not all villagers had an Idiom. But hunger and survival have a universal language, you know that. They don't need words. Nor does kindness." It was the confused man's first smile, John noticed, and smiled back.

The visitor, encouraged, continued, "Often, I felt inside that I was reliving my own past, in the past I was searching for in that magical land, the land of the Deer Stones. I felt very much at home, wherever I went." John reckoned this "lost" wayfarer had his finger on his inner "self."

"Years passed by – I lost count. One day I met an archeology team working on a Deer Stone site. They were researchers – Chinese, Turkish, Indian, American. Their professor looked German. They were incredulous when they heard my story. "Welcome to the new world, old man," the professor said, and he kept smiling at me, for some reason. Name was Muller. He asked if I'd like to go back home. I said I guessed I wouldn't mind doing that, but I had no money and didn't want to go to LA anyway. He said not to worry and arranged for me to fly to New York."

"Nobody helped you when you arrived in New York?" John was intrigued.

"Once I was out of the plane, I just kept walking. Nobody asked for my passport. Since I'd lived in New York before, I thought I'd find my way. So I didn't ask for help. By the way, it was an incredibly short flight. I was in New York in less than three hours from Mongolia! But I was shocked – New York has changed so much. I don't recognize anything here."

"So how did you get to our school?" John hoped to help the

old man create some logical sequences, sure that the visitor had *much* to catch up with.

"I kept walking. It seemed I was walking in an endless Central Park. But there were no cars, no high rises. Only single-family homes with acres of land around. Then I saw these two young lads." The old man, relaxing into the cushioned chair, let his voice fade as the memory overtook him and emphasized the dazed look on his face.

"I can fill you in on that, the whole landscape story, later. First let's get you some food," John said. "I've asked our superintendent to come meet you and get you to the cafeteria while I close up a couple of things here. He was as interested as I was, and am, to talk with you. I'll see you at lunch in a few minutes. Oh, here's the super now."

John rose and extended his arm to the weary visitor, preparing to make introductions, and then caught himself. "By the way, the current year is 2084. I'm sorry, but I didn't ask your name, sir."

"Adam Smith. They call me Adam Smith," the old man muttered, still bewildered, turning his blank gaze from his worn shoes to John and the room around, then to the superintendent. He seemed to be trying to wake up from a dream.

2 Three 'M's

"We welcome Anton to our class. Hello, Anton." Sophie reached to shake hands with Anton. All twenty children waved hello with their little palms up in the air and broad smiles on their faces. All except one: Shiraz. He had lost his pet, his ant Tillie, that morning and was still upset. His big sister, Shehnaz, had thrown out his pet ant while cleaning the table at home. She had apologized for her unforgivable, of course unintended, act; but Shiraz's pout refused to budge.

Sophie was the head of Three Ms kindergarten for children ages one to four. Anton had been home-schooled till he was three, and had come to Three Ms to graduate, so he could be admitted to regular school. The huge room looked like anything but a classroom. Wide windows set into a curved glass roofline gave the impression that people in the room were sitting under a tree, a sort of open-air hall. On one of the walls was painted a collage of trees and colorful flowers and birds, with an overlay of the school's mission:

Three Ms
M for mathematics − pure science
M for music − pure art
M for meditation − pure force
Three Ms converge as One Force
The Energy Essence
Stay Awake!

"Anton, could you tell us about yourself and your family?" Sophie asked. "Yes, Ma Sophie," Anton responded, having been instructed earlier by Kumar that all female teachers were addressed as "Ma" and male as "Pa." "My mother's name is Ella, my father is Samir. My brother is thirteen and his name is Kumar. Our last name is Pundit."

"Do you have a cat?" red-haired Amber asked.

"Not anymore. We had Missy, the cat."

"She died?" Amber was quickly in tears.

"No. Missy got too close to Marlow, our dog. My mother says often pets forget who they are. Marlow licked his paws like a cat, and Missy started growling at everybody. So she was sent to Mrs. Boats, who loves cats. She has five already. Now we have only Marlow." The whole class laughed, except Shiraz, still feeling the pain of a lost pet.

"Do you count up to a thousand, and add and subtract?" Melanie wanted to know.

With a twinkle in his eyes, Anton said, "Actually, we all can count up to infinity. After one hundred it's all easy. I do only three-digit additions and subtractions. Do you do more?" Anton was eager to find out how far behind his classmates he was, starting out.

"You're doing well, Anton," Sophie said. "Tell me about music. Do you have a favorite instrument that you play?"

"Flute, Ma Sophie, flute. I love it. Play it day and night whenever I'm not at a ballgame, or doing math."

"Or sleeping, right?" piped in Kent with a shy smile. Sporadic giggles arose.

Suddenly Shiraz called out, "How long can you hold your breath, without thinking?" He was getting interested in this newcomer.

"One minute, sometimes forty-two seconds," Anton replied

and returned the question to Shiraz, "Can you focus longer?" Shiraz shook his head No.

"Thank you, Anton. Okay, everyone, let's start with math." Sophie opened her electronic tablet. Some students opened their own tabs eagerly, others reluctantly, wanting to talk or sing instead. Only the youngest, the one-year-olds, were without tabs; for them, it was a natural naptime, a sort of meditation. They were accustomed to closing their eyes and resting in the hum of voices.

For the active kindergarteners, Sophie sent different additions and subtractions, a different set of sums for each child according to his or her level. They calculated the sums on their tablets. Younger ones counted the colored pebbles that appeared on their screens, then electronically sent their answers back to the teacher. After completing the exercise, each child was required to sit silently with eyes closed, "meditating," till she said "Slowly open your eyes."

That was the routine practice. For Anton, in-class group meditation was a new experience. His big brother had repeatedly reminded him of the proper behavior in class. "It's not your home, remember. Mom and Dad are lenient with you," Kumar had said "twenty times" in two days, lest his little brother goof off on the first day of school. Anton had a lingering smile when he opened his eyes at Ma Sophie's call.

Meditation had become a mandatory practice in all Three Ms worldwide by 2025, having been used successfully in schools and even prisons during the early part of the 2000s. Advanced research in consciousness, which expanded with these preliminary projects, demonstrated that meditative habits considerably enhance an individual's awareness. Soon after its success in Three Ms, all schools had adopted meditation, since improved performance in life in any field – from psychology or painting to sports or Space research, marketing or governance – had been established.

Sophie looked around. "Well done, class. You did your sums well. Does anyone want to share what you saw or felt during your meditation?"

"Ma Sophie," Amber said, "I saw this huge swan-like bird flying, I was on its back." Her amber-colored eyes were fixed on the swan painted on the wall.

"That's awesome," Shiraz said, staring at Amber.

"You must feel wonderful, Amber," Sophie said. "Does anyone else want to share?" All remained quiet, looking at each other to see if anyone was ready to talk.

Anton said, "Ma Sophie, a very bright blue ball kept going round and round."

"That's funny," said Amber. "My swan was headed toward a blue round." All of them listened intently.

Shiraz spoke up, smiling, "It seems like a ballgame. My ball was yellow, gold." The children laughed in delight, and Sophie joined in.

"Stay Awake" floated in the air.

Sophie dismissed the class for lunch break.

"Anton, let me guide you to the cafeteria," Sophie said.

"Thank you, Ma Sophie. My brother is in school, so he took me around yesterday. I know where it is."

Anton headed toward the cafeteria. Sophie waited to see that he was going to the section for Three Ms children.

"Hello, young man, our paths do cross, don't they?" Anton heard a gruff voice and looked up to see the strange old man from that morning, now walking with the school superintendent, also headed toward the cafeteria.

"Hello, sir, are you well?" asked Anton with a curious polite smile.

They shook hands, their eyes deeply staring into each other's eyes.

Both stood speechless. A strange, indefinable energy seared through their beings, young and old: Adam felt young, Anton looked ancient.

As he watched young Anton disappear into the cafeteria, Adam felt a new timelessness, a tremendous new liveliness, in the banners he'd just seen outside the superintendent's office, with words he'd somehow spontaneously memorized, probably because he was grasping at any detail that could tell him where he was, what was happening. Anton's hand had somehow transmitted to him the energy of the banner's quote from Pythagoras: "There is geometry in the humming of the strings, there is music in the spacing of the spheres." Adam wondered what musical instrument Anton was likely to play, since the school obviously focused on this: the second banner had declared that children who play a musical instrument can perform more complex arithmetical operations. The third banner had displayed the school system's philosophy that the three intersecting realities of the pure science of math, the pure art of music, and the pure force of meditation created the one Energy Essence — a philosophy derived from the earliest Three Ms experimental schools a century earlier, created from the traditions of a meditation teacher from India who brought new realities to the West through its younger generations. It was a new world, Adam felt at a deep level — tiny children, in some kind of post-New York, engaged in what used to be hidden esoteric practices and wisdom. He nodded respectfully to the small child and turned back to the superintendent, resuming their guided tour to the cafeteria, making plans to meet again in a few days when the superintendent's schedule opened up, after Adam had rested.

Exhausted as he was, he looked forward to lunch with John Sargent, to see if he could fill in some of the gaps.

3 Adam Smith Adapts

Sipping coffee, letting his food sit for a moment while he delivered the biggest news, John Sargent calmly launched into a general review for the visitor. "Since 2020, when you left home, Mr. Smith, things have changed enormously. The world has turned upside down, inside out. This is the *new* New York City. Formerly, this stretch of land was a part of Connecticut. It's an homage to the original City, an icon of the United States, which was lost in the floods and storms of 2025." John looked down to check details on his wrist pad, then glanced at Adam's reactions.

The stranger was aghast. "New York City was destroyed, lost, drowned?!" Adam's voice came from a constricted throat; his raised eyebrows seemed to shout "Incredible!"

"That was, say, five years after you left. But after the nuclear accident of 2045...." John kept his statements matter-of-fact, without mixing in emotions, so as not to disturb the time-lost traveler even more.

"What are you talking about? *Floods*? And then a nuclear *war*?" The old man was on the edge of his chair, his face contorted with confusion and anxiety, his voice shrill and urgent. "Are we under Communist government? Is Russia ruling the world?"

John laughed heartily, hoping humor would disarm some of the visitor's panic. Adam Smith, out of touch with reality, sounded even to this trained counselor like a crazy old man from another planet. "Oh no, no, no ... at present no *one* country is ruling over any other. By the way, it was a nuclear *accident*, not a *war*. In fact, we have *no countries* anymore. Former nations are now considered 'regions' or 'territories'. The United States is not a *country*, it is a *region*, one of the seven Regional Units – RUs – of the Global Union, which we call the GU."

Dazed, Adam wanted to make sure he'd heard it right. "So China and Russia are also Units, not countries?" He stared at John with wide-open eyes.

"Yes. The entire globe is divided into Regional Units. Professor Muller in Mongolia could arrange for you to come back home easily since the entire world is centralized under the management of the Global Union Council, the GUC."

Letting this unbelievable reality sink in, after a few seconds of silence Adam spoke again. "Now I understand why nobody bothered me in Mongolia in all those years of wandering. Neither did anybody at the airports in China or New York. You call them drone ports now, I guess?" Both men alternated eating their lunch and talking.

After some silent dining, while Adam's eyes surveyed the scenery outside the huge glass walls that surrounded them, he finally asked, "By the way, what is this 'Stay Awake' call I keep hearing? A political slogan, from what you called the GU, or something religious?"

"It's extremely complex at first, Mr. Smith, though I'm sure you'll come to understand it very well. It's neither religious nor political. In fact, it's scientific, based in the recognition of the universal energy pervading all existence. It is a constant reminder for awareness: 'Stay Awake.' It overlays *all* religious traditions, a reminder to all to be *aware, awake, alert*. It sounds all over the world six times a day during waking hours, from five a.m. to eight p.m. in each zone. This has been sounding for the last twenty years, maybe more. Didn't you hear it in Mongolia?"

"I was in a remote desert most of the time," Adam explained. But then he quickly added, "Wait a minute. Now I get it. My herder families waited for the chief's electronic serekh! That was it! Never did understand it. I thought it was some primitive custom. At regular intervals they got this signal, something they called serekh. People regulated their daily activities by that call."

"You know something?" John was excited. "Serekh in the Mongolian language means 'awake'. I just found it on a search site." Looking at his wrist pad, he was really pleased.

"Really? It all fits in now." Adam had been absorbing new information with as much fortitude as he could muster. So much had happened in one day, in less than ten hours! He said to John, "I'm tired. I need to rest. Could you guide me to a place to spend the night?"

"I'll arrange for your stay at the local guest house, not far from here, where you can stay as long as you wish. By the way, if wanderlust prompts you to move again, you'll find such guest houses anywhere on the globe. You'll get food, shelter, and medical help everywhere, at no cost to you." John wanted to make sure Adam Smith knew the basics of living in 2084, especially at his age.

"Does it mean I'll be on welfare?!" Adam nearly shouted, staring at John in total disbelief.

"Why are you so upset? Worldwide, no one suffers from lack of money. All are provided what they need to live. So in a way, we are all on welfare. And it's a good thing, isn't it? It reflects intelligent management by the GUC." John Sargent – speaking of the only world he'd ever known, since he was only thirty-five years old – was proud of this human achievement. Welfare for all. All shared the Earth's resources without private profiteering or control. He could not comprehend Adam Smith's strange aggravation, as if welfare were a detestable condition.

Seeing the blank look of disbelief on Adam's face, he elaborated. "Everybody on the globe – old and young – has food, shelter, healthcare, education, and amenities for travel and community life. People who are a hundred years old, or older, usually need guest houses. That's part of the Gratitude Program in all seven Global Units. We're grateful to so many among the older generations for their service and wisdom. Most of the elders who'd been responsible for the devastation, if they survived at all, had lost loved ones as well as empires, fortunes, and fortresses – even ocean liners. Some are still in extended stays in accelerated-evolution retreats, and some 'graduated' when they transformed. We can afford to be generous in spirit toward them, even if 'service' and 'wisdom' was very late in coming to them. The age for the Gratitude Program varies according to each region. In some places, it begins at age ninety, or earlier. Why are you so shocked?"

Both saw that each had placed a napkin on the table and both were ready to leave. John rose and moved towards Adam's chair, extending a hand to help the increasingly dazed Adam get up out of the chair.

It certainly was a strange "brave new world," Adam thought as he reached for John's helping hand.

＊

John Sargent's assistant, Ng Lee, asked the shaky Adam Smith if he could walk to the drone park, or would need a motorized cart. Ng Lee was to take him to the nearest guest house.

"That's one thing I can do, young man. Walk. That's all I've done in the eighty-four years of my life: walk," Adam said, laughing, to the shocked Ng Lee who'd been sure Adam was over a hundred.

"So what do you do here at school, Ng Lee, what do you

teach?" Adam asked as they made their way to the drone.

"I'm on the tech-support team," Ng Lee said, "We're a team of four, for the entire school system, from K to eight, including the Three Ms preschool."

"So you have other tech-folk, besides you, for the high school?"

"High school?" Ng Lee didn't recognize the term. "After Three Ms preschool, we have the school, from first through eighth grade. After that, university and research, for those who want to go deeper into any field. Many follow their vocational passion. For example, I became a tech-support person, which these days is a pretty comprehensive full-time occupation."

"Of course," Adam said politely. He thought of Anton and his smart brother who had helped him that morning. Maybe everybody is extra-smart now, Adam thought, to be able to graduate from school in eighth grade, at age thirteen or fourteen.

"Here's my drone. Let me help you in, sir." Ng Lee settled Adam into the passenger seat.

Flying over what had been New York City, from 1500 feet up in the air, made Adam speechless. No high rises, no Empire State Building, no shopping malls, no Park Avenue. All he could see were wide lush green neighborhoods, with houses spread out over miles and miles.

"I cannot conceive of New York City without its skyline … no high rises!" Adam said. "It looks like a gigantic Central Park, with tiny houses."

"Oh, we have *Old NYC*, recreated in our amusement park. We love it. The entire old historical city is there, on a smaller scale of course, built by our engineers and tech people." Ng Lee was all smiles. "I often take my children there. They're crazy about the Coney Island roller-coaster ride. *Old NYC* also has one of the best historical museums in the world today." Ng Lee could sing the glories of technology till the cows came home, or drones stopped vibrating.

Adam, after six decades of roaming in the desert on the other side of globe, was trying hard to adjust to the view of a reincarnated New York City gliding below him. "If so much of New York was destroyed by the rising oceans, and all those storms, how come you have such vast green sprawling neighborhoods now?" Adam was mystified.

"If I remember from my first-grade history class, after the floods and climatic disasters, the First Call was the Green Earth project." Ng Lee turned to Adam to see if he was listening or dozing off.

"What do you mean by 'the First Call'?" the groggy passenger asked.

"All destroyed land that could be reclaimed, that hadn't sunk under the ocean-floor quakes or stayed flooded, had to be reclaimed. There was a lot of biotech involved."

"Flying in drones is a strange experience for me," Adam said. "Back in my day, before 2020, drones were unmanned and remotely operated. Nobody travelled by drones. People flew in planes."

Ng Lee's tone was patient, helpful. "Most drones aren't unmanned anymore. We call them drone-planes. It's like talking about a car's 'horsepower', even after cars replaced horse carriages."

They arrived at a large single-story complex beneath them with "Shanti Lodge" written across the roof.

"Here we are, sir. I'll walk you to the reception hall."

Adam quietly absorbed the new world as they strolled toward the entrance of Shanti Lodge.

"Welcome, sir," said the young receptionist at the front desk. Adam profusely thanked Ng Lee, who left after a warm handshake.

"Please have a seat," the receptionist told Adam. He sank into a plush chair.

A few minutes later a concierge approached Adam and offered to guide him around the facility. Adam noticed that no one he'd met thus far looked older than thirty-five, and most were in their late teens or twenties.

Two hours later, after a spa treatment and a sumptuous healthy meal, Adam felt literally reborn. In the community lounge he looked for a newspaper to catch up with lost time.

"Do you have today's *New York Times*, madam?" he asked the woman at the desk.

"Yes, sir, here it is," she said with a smile as she handed him a small electronic tablet. "You'll find world news in all languages on this tab." Adam looked at the palm-sized instrument in his hand, noticing its similarity to pre-2020 cell phones.

Ambling towards the nearest cushioned chair, by a table with a vase of lovely flowers, he tried several buttons on the tablet but made little progress in educating himself about the New World or New York, 2084. He sat and leaned back. He dozed off.

"Sir." Adam was awakened from deep sleep. Somebody was touching his arm.

"What?" Adam stared at the young woman, who smiled gently at him.

"May I lead you to your room, sir?" The girl's voice sounded like a gentle jingle. She began walking a few steps ahead of him, and he was happy to follow.

"The living quarters are at the other end of the complex, sir. Let's take the trolley. It will save time," her jingling voice said.

At the end of the main building was a longer structure, separated by a beautifully landscaped garden and a little pond. Jingling Voice led Adam to his room. Before she could explain the facility and its workings, Adam had collapsed on top of the luxurious king-size bed and was asleep.

Smiling, the girl left quietly and closed the door behind her.

4 Nuclear Accident 2045

The early-morning hour of January 10, 2045, was foggy, cold. The sun had disappeared, or so thought Dimon, twenty-three years old, second in charge at the nuclear plant in Negev, Israel. He was despondent on this bleak day.

Why were his parents so old-fashioned, so close-minded? Holding on to old history and traditions when the world was hurtling into Space with such ferocity! Ironically, his parents were considered progressive in their social circle, and among the Jewish community at large.

They were in love with their country. They named him, their first-born, Dimon, after Dimona, the village known for its nuclear power plant. It was also his great-grandparents' first home upon migrating from India to Israel in 1950, two years after the formation of the nation of Israel in Palestine. Having a nuclear plant in their home town was a matter of national pride for them. Having nuclear energy was also empowering for the new country surrounded by hostile nations. Dimon's parents encouraged him to be a nuclear physicist. He enjoyed it, got his PhD at twenty, and won this highly responsible position at age twenty-two.

Nine decades after the family's arrival, now, in 2045, his parents refused to let him date Ayesha, a Muslim. How could they have a say about whom their son could love and marry in this day and age? In other areas like education, scientific research, and politics, his parents and grandparents were community leaders, but they still managed to carry what he considered to be antediluvian thinking about their son's dating partner!

Last night there had been a shouting match at home. "Muslims are anti-Jews," Dimon's father, Aaron, said in harshly controlled tones. "What kind of children you will raise?"

"And what about our prayers?" his mother, Reba, asked, more softly but still intense. "Who would observe the daily prayer rituals every morning and evening? You? You're a man. Men don't do it. It's been women's duty in our families for hundreds of years, forever." Reba, raised in Israel, still upheld the centuries-old traditions, as taught by her immigrant grandmother.

Dimon had to shout them down. "This is *twenty*-forty-five of the Common Era, mother, not *forty*-five." When he was angry, Dimon addressed her as 'Mother' – not the usual 'Mommy', which had been his first spoken word, a sound that had sent Reba into ecstatic joy at the time.

"Ayesha is not even religious, any more than I am. Just because her grandparents were Muslims, I can't date her? She doesn't care that my parents are Jewish. You must be...." He'd been about to say "crazy," but stopped.

"All right, you can date her," Aaron relented, "but never think you can marry her." Dimon was furious.

~\'/~

Dimon had been hired to assist the chief, Mr. Rabin, at Nuclear Central. It was quite a prestigious position, especially since the deputy position had been given to a young graduate! It required not only a superior technical, calculating intellect, but an intuitively judicious mind. Everybody at college and at the nuclear division admired Dimon's excellence. His family was thrilled by his exceptional recognition.

This morning Dimon saw unusual spots on his monitor, on areas in the region under constant surveillance. Since the facility had been established almost seven decades earlier, various neighbors had entered and left the spotlight of surveillance and automated defense. Heroic efforts had been made to restore and improve the communications and operational equipment damaged by the flooding and storms of 2025, so that any dangerous activity, anywhere nearby, could be detected and responded to – by the robotics and/or by human intervention.

What was that? Dimon's fingers and eyes moved quickly over an array of high-tech gadgets in the control room, one monitor after another lighting up with unfamiliar patterns. Dimon called his boss, Mr. Rabin, using his private code.

"This could be an emergency, sir," Dimon said in a loud, trembling voice. "If the screens are right, we may be facing annihilation. It's *every*where." Dimon's eyes popped, zooming from screen to screen. Then a brilliant dazzle filled one monitor, which quickly went blank, black. And then the sound, an explosion in the distance, another in quick succession, and another, closer and louder. The nuclear roars combined and reverberated in the single remaining split-second of Dimon's awareness. In that instant he heard "I have become Death."

One hundred years after Hiroshima and Nagasaki. History reported that in 1945 few had anticipated the horror of it. Oppenheimer, chief scientist of the Manhattan project that had created the bomb, had said, watching the glowing mushroom, "I have become Death," quoting Krishna's words from the Hindu holy book, the *Bhagavad Gita*.

A hundred years later, 2045, Dimon instantaneously *felt* the same words, never having imagined in all his studies that he would ever experience this agonizing enlightenment.

On a Full Moon night, the Dead Sea looked deader. Dull gray salty waters paled by silver rays cast a weird aura. A solitary visitor, roaming in the night like a living ghost, sighed and stared at the salty puddle. He remembered it had once been a lake called the Dead Sea.

The nuclear blasts the day before had burned, evaporated everything for hundreds of miles around. How could he be alive? With squinting eyes, he tried to look at an object moving toward him at some distance. Was that another man, alive? Was it a ghost? What was that thing moving?

He did not know where he was. The last thing he'd known, he was tending his goats in a remote village.

⁓✶⁓

The whole world woke up "seeing" the nightmare on their phones and tablets: flying and melting bodies, buildings collapsing to ash, disintegrating animals and acres of fields, in the last phone-photos most of the senders would ever take and send, long before the news media relayed them.

The following morning, the devastating news reached Japan first – ironically, since the Japanese had been the first and only victims in 1945 – as the Sun awakened them. Inconceivable satellite pictures of horrifying details flowed into every home from Siberia to Alaska, from Greenland to Argentina and Australia, flashed on each kitchen table of the world. What happened miles away was their own reality, even in the early moments, before the effects circulating in the atmosphere would change the shape of life for them all.

Towns, cities, villages across both hemispheres increasingly succumbed to the devastation of the explosions, drought, floods, diseases, and starvation. Satellite pictures of "the blue green-marble" transformed into gray, black rock. All over the globe, unspeakable agonies tore up communities.

Economies tumbled. Political breakdowns persisted. Millions roamed in search of food, water, and shelter.

Technologically intertwined, with startling new cyber-capacities, the world suffered together. No pain was isolated.

Within weeks, holograms began flashing in the skies around the world. The most overwhelming was that of a grieving mother holding the burned body of a five-year-old child, his skin hanging flailed and loose, eyes bulging, face scarred. Text glimmered under it:

> *Step into the heart of this mother. Tell us if you have not seen this mother where you are. She is everywhere on this Earth, in body or in image and imagination.*

Watching it overhead in England, people cried bitterly. And in China, in Chile, in Sweden, in Australia, all over the world, everywhere.

From America more holographic images floated:

> *No distinction between "us" and "them".*

> *Their pain is ours, and ours is theirs.*

> *We are all One humanity.*

A young poet's song flashed around the whole world in different languages:

> *The tango of Compassion and Suffering is the dance of our life.*

Something shifted, again, in the world-mind of humanity, twenty years after the rampaging Earth had generated floods, earthquakes and storms that had killed millions. The world-mind had struggled to recover. And now this, erupting from what some bitterly recalled had been known as the cradle of civilization. All the false pride of bravado and aggression seemed to have turned to ashes, along with the buildings, the bodies, the farms. Overwhelming compassion for the agony of others became the primary self-sense of the billions who remained. And it kept deepening as more pictures of reality kept streaming in. It was not "others'" pain anymore.

Among the scattered messages that flooded communications from everywhere, it was reported that even hard-core criminals in prisons cried. Some of the reporters who'd specialized in prison work – especially those whose philosophy included the concept that in some ways, especially after the floods, most denizens of Earth were prisoners of a sort – retrieved language from earlier feature stories emphasizing that meditative practices in prison rehabilitation programs played an important part in awakening compassion. These specialist reporters would provide a disorganized roving "think tank" for the creation of a new planetary society, one that arose from compassionate self-awareness, even in the prison of the disastrous times.

As people around the world struggled to make sense of what had happened, across the long course of their devastation, they inevitably invoked memories of the horrors of the floods that now seemed terrifyingly recent.

People remembered that in 2025, the cries of a horrified nobleman in England had been no different from the piteous cry of a fisherwoman in Bangladesh when she saw her sleeping children swept away in the furious watery dance of the bay.

The agonies of the rising tides, of the nuclear ash, had reckoned no race, gender, class, culture, or nation. Millions of lives had been lost, in two great cataclysms and the times between.

Homes big and small, huts, palaces and temples, industries and commerce, art and architecture, museums and academic research centers had sunk under the water. And what was left, or rebuilt, was now being incinerated or irradiated.

5 When We Dead Awaken

The 2045 nuclear cataclysm shattered the entire world into pieces. The interdependent world had become so tightly knit, a disaster in one area impacted all in widening ripples.

A snippet of a New York Times op-ed of August 11, 2045 read:

> *Pandemics, death and pain, the multi-headed monster, crushed to dust all in its path: the rich and the poor of all colors, sizes, nationalities, and beliefs have suffered. The nuclear explosions have been a great leveler. The unspeakable devastation has resulted in unprecedented migrations … in fact, to nowhere. There is no promised land, at least not one that is visible. Interdependence has made national boundaries meaningless, redundant. Chaos prevails.*
>
> *Those who survive wonder if they had a nightmare. Are they really alive? A growing number of survivors have woken up. They have heard the heartbeat of agony.*
>
> *At the deepest core of the dance of death a ray of hope has arisen.*
>
> *Out of this deluge emerges the basic core of humanity: compassion and hope. Visionaries around the world, using their phones, videos, and websites, have decided to meet at Mt, Uluru, Australia. They are men and women of all races and nationalities – scientists, politicians, econo-*

mists, philosophers, religious leaders, social workers, aca-
demics, farmers, traders, musicians and artists, with the
only common trait: compassion.

On August 15, 2045, world leaders from everywhere – the United Nations, the World Trade Organization, NATO, the Americas, the Pan African Nations, the Middle East, and South and Southeast Asian Nations – met near Mt. Uluru in Australia to address the issue of global peace and harmony – which seemed the only alternative to conflict and competition. Key to the discussions was a universal realization that without technology, such an awakening of the shared mind of humanity would have been impossible.

August 2045 became the foundation of "Resurgence," the universal awakening. Plans were drawn, announced, and implemented. Social and community leaders bloomed all around the globe. Research in every field coordinated the interwoven development of innovative ideas, devices, and projects. The world went through a cleansing and regeneration. It was not easy. But it was possible.

Much the way the United Nations was created in 1945, in the exhausted reflective moments after the second world war, a hundred years later the Global Union was born. Those who participated in the design of new forms, beyond national boundaries, would always recall an indescribable feeling of unwavering, irrevocable connection, an ephemeral consciousness that enveloped their awareness and rippled out to all who heard the plans.

The vision was recognized and experienced at first by those who were actively participating, near the center of the new human reality. It was envisioned that over the years, eventually, a shepherd in the remote mountains of Afghanistan or Mongolia, a dweller in the remote rainforests of Brazil or the Gobi desert, the fishermen of Papua New Guinea, would feel the impact.

One of the new-era reporters sent a message about these remote members of the human race, a message that was picked up by most news hubs, in a voice that might have been ignored or silenced in earlier years:

> *Their tiny voices are our source of hope. It has become a collective call of awakening, reaching every dark corner of the Earth. The great leveler Death has awakened the Living. We now know the real truth, the essence of Life.*

A poet from Mali in Africa declared:

> *The daring stride of monster pain*
> *Evoked a reign of compassion.*
> *Awakened, young and old around the globe,*
> *Armored with technology and courage,*
> *Infused compassion into all.*

People not only *read* and *heard* the poet's words, they deeply *felt* them in their beings. All their images – of the world, of themselves – had been shattered. Without the comfortable coverings of delusional confidence in their power over the environment, which lay in ruins, they existed in a raw, vulnerable state. For some, a numbness persisted. For some, the inner and outer annihilation was so total that their bodies gave way into the peace of death. For some, the liberation was energizing. Together they discovered their shared fates, their shared losses and fears. New forms of recognition began to percolate through their battered psyches. Gradually, or in some cases instantaneously, they saw themselves in the eyes of others, saw themselves *as* the others, and the sense of there being any "others" at all began to dissolve. Genuine compassion, an unprecedented emotional and intellectual experience for many, developed an awe-inspiring quality. In small groups at first, then expanding, an awareness of the unity among them, as them, burgeoned into an unfamiliar joy, an openness to move and be moved – a sort of transcendental awareness.

The surviving humanity then declared, "We dead are awake." They had been transformed. They had become beings who could understand the spirit of Mt. Uluru, wanting to live in the new way. They realized the only way out of the agony was to *move up, since there was no room to go farther down.*

The transformation extended deep into all peoples, not just leaders and artists. The floods had been the beginning of the time when all of humanity acknowledged reality and got engaged in global revival programs. Equipped with technologies that had expanded to reach most populations, the enraged and deprived peoples of the world found a new way to survive. Their imaginations lit up in the dire circumstances.

One small community self-generated in the wreckage of a great ship, scattered across a rocky promontory. The ship had run aground in a forest of underwater skyscrapers, its equipment and supplies thrown onto the rocks.

⸝⸜

Sandra Attenborough shifted her weight on the pile of soggy blankets she used for a cushion. Leaning against a gnarled twisted shrub that grew from the rocks, she let her eyes drift to what they were calling a 'harbor', an ocean inlet surrounding them. Her gaze settled on jackknifed radio spires straggling up from the tops of buildings, barely visible above the waves. They seemed as broken as she feared her ankle might be. This sitting, this place, seemed all that remained of life, since the memory of being dragged up the cliffside on top of a duffle bag was only the faintest diaphanous image floating in an illusion she used to be able to call the "past." What in the … were those *dolphins* swimming among the towers? How many days had she sat there, receiving gifts of fresh water and bits of food from the scurrying crowd of people who'd gone inland and sent emissaries to check on her? When should she stop struggling to survive, and just let herself dissolve into this watery new world?

The thought of dissolving suddenly felt appealing. Extremely appealing. Some part of her wondered if she were entering into delirium, maybe dehydration. Strange: it was no longer odd that dolphins were swimming among the tops of buildings. The edges of everything became fuzzy, the objects themselves shifting into shimmers, insubstantial. A bizarre hilarity seized her – again, a feeling like some distant aspect of her that was not her, simply a noticing, in a universe that was made entirely of shifting patterns and colors of light. Her lips curved into a faint smile, knowing she could sit there forever and not care, simply dissolve into the nothingness the world seemed made of in its deepest reality.

She sensed a presence moving toward her from below, and let herself sense it without turning her head to see. When it was very close, she turned and looked up. It was a pair of young children, from the gang who'd formed a team to get things done. Their forms looked fuzzy too, shimmering. Staring at them, wondering if she could focus, or if she wanted to, she gradually sensed their outlines and the package the boy was carrying. From within her, an overpowering and completely unfamiliar love welled up and she felt it rocketing from her eyes into theirs. In their eyes were sparks of recognition and response, a twinkling, a hello-at-last. She pinched off two tiny blossoms from the gnarled shrub and, smiling, handed them to the children as she received the food-and-water ration.

She had only ever sewed on missing buttons or repaired the hem of a couture gown, yet soon she found herself expanding as the seamstress of the makeshift village, able to be helpful even with a damaged leg, still drawing on supplies from the wreckage. A flicker of surprise and relief accompanied her awareness that she was able to contribute in her brokenness, transitioning into her ability to sense that every one of them was broken in some way, still shining, still contributing, with a tenderness originating in the heart that knew no boundaries, infused every wound in themselves and everyone around them. They swapped what they could do or give in exchange for what they needed. Sandra experienced the depth of this sharing in waves of realization, until the notion became obvious, the way creatures and plants exchange oxygen and carbon dioxide.

⁓ᐧᴵᐧ⁓

As they evolved into a complete culture, the people used tools that were handy: words, paint, music, ship supplies, community collectives to help the sick, suffering, and needy — tools of endless variety, supported by scavenged and salvaged electronics, cyber-instruments, and transmission equipment, tinkered together and programmed by young people who'd trained for a completely different future. In the rebellious humor of the time, some joked that they were "reinventing tech support." They already knew that the exponential growth in technology had made it possible to co-create, and now they were finding it also made it possible to empathize: it had been destruction that motivated compassion. It was the victory of the divine in the human — on a small scale at first, as technology caught up with the new mindset, as the healer-bot and barter-bot algorithms were loosed into the system. Two among these survivors, who communicated silently – and who were so adept at disguising their identities in the cyber-cloud that their names are lost to history – knew they had a larger vision in mind for the planet's benevolent, decentralized, electronic future. And that it would develop very very fast.

6 Resurgence 2045

The scene facing the new-world-designers near Mt. Uluru was unprecedented in human history. The earthquakes and rising sea levels from 2020 onward, the 2025 floods and storms, had claimed the lower island nations and many of the thriving cities along the oceans' shorelines around the world. Most financial hubs in each region had been engulfed. The 2045 nuclear accident was continuing to destroy physical and organizational infrastructures worldwide.

The idea that the entire world, represented by delegates, would meet in one place in the chaos was called miraculous. A host of surviving wise minds from everywhere congregated in Australia – many in person, most through technology and social networks that were intermittently operable.

It was like a global family gathering, deliberating the next move, each aware of the others' pain. Hope and firm intent guided each heart and mind. "None used the word 'soul', but each was speaking from there," said a wise old Aboriginal woman in the crowd, witnessing the unusual event near her sacred Mt. Uluru.

Spurred by the natural human instinct of preservation, extended from "me and mine" to "all," the gathering reformulated the code of civilization. Since former national boundaries had been wiped out by the devastation caused by the watery takeover of 2020 – 2025 and the nuclear disaster of 2045, the gathering came to a consensus that each former country would be named a

"Regional Unit" (RU) of the Global Union (GU).
The new Global Union had seven Units:
Unit 1 North America
Unit 2 South America
Unit 3 Europe and Russia
Unit 4 Middle East including Turkey,
       the -Stans of the former USSR
Unit 5 Africa
Unit 6 Asia: East, Southeast, and South Asia
Unit 7 Australia/New Zealand and the Pacific Islands.

Now people of the world were global *denizens*. Old national identities were retained only as *cultural* identities, not citizenry. Each Unit kept its old name, its art, literature, music, seasonal celebrations, its regional customs and traditions. Local languages continued to grow, interacting with each other, as they had since the beginning of time. Now AI technology was the great enhancer.

At the pragmatic level, a first priority, coordinated among all Units, was treatment of all life to recover from the radiation challenges from 2045. Biotech interventions and genetic-repair research were among the urgent responses that would change the course of human biological evolution.

At the level of the newly global collective consciousness, a message of "Stay Awake" floated in the air every four hours during waking hours in all Regions, a mandatory global practice documented nowhere! It was universally honored, but nobody found a written record of it anywhere in the world. Nobody challenged it.

"Stay Awake" was a universal call. Everyone, including those who did not understand English, also used "Stay Awake" – just as everybody around the world understood "Thank you" or "internet," the call belonged to an emerging universal language. Some remote natives fused their own traditions with the new, as Mongolian peasants did in the early days of the great change.

With the new universal *language* emerged new universal *concepts*.

People learned to stand outside their boxes, expand their vision. They did it with the help of artificial intelligence and its deep-learning technology. With the help of AI kits with specially designed algorithms for biofeedback, schools introduced programs to modify natural instinctual fears and replace them with an impulse to trust, followed by careful perception and considered responses. They defused the instinctive aggressive stance by cultivating the capability to "de-center," to look at life from others' perspectives. People learned to stop stereotyping and labeling others. Then they could start a genuine dialogue with the "other" – both the inner and the outer other.

"De-center, De-label, and Dialogue" became the famous three Ds – part of every school's curriculum.

"Cooperate and Communicate" was the next natural stage. *Love* and *Compassion* became foundational elements of the next evolutionary step.

But no one culture or person overpowered "others." Not only *hegemony* was rejected, even *homogeneity* was. Only *harmony,* among different voices, would prevail. Empathetic hearts and minds, aided by empathetic technology, generated a new era: the Resurgence of 2045, a transformation umpteen times more enhanced, in a radically short time, than the European Renaissance that stretched from the fourteenth to the seventeenth century.

Harmony among different voices extended into the governmental sphere, in a system of inter-Unit relations formulated by the Global Union Council. There were subsystems for economics, commerce, healthcare, climate, scientific research, defense, and the judiciary. Did it work? Largely. Always? Often. Everywhere? Mostly.

With these principles and inner experiences as the basis of a new reality, historical structures of society dissolved into new forms that included humanity's shared realizations. Major world religions (Hinduism, Buddhism, Jainism, Judaism, Christianity and Islam) and local religions and traditions – everything from Mother-Father God to Yin-Yang and the Nature religions – were overlaid by the scientific concept of the all-pervading force of energy. People began to refer to *Essence Energy,* sometimes calling out "EE" as a greeting to one another.

Because the new understanding of multilevel life was so unfamiliar to so many, scholars helped in the transition by clarifying the paths along which humanity had traveled in its search for expression of subtle truth in the material plane. The scholars, in preparing pamphlets to be cybernetically distributed worldwide, put the new understanding in the context of what people had known before. All were absorbed as one unifying Force of Spirit and Matter, known as EE to some and TattvaShakti or TS to others – depending on family history or present company. Because so many communities had adopted TS, with its originally culture-specific understanding, the pamphlet also included an explanation: Tattva refers to the 'Essence', all-pervading energy, the scientific concept of Space – the entire cosmic reality, the stuff that all life, including us, is made of. Shakti is 'Energy', the 'Force', which mobilizes Essence. Many ancient scriptures gave form to this seeming abstraction through stories of Shiva and Shakti, male and female principles, for the masses who could not comprehend abstractions.

7 Yale University

After the boys left that morning, Ella completed activating her robot Kelley for daily chores: cleaning, rearranging closets, watering plants, on and on. There were no extras today she could think of, as her mind was set on an important university project.

"Bye, Samir. See you in the evening. What time will you be home today?" Ella walked toward her drone on the terrace.

"I'll be back by four, perhaps before you," Samir called out from the bathroom.

"Check with Shreya," she said, remembering. "Be sure Anton's favorite pakora came out right. Taste it. Let her redo it, if she needs to. See you later." Shreya was their robot-cook, master of the world's cuisines. Ella and Samir had programmed her with family favorites to suit each one's personal taste.

At the university, Ella, a gynecologist, was the coordinator of three other divisions for joint research programs: Dance, Physics, and Civics. She had specialized in all of them as part of her training. Although interdisciplinary programs had been increasing since the last decades of the twentieth century, the dramatic advances in technology and AI meant that the lines between disciplines were blurring faster than ever, interlaced with algorithms that organized and directed ever more sophisticated sets of data gathered from the professions and the practices, so that they could be seamlessly commingled.

After the Resurgence, all over the world at all universities, distinct academic branches had begun integrating their programs. Physicists were artists, photographers, even athletes. Students could create their areas of combinatorial specialty. The focus was on creativity, self-expression, and community. Regional, cultural, and genetic peculiarities often shaped individual choices.

There were no fixed modalities, monopolies, or competition, except with oneself! Excellence was the aim. Cooperation was the way. That was the behavioral code worldwide. Reality, however, did sometimes lag behind, needing time to catch up with the highest ideals of global cooperation.

Dr. Ella Pundit, from the US region of GU-1, was a name to reckon with in all Global Units. Her illustrious maternal lineage and heritage had made her who she was. She often said that her great-grandmother, Ella Huston, had been a patron of the arts and had founded a Global Unity Hall at Yale, in Connecticut, in 1950. Her grandmother, Ella Smith, had been a pioneer of Global Oneness as a young Yale Dance and Music major in the early 1970s. Her mother, Dr. Ella Singh, also a gynecologist, in 2052 had introduced the controversial Fetal Gene Enhancement procedure, which was built on the radiation-repair research that had accelerated after 2045. Ella had inherited, it seemed, four generations of visions to build the future.

However, today, October 4, 2084, Dr. Ella Pundit was agitated.

The very old DNA controversy was raised, again! The issue was the new Fetal Gene Enhancement chip. As a young scientist of twenty-two, in 2062 she had argued vehemently and rallied in its favor in New York. Men and women had demonstrated in its favor near city halls and on university campuses. What her mother had advocated in 2052 was settled by 2062, after fierce worldwide debates.

In fact Ella had used FGE for herself. Samir had encouraged her to have an FGE child. "Why not?" he'd said. "Be the practitioner of what you preach, Ella. You will make your mom proud."

They had Anton, an FGE child, when Ella was in her forties.

Why, now in 2084, was someone from GU-7, from Polynesia, questioning the process? She would be the one who'd have to answer. Yale University was the central division for research and enhancement worldwide. And she was the chief researcher in the field.

Ella hurried to talk with Dr. Sarah Huan Ling, her colleague and friend, to organize her thoughts about the GU-7 problem. When she found Sarah in the corridor, she asked point blank: "Why do you think people are questioning FGE again? It's been in practice for nearly twenty years."

"Is it again from GU-7? Polynesians displaced by the floods?" Most of the Polynesian population had relocated to New Zealand, where ocean-floor earthquakes, the shifting of tectonic plates, and volcanic activity had pushed again to the surface much of the land mass that had disappeared in the 2020 – 2025 floods. In 2045 the deserted new space was repopulated by displaced Polynesians, who were proud of their cultural heritage and reluctant to let go of old traditions, which had little to do with science.

"You know, Ella, we always have to work hard to convince the proud Polynesians. Mind you, I totally understand their reluctance. But we need to be creative to convince them, personally, not remotely by tech communications. It's time for someone to go there and explain what the FGE *really* is, and is not. They're struggling to keep up with the cultural mix of past and present."

Ella agreed, sighing with relief. "You're right, Sarah. Do you have some ideas?"

After thinking for a moment, Sarah perked up. "I have a suggestion. Why don't you go to New Zealand? Maybe this winter. When schools close here, they'll have summer over there. You can take your whole family, if Samir is free to go over the holidays. Anton is living proof of the potential in FGE research. And Kumar will have his graduation gift." Sarah's intuitive gift for working out a family vacation, celebration, and work plan for Ella still amazed her friend, even after years of knowing each other.

"Good. It's settled," Sarah said enthusiastically. "Let me think out loud a minute about what they might approach you with when you go. You know many in that area still harbor the old twentieth-century notion of designer babies, genetic engineering for gender or looks. Remind them that that primitive approach is prohibited by GU policy. You can tell them that the prohibition is part of our professional oath. You're so good at convincing people, I don't have to coach you."

"Well, thank you, Sarah." Ella as usual was thinking fast. "I believe they need to be reminded of the gene enhancement for healthy competition in sports – of Olympic standards for excellence, not for unhealthy rivalry or monetary gain."

"While you're on that topic, maybe you'll want to emphasize cultivation of bioenergy arts like qi gong. Some of them still may call everything martial arts, even though they realize karate and kung fu, as much as t'ai chi, are about expansive integrated mind-body-energy consciousness first – without the need to use that potential for destruction. I know, with two of your own children in training, one of them FGE, you're completely aware of the ways our 'new design' genetics focuses not on competition but on enhancement of our consciousness. So that they're fresh in your mind as you're preparing your remarks, what are your three Cs?"

"Concentration, Courage and Consciousness," Ella announced, laughing, "our evolved version of grandma Ella's three Cs in 2001 – Conflict, Cooperation, and Compassion."

"Brilliant, now get ready," Sarah said as she turned away and left Ella to ponder and plan.

Ella was elated. She dashed to her office and searched for her old online file for "Fetal Gene Enhancement, AI-2080," which had been her largest proposal for AI devices. It read:

> *Fetal Gene Enhancement (FGE) is a voluntary proce-dure for women in the second trimester of pregnancy. After determining the genetic code of the fetus, both parents may opt to enhance the good genes by chip implants. The procedure must be used only to enhance the benevolent genes, the life-enhancing ones, including telepathy. At least three medical experts must approve the findings and the procedure. The mental and physical health of the mother and child must be the primary criteria.*

Ella felt again her great confidence in the twenty-year-old project her mother had initiated, encouraged by the fact that the technique had been fairly widely used in most Global Units for at least the last ten years. For some, the enhancement was not as important as the process for deleting or decreasing the so-called unethical genes, a technique practiced alongside enhancement. She started mentally composing a slide presentation that would help the doubters.

People from Polynesia, she thought, were proud of their cultural heritage to a fault, leading them to question the "morality" of the procedure. She would have to use her much-admired people skills to the max.

Ella relaxed and decided to take a meditative nap on the office couch to process it all. Listening to her favorite stringed instrument, the *sarangi,* on her player, she fell into a deep sleep.

8 New Tonga

"Listen, you're not getting designer babies, made to order. That was an idea of the twentieth century. It was self-centered and also immoral, if you ask me. It was wish fulfillment for the parents. This is different." Dr. Ella Pundit was addressing a crowd in the New Zealand region of GU-7. With native Maori and white New Zealanders were Polynesians in big numbers to hear about the still-controversial FGE procedure.

The audience was checking Ella's credentials on their Universal Connector handsets.

"Are you suggesting this is not the parents' decision?" asked one of the men.

"It is the parents' decision," Ella responded. "You're right to raise that question. But the decision is rooted in the genetic structure of the fetus, not parental fancy."

Apparently unsatisfied, the old man persisted. "I see it as the beginning of another phase of racism and bigotry. Do you promise there would not be another class system created by the smart ones, who are also often power-hungry?"

"You're right again, sir, about human nature. Back in 2001, many such concerns were raised, rightly so, since the world was furiously divisive and self-centered during that era, an era that lasted millennia. National, racial, and ideological bigotry predominated. Economic superiority, and its inherent control, decided everything in life from family to government. Entire cultures' dependency on money, and thus the politics of money, led streetwise advisers to explain to the candidates that no other issue mattered, saying, in sum, 'It's the economy, stupid.'"

Ella's voice retained its friendly, gentle tone, clear of confrontation. "Our *ancestors* lived in times of strife," she said. Killings and hatred were rooted in race, economies, competition, and religious identities. But today, almost forty years after the Resurgence, we live in a different world. We have evolved. The FGE program has also evolved. Now the intent is human *enhancement*, not exploitation, not egoistic self-absorption, but communal growth. It's rooted in the most humanitarian and *evolutionary* approach ever."

A woman raised her hand and asked, "Is it true that in the last sixty years we Earthlings have evolved technologically faster than we did in the 600 years before? We call it exponential growth in technology. But have we evolved spiritually?"

"What do you think?" Ella responded with a smile. "Do you think we live in a more compassionate society? A more humane world, now in 2084, than, say, in 2001?"

"Sure we do. But is that spiritual evolution?" The woman sounded unsure.

"Mummy, can I ask something?" piped little Anton, who was listening intently. Ella was surprised, and Samir tried to hush Anton with a finger on his lips. Kumar was tickled and embarrassed. The audience's curiosity was palpable.

Ella said softly, "What do you want to know, Anton?"

"Being kind to someone, even if you don't like him, is called 'compassion', my teacher said. Is compassion spiritual?"

The audience burst into laughter. Everybody seemed to relax, including Anton. He intuitively recognized the laughter as the kind that always cracked up the grownups when they shifted into some kind of cosmic zone. Sometimes he even heard it through the wall of their meditation room, when the grownups were "supposed" to be being quiet.

"By the way," Ella continued, "let me introduce my son, Anton. He is four. He's the product of the latest FGE research." Some in the audience clapped, some waved at Anton approvingly. A few faces were serious.

Ella resumed her planned talk. "Since 2020, and especially after 2045, there was accelerated growth in genetic research. One could determine the natal characteristics of the fetus, not just for diseases and disorders – that kind of research continued and expanded – but for spotting positive traits. The ones considered positive, for example, might include capacities for music, art, sciences, athletics, mysticism, telepathy, a long list. Creativity in these areas could be enhanced by chip implants. Likewise, the negative tendencies – greed, cruelty, domination, hatred and so on – could be diminished or eradicated."

"Did Anton have more than one quality enhanced?" a skeptic shouted from the back row. "Which ones did you choose for *your* son?" His sarcasm was obvious.

In a calm voice Ella responded, "Yes, we selected the one that included all others: the 'consciousness gene' as it's called in scientific research. The point is to enhance what the fetus *already has* in his or her genes, to give the child the best opportunities. It's like sending your child to the best school, or providing the best home that you can. Adopted on a large scale, it's a progressive tool for humanity at large. 'Enhance the child, advance the society' became our slogan, as many of you well know," Ella said. Anton looked at the questioner with a gleeful smile.

A teenager in the audience raised her hand. "What does your *older* son think of his brother? Does he think Anton is kind of 'special'? Is he jealous?"

Nearly-fourteen-year-old Kumar smiled. This graduating vacation in New Tonga was turning out to be quite different after all, he thought. Mummy's lecture was just a thing to be over with. After that, sailing, swimming, rafting, and whatever else the land offered was what he was looking for. He didn't react to the question.

"Why don't you respond to that, Kumar?" Ella gave him the microphone knob.

Kumar summoned up the will to respond. "Well, it's difficult to be jealous of this little angel. I have tried, mind you." Laughter rippled around him. "When I had been the only child for nearly ten years, I could not understand why I had to share my parents with anyone." The surrounding laughter got louder. "My parents explained to me their intent. They wanted to support the FGE project by action, not just words. I saw their point. Today I'm a social activist, interested in generational links and evolution. This visit to New Tonga is my graduation gift. I'm looking forward to university next semester. I love my little ... *bro,*" he said, winking at the little one and ruffling his hair, "although he tires us with his perpetual questions." Anton pouted, with a "leave me alone" look.

"You're the only one who hasn't said anything, sir," said a man who'd been quiet thus far, addressing Samir. "I'm sure that without your support, your wife would not have succeeded. Are you also a medical doctor?"

Samir got up, took the micro knob from Kumar, and said, "No. My wife's world is on Earth. Mine is in Space. I'm an astrophysicist. I scan the cosmos."

From the podium, Ella could see a few smiles in the audience. Samir continued, "Today in 2084, the concept of interconnecting Earth and Space is real, not just a philosophical thought of nondualism, which ancients of my Indian heritage call advaita, the 'not two' they spoke of. As an astronaut and scientist, I can say that we live interconnectedness *physically*, not just *spiritually*. My wife and I are *humanitarian* scientists. As some of you know, I believe the 'science-spirituality divide' is yesterday's story. Today, toward the end of our century, we *feel* this truth in our bones. Not only do we *know* it in our heads, we know it in our hearts." Samir, the astronaut, was flying off into Space with his words, once again. Ella had to check him often, especially in company or at public gatherings, when he sometimes reiterated platitudes.

"If any of you have questions or doubts about the latest FGE program, please feel free to contact me," Ella concluded.

Vigorous clapping made Ella feel her visit to the island of New Tonga had been a good move.

9 Adam Wakes Up

A cool breeze wafted the fragrance of jasmine through Adam's window. It woke him. He thought he was out in the wilderness. No...! With a faint smile on his lips, he touched the smooth sheet, smelled the fluffy blanket, and closed his eyes again.

With a gentle knock the door opened. Jingling Voice, carrying a breakfast tray, walked in. Adam was too sleepy to notice she hadn't asked permission to come in. "Good morning, sir. Here is your breakfast. Enjoy your day!" Leaving the tray on the center table, she started walking out.

"Miss, what time is it?"

"Eight thirty a.m., sir," she jingled, and left the room.

Half an hour later, refreshed and well nourished, Adam walked through the lush garden of Shanti Lodge. He saw a young girl tending to one of the plants. "What are you planting, daffodils?"

"It's cactus, sir," she answered, looking up at the old man.

"Cactus? Here in New York City? Why?" Adam's surprise was starting to feel like his normal state of being.

"We're experimenting on transplants in our horticulture section, sir," the girl explained, being especially courteous to one so old.

"What's your name?" Adam hoped, as always, he could learn more about the new, transformed world, and maybe she would help.

"Genevieve Arnold. You can call me Geanie."

"My name is Adam Smith. How old are you? What grade in school?"

Genevieve answered as she rose to go to her next planting site.

"I'm twelve. After graduating from school next year, I want to focus on the Green Planet research program at NYU. I've already started my biotech research." Adam was astounded. Geanie, who looked eight, was already graduating high school?

As part of his ongoing 'awakening', Adam was learning to hide his feelings, whether shock, astonishment, confusion, irritation, admiration, fear, joy, or whatever else might arise as he coped with his disorientation.

"What will you focus on, do you know?"

"I'm passionate about music," she smiled. "Violin especially. With my friend Nushka's mathematics, we want to experiment on enhancing vegetation growth." Adam thought he was hearing a fairytale from a possibly mixed-up child. But he resisted saying so.

"Have you shared your ideas with your teacher? What does he or she say?"

"Oh yes. Pa Soham, that's my teacher, told Nushka and me about similar programs all over the world. We researched online. Now we have a worldwide network on such projects. It'll be easy to focus."

Adam realized he couldn't comprehend this 2084 field of knowledge with his 2020 mind. He changed the topic to something he thought he understood.

"Do you have a boyfriend? Do you date?"

Geanie burst into laughter, so loud that a little swallow in the hedge turned its head and froze, sensing danger, wondering if it should fly away. "You're really old, sir," she said, but instantly apologized. "Forgive my rudeness, sir."

Adam said kindly, "It's okay. I'm from another time, in the most literal sense. Don't worry. But tell me more about you."

"I've read about old-time dating, and I've heard old family stories. Wasn't online dating fashionable at the beginning of the century, especially in countries that're now Global Units 1 and 3? I think I read that it was around 2020 or so, that the social networks radically advanced and morphed, making such 'dating' obsolete. That was about the time people started confirming their mates online, worldwide, even before they met. One of the commentators said that romantic involvement was reshaped by technology."

Adam was still adjusting, not just to the new concepts, but to the fact that a twelve-year-old was so articulate, so advanced in her thinking. Yes, he remembered, before 2020, he himself had had a few heated arguments with his parents about his social life, as did many young people in those generations. But Geanie's world was like being on another planet. In fact he was on another planet, in most ways that mattered.

"What does this reshaped romance look like?" Adam thought he'd let his curiosity keep flowing, as long as Geanie would tolerate him.

Geanie struggled. How could she describe the new ways without being rude to this Methuselah? Her grandfather at ninety-five looked much younger than this guy. So he must be 120, at least, she thought.

"Would you like to come to my school? Our social counselor, Ma Katherine, might explain the current practice better."

"That would be helpful. Could you set up a meeting with her?"

"Sure. I have to go now," Geanie said, moving toward the gardening shed. "I'll let you know. You can find me here most days during this season."

Adam walked to the pond with the multicolored fish. Around it were bright chairs of many colors. Light musical notes flowed from nearly invisible microphones. On one side of the pond was a rose garden. He had never seen a jumble of colors in one rose. A huge lush sycamore shaded the pond. Adam sank in a cushioned chair, looked up at the blue sky, and dozed off.

"Mr. Smith, sir." He heard the jingling voice coming his way to fetch him. "It's time for lunch, sir. Will you prefer to come to the dining hall, or to eat in your room?" she asked gently.

"Oh, certainly in the dining hall. I want to meet other residents," Adam said. "Will you guide me to the hall?"

"With pleasure, sir." She extended her arm.

Adam held her arm and was shocked. Jingling Voice was not human. She was a robot.

Less than twenty-four hours in this brave new world seemed harder to wrap his head around than roaming for sixty-plus years in a foreign land.

10 Global Union Council

Soft rain, mixed with early-morning dew, covered Mani Dweep with hazy air like a gossamer veil. Scattered rays of sunlight twinkled in drops of water on the leaves, lending magic to its English name of Gem Island.

This morning Chou Li and Amir Khan were practically racing to the Security Division. They'd been awakened, while sound asleep in their warm beds, by the vibrating ISCs, the internal systemic chips implanted in their left arms. A vibration alert like that meant trouble, big trouble, somewhere on the globe, or anywhere in Space or the Galaxy. No time to speculate. They were reacting to a warrior instinct from the beginnings of humanity, known for centuries as "do or die," now evolved into "save or sink."

"False alarm." Chou and Amir heard Buddhi, their lovely robot, as they hustled through the door of their office. Sitting cross-legged on the desk in short dark pants and a black-and-white striped shirt, Buddhi smiled. "It was a faulty galactic signal," she said. "From Venus." Both Special Astronauts slumped into their chairs, relieved, saying, "Yesss, Essence Energy!" (Only the great-grandparents still said "Thank God.")

Geologically, mathematically, and metaphorically, Mani Dweep in the Indian Ocean was the center of the Earth. As such, it had been developed as Earth's Galactic Intelligence Center. The world's best planners, architects, engineers and scientists had worked on it laboriously for two years, from 2045 to 2047, to complete the plan – then four more to build it.

Since 2045, the year of Resurgence, Mani Dweep was also the new administration center for the Global Union Council (GUC) the Humanitarian Center, and the Research and Security center where Chou and Amir worked. It was also headquarters for the Judicial Center, which had two divisions: one created and revised rules, the other resolved conflicts between Global Units. Domestic judicial divisions were under each Global Unit's jurisdiction, located in their territories worldwide, not centralized in the Council.

Distinctions between central and local management were developed in several areas. Each Regional Unit, each former nation, was autonomous as far as culture, language, education, arts, worship, and local organization. And yet all Regional Units were required to follow guidelines for geological, climatic, political, economic, and trade relations formulated by the central GUC.

Coordination of the activities of the seven global Units was centered in the Council offices, organized by specialized inter-Unit divisions, which intertwined with each other in interdisciplinary activities. The range of focus areas that could be mixed included education, social issues, and commodity exchange, for example, and a host of study and practice areas such as philosophy, arts, literature, and music. All held their annual GUC meetings here. Representatives from all RUs came to report and make new plans for the future.

The busiest administrative office was the Technology Section, which included artificial intelligence, Space research, and inter-unit communications. They provided data, algorithms, and the newest technologies to all divisions and their cooperatives around the world.

Mani Dweep, in essence, was the heart-center of the human universe, the appropriately named Gem Island, sparkling in the Indian Ocean.

The original Maldives Islands had sunk in the floods, and yet were still considered the inevitable and appropriate center for the new organization of life on Earth. Instructions were programmed into the AI by specialized robotic engineers to create the foundation, using mathematical calculations in geology and astronomy that would ripple into the town planning of Mani Dweep. The result was an array of thousands of huge metal tubes, of different heights and widths, jutting out above the ocean surface – the shortest 200 feet above the water, the longest 800 feet – all interlocking in flexible modules that could respond to any future shifts in the ocean floor. The tubes themselves contained an integrated range of essential technologies – wires, plates, chips, and devices. Since Mani Dweep was going to have a much larger land mass than the original Maldives, the tubes were placed diagonally, rising from beneath in inverted triangle configurations, with points converging below the surface on the original land mass, and the larger base of each triangle high above the water – much like a massive inverted pyramid.

Planners designed a magnificent multilayered terrain with a rolling landscape on the top visible layer – complete with red rocks, green valleys, and blue lakes. The created land was dotted with assembly halls, research centers, and homes with gardens. Each construction was an architectural masterpiece, product of the best of artificial and natural engineering skills from around the world. It was virtual fairyland magic.

Designers created four basic elevations in the terrain: the lowest, foundational level included homes for GUC personnel, with schools, playgrounds, and shopping areas. On a nearby hillside was the Mani Dweep City Hall. Further away and higher up were the GUC offices, halls for conferences, and global meeting facilities. The highest level, a little distant from the central town, contained the Galactic Space Research Station. Its height provided clear access to all other Space installations around the world, especially the one near Mt. Everest, the highest peak on Earth. Chou and Amir worked at this Space station, their houses resting on the terrain nearest the ocean.

~\/~

Now relaxed, after the urgency of the false alarm had cleared his system, Chou asked, "So where is Zainab going for vacation this year?"

Amir, who never tired of bragging about his only daughter, chuckled with enthusiasm. "You know Zainab, she'll surprise us. Her mom is getting restless as she scans her mind. But I'm ready to be surprised by any of her stunts."

"You call them stunts? I'm impressed by her zeal for search," Chou Li said. "I call it 'search' deliberately, not 're-search', considering her history. Last year, a Siberian oil venture, and the year before, didn't she go to a Tibetan meditation camp? She always steps into the unknown. She always searches."

"Well, Mandy scanned her mind," Amir confessed, confident he could share information about his wife, Mandy, a consciousness research specialist who used her skills and maternal care to create a role for herself as the snoopy mother. She had scanned her daughter Zainab's mind. "Mandy says Zainab is juggling three ideas: scaling Kilimanjaro, going on a Venus Space exploration, or attending the *Bhagvad Gita* study camp. I'm happy with whatever she decides to do. Why cramp your life at that age? She can do any of those things under the sponsorship of her university program in Germany, even with an undecided major. But I have a feeling she may go to South India in GU-6. She's been meddling with consciousness, and her professor introduced her to Sri

Aurobindo's concept of supramental consciousness. So who knows?"

Amir sighed. "It exhausts me just thinking about all that. And it's been an exhausting morning. I believe we're entitled to go home and get some more sleep"

⚬

Xi was fast asleep when Chou Li reached home. Parking his drone on the roof hadn't disturbed his eight-year-old son.

Peeking into Xi's room, Li noticed his son's dream. Deep, deep into the dark ocean, Xi was fighting a dragon-like sea creature. Anxious, the father shook his son to break the nightmare. Xi, groggy, hugged his father. "Papa, no ... I was having fun killing the dragon, like in great-grandpa's old, old, super-old Ninja game. I was not scared!" Chou Li was tickled, but kept a serious face and said, "Okay boy, wake-up time. No more dreaming of Ninja games. Get ready for school. Is your drone-bike fixed?" Chou knew his son's mechanical skills, but did not trust his playfulness, which sometimes left mundane tasks undone.

"Yes, Papa, I fixed it last night," Xi said in a rush, distracted, his mind already on a new venture with his school friend David. Since David's mother was school principal, "violating" regulations was exciting. In fourth grade they were taught how to develop their innate telepathy, a new subject for eight-year-olds. All were at different levels of telepathic capability, depending on whether the child was FGE or not. Xi had always loved the meditation practices, begun in preschool when he was two, and they may have given him a head start. Since everybody was at a different telepathic level, the game to "cheat" became more sophisticated, more exciting. Xi could hardly wait to get to school.

When Chou's wife Fe had died two years ago, he was devastated. How would he raise six-year-old Xi as single father? Being the head of the Galactic Security division, Chou dealt with unpredictable work hours. It was overwhelming. But with robot Kelley working around the clock, it had not been so

11 Stay Awake

The wake-up alarm rang in Nye's head. It was different from the constant reminder "Stay Awake." On this spring morning, Nye Tee woke up with what he thought was a brilliant beginning for his presentation at school. He could not resist looking at his writing on a notepad, completed the night before:

> *What happened to all those old religious traditions? There were so many at the beginning of the century − at least till 2020 − six or seven major religions with subdivisions, some claiming absolute authority. People had killed each other in the name of religion for several millennia.*

Ten-year-old Nye smiled to himself. "So ridiculous, to kill for ideas. Pa Soham will absolutely love my approach." Like many of his classmates who took specialized courses with Pa Soham, he had felt their teacher's innate rebellious quality that, maybe ironically, ferociously spoke of *peace*.

While showering and getting ready, Nye could not stop thinking how humans could've been so devoid of common sense for so long. How could they not perceive the scientific data staring in their faces? Everything, including the cosmos, was interconnected by the universal Force. It was basic knowledge for *Homo sapiens*. You don't have to be extra-intelligent to grasp the evolutionary process. It's so exciting. But why so *long* to evolve? Worth further research.

"Ma, have you thought any more about my idea for the new project I'm doing for Pa Soham's class?" Nye asked his mother, Susan, over breakfast. "I have a new title, by the way: "How Religions Collapsed and Humans became Gods."

"I didn't want to discourage you, but since you ask, I know you know that that's old news, dear. At least forty years old, if not more."

"But didn't they once believe God created man in his own image?"

"That was one of the prevalent old traditions, yes, not everywhere, but in some powerful cultures we inherited. But, as you're apparently discovering, a great many philosophers and psychologists knew it was man who created God in his own image. They understood that humans needed religion for protection and growth, so they came up with various beliefs. So what's your point?" Susan sensed that all her teaching specialties – Science, History, and Civics – were involved in this one topic, maybe not a surprise coming from her own son.

"Well, I want to work on evolutionary stages in *all* dimensions, including the project I'm doing in your class. My target topic, in all these areas, will be how technology in the twenty-first century sped up evolution. When did *Homo erectus* become *Homo sapiens*, Mum? What time period?"

"In Neanderthal times, around....You know that's the 'missing link' of evolutionary theory, don't you? We covered that in class."

"I do, I do. Since humans are hard-wired for growth and creativity, unlike all other species, didn't someone years ago say 'The Singularity is near'? – meaning that technology and humanity's minds and bodies were about to merge?" Finishing his juice and getting up, Nye said quickly, "I need to run, Mum. See you tonight." He grabbed his backpack and hurried to his drone.

Susan smiled at her son's passion and got busy activating her robots for the day's work around the house. She heard her UC handset ting.

It was a text message from Abhishek, one of her students, Nye's classmate and best friend. He'd typed:

> *Do you think this is acceptable for my history project, Ma Susan?*

> *How Democracy Died: The real questioning of democracy started in the year 2016, the year the people of the United States elected their President. He violated principles of democracy because he was not for the people, or of the people. He was all about personal gains for himself and his ilk, the multimillionaires, but claiming he was for the downtrodden, forgotten, white middle class. There was no hiding his constantly changing statements openly played out on his tweets. Books were written about his mental inadequacies.*

> *Many thought he was unfit to be a President. Different factions of the media were engaged in perpetual analyses of his stunts. Many in his own conservative party could barely tolerate him. Ironically, totally inadvertently, he triggered an ideological revolution. A movement initiated by enraged common masses of informed people trumped the unfit President. Perhaps his coming to power was good, in that he became Americans' "Stay Awake" call. That was the beginning of Revolution 2020 that initiated the change from a degenerated form of democracy, giving rise to our current system projected in "Energy Essence," a scientific concept of interconnected Oneness.*

12 Parlor Chat

"Hello, I'm Julia, and you are?" A graceful, meticulously dressed woman caught up with Adam in the corridor leading to the dining hall for residents of Shanti Lodge. As she was about to pass him on the way to lunch, she'd smiled in greeting and extended her hand for a handshake.

"I'm Adam, Adam Smith," he said, glad to meet such a classy lady, accepting her proffered hand. She waved toward the entrance to the dining area, an invitation.

"Where are you from? Did you just arrive?" Julia continued as they walked to a table.

Adam's words were slow as he formulated a response. "Checked in last night. Originally from LA, but right now from China." He pulled the chair out for Julia. A little surprised, she acknowledged the ancient courtesy with a gentle quizzical smile.

"China? That's GU-6. What brings you to New York?" Julia's curiosity was polite, if a bit focused, about this man who looked unusual in these environs.

"Exploring the new world," said Adam with some enthusiasm.

"Why 'new'?"

"I'm returning to the US after sixty-plus years," he said casually, then shifted into his current interests. "Would you know the time of mass at Saint Patrick's on Sunday?"

Mildly shocked, now Julia was perplexed. How to respond to someone who seemed genuinely lost in time? "I don't think Saint

Patrick's is active anymore, Mr. Smith."

"Oh yes, now I remember. Maybe it's in the *Old NYC* museum now. My drone pilot told me about it. Is there any other place of worship in this new New York?"

"Attendance in places of worship," she replied kindly, patiently, "like churches, synagogues, temples, and so on, had been thinning from the beginning of the century, as you know. During the floods, the earthquakes, and then the nuclear disaster, they became places of refuge, more than worship. After the Resurgence, churches in their old forms became extinct. Now it's all EE, Essence Energy."

"I've heard of EE, but since you mention it, I'd like to hear more. Way back, I heard of TM, transcendental meditation, taught by an Indian guru, was it? A relative of my father's joined it. It must've been in the 1990s, I guess." Adam's eyes were dreamy, empty of certainties.

Julia couldn't control her laughter. "Mr. Smith, I'm delighted I've met you. I'd be very happy to help you when we're not so hungry. We'll have to have a long conversation some other time. How do you like the soup? The food here is very good. Do you plan to be in New York long?"

"I guess I will," Adam said slowly, but his brain was working furiously, trying to process ever-thickening clouds of new information.

Julia finished her salad entrée, set her napkin on the table, and said, "I don't want to be impolite, but I have a lecture to go to at the 92nd Street Y. Do you mind?"

"Of course not." Adam's impulse was to keep the conversation going anyway. "What's the lecture on?"

"'The Resurgence and Inter-Unit Relations.' It's by Dr. Igor Myanowich. He's an eminent galactic cosmologist from Russia, involved in the global network."

"You work in the same field?"

"Sort of a related field. Everything is related anyway, as you know." In fact, Adam did not know. In his younger days, many academic fields had become interdisciplinary in various universities, but he wasn't sure this was what she was talking about. "My interest is in integrating EE and the new galactic findings," she said. "I teach at George Washington U."

"I won't hold you up, Professor," Adam said, smiling, as he rose from his chair. As Julia also stood up, his wish to continue learning from this new source took another form: "Can I find more information online, to catch up on EE?"

"Sure. If you give me your contact info, I can send you some targeted links to explore the field at your leisure, read up, go to events. If you don't have it with you now, find me at breakfast in the morning. I'm leaving in the afternoon for DC." Julia smiled, shook his hand, and left.

Adam sat back down at the table and stayed for a long time. "This is truly a new world. Awakened? Or awkward?" he mumbled to himself.

The antique grandfather clock chimed and simultaneously he heard "Stay Awake" in the invisible cloud.

13 Treasure Chest

Kumar ran into the classroom to show Jack what he'd found in his father's 'treasure chest'. That was the name astronaut Samir Pundit's family had given to his box of old papers, cards, trinkets, tapes, videos, and souvenirs. According to his wife Ella it was all clutter. Samir treasured tidbits from his research in Space travel – evoking the future – as well as family archives tracing his past. His treasure chest contained ancestors' writings, medals, social service records, clippings, and awards for academic achievements. They were gold nuggets for him. Attached to each item were Samir's comments under "Why do I treasure this?"

Kumar, rummaging through the chest, had chosen a particular set of materials, photographed the label, and transferred Samir's digital recording to his own UC, elated at the prospect of sharing this find with his friend. The 'nugget' now in Kumar's handset read:

> *This was February 2018 – SpaceX Falcon Heavy Launch with a dummy and Tesla to drive around Mars! Elon Musk's private commercial enterprise, much cheaper than NASA's ventures.*

Before class, he stood next to Jack and opened up his backpack to retrieve his UC. "Look at this video, Jack. Elon Musk's video of the launch. People are so excited. They're jumping, yelling, grinning like crazy. Could you imagine the time when people went nuts about individual Space travel? What's the big deal? We *vacation* on the Moon, on Mars."

Jack viewed a few seconds of video. "Look at this reporter," Jack said, staring into the screen. "She can hardly speak. She's out of breath, shouting and bouncing up and down, just watching a Space launch. Funny."

"I know. What a change from 2018. Hard to believe it was only sixty-six years ago."

Kumar pulled a piece of paper out his backpack. "Look at this, also from Papa's treasure chest. It's a poem by a fifteenth-century Indian poet. This guy seems to have known about Energy Essence 700 years ago. And in his time, it was already 2,000 years old. Read it."

Jack glanced at the poem, but his attention was drawn by yet another "treasure" visible in Kumar's open pack.

"What is this?" Jack pulled out a photo with a written label attached. He read Samir's note:

> *The first-ever Space travel of a living being, Laika, a dog, in 1957. My great-grandmother Jankima was 21 years old in 1957, and this triggered her imagination. She wrote a humorous story for a local newspaper in her hometown in India, a comic story of college kids planning a vacation to visit relatives on Mars and the Moon. Now, since the 2050s, visiting other planets is part of everyday life. Did grandma Janki envision the future almost 100 years ago?*

"This is amazing. Your father's treasure chest is like a missing link between the past and the future."

Soham, Headmaster of the school, entered the classroom and took his seat. Students reached quietly for their cushions and gathered around the teacher. They sat cross-legged and closed their eyes when Soham rang the bell – for a five-minute meditation to start the day, as always. At the end of meditation, Soham rang the soft bell again and began the class discussion. "Let's begin with the theme for your graduation thesis. Who wants to go first?"

Every year, Soham's eighth-grade graduating students were required to describe what they wanted to accomplish in life, why, and their preparation to achieve their goal. This included career, hobby, activity, service, governance, family, spiritual dreams and goals, or any combination thereof. If there was no clarity or defined vision yet, a student had to write about why not and how he or she wanted to address the issue. The project had to be descriptive, insightful, an honest inquiry deep into one's mind and soul.

Jack signaled Kumar to go first with a jerk of his head and a movement of his eyes.

"I have some thoughts, Pa Soham," Kumar started. "In my father's treasure chest, almost this high now…" Kumar indicated his chest, and the class laughed, "I found these two items. One is a poem by a fifteenth-century Indian poet and another is a video of the first Falcon Heavy Launch from SpaceX in Florida, dated February 2018. It was the first private commercial Space-travel launch in the world. The two pieces are 700 years apart."

"So how do you connect the two? Besides, how do you relate the items to your future?" Pa Soham did not tolerate mere entertainments for graduation papers.

"Of course plans for my future will emerge as I expand my thesis," Kumar said confidently. "I want to show the connectedness of the past and present, science and spirit, father and son, east and west, poetry and Space flight – not as opposites but as the essential continuum of life on Earth and in the cosmos. The vital Force, Shakti, breathing in father, son, and grandmother as Energy

Essence, connects them with the entire world. The personal as universal."

The class applauded, with Wow on their faces.

"Can I see the poem?" Soham asked. "Do you have it with you?" Soham was aware of the SpaceX launch of 2018, but was not sure about the poem, despite his background in Vedic studies and the Indian blood in his veins.

"Yes, I do. Here it is." Kumar pulled out the poem.

"Are you interested in hearing it?" Soham asked the twenty around him.

A resounding chorus of "Yes" settled it.

Kumar started reading his father's meticulously handwritten note:

> *Found in great-grandma Janki's papers. This is her own translation of her elementary school prayers, which they sang every morning before classes began. It was a poem by a 15th-century devotee of Krishna, Narsimha Mehta, titled* Akhil Barhmandama *("In the Infinite Space"). Jankima presented it to her class at Columbia University, in New York, where she got her PhD in 1977.*

> *Pervading the Infinite Space, O Hari (Krishna)*
> *You manifest your Self in varied forms.*
> *You're the One divine spirit in all living beings,*
> *The luminous essence of Light.*

Kumar added, "This poet describes, in the fifteenth century, what we in the twenty-first century perceive as Force in Essence Energy, cosmic reality, TattvaShakti in Sanskrit."

"That's so true," Soham agreed. "I like your approach of *continuity* and *evolution* in both personal and universal contexts. Who wants to go next?" Soham wanted to hear from at least half the class that day.

Valerie spoke up. "I will, Pa Soham, if I may. I see my career in social work. A lot of footwork, active participation in awakening people. Since the Resurgence in 2045, we've developed enough institutions for scientific, social and civic education. But many in remote areas of GU-6 and -7 do not, cannot, fully utilize them, despite their internal knowingness and energy. I want to explore those through *their* storytelling, their musical and theatrical performances, and connect those traditions with current technology. My paper will describe specific areas and findings. I'm still working on details."

"Very good project. That's much needed, Valerie. Who goes next?"

"I want to work with *new Pangaea*," said Jack, "the new surviving world after the rising sea levels of 2025 and the nuclear devastation of 2045, all of which got further distorted with all the tectonic shifting and volcanoes. Basic issues related to housing, schooling and healthcare have been addressed. With universal income worldwide, people have better lives and facilities, but not always *real inner transformation*. So I want to explore the nature of that gap, to bridge it."

"Great, Jack. Universal integration and wholeness makes for completion. But I need specifics, not just generalities. Are you clear about that, Jack?"

"Kumar keeps me on my toes, Pa." Jack smiled and pursed his lips.

"Good. Anybody who is yet not clear about the assignment?" Soham surveyed the room.

"Pa Soham, I want to chart the robotic evolution," offered Chris Ip. "Which track should I follow to make the robots *conscious*?"

"That's extremely important, Chris. I encourage you to do it. If you want to pursue this, beyond mechanical higher awareness of measured information, by which I mean data, come see me about the higher dimensions. But for these initial inquiries, look it up and pay attention when you see references to the evolutionary path called 'To Singularity'. Run a search for "Kurzweil." Any more questions?"

The midday "Stay Awake" sounded.

"Aye, Essence Energy," all of them said in unison and then headed for their next class.

14 Five Trees Complex

"Mrs. Alvaris, I need to move from here." After a week's stay at the guest house, Adam asked the kind lady at the desk for a referral. "This has been a wonderful place to rest and recuperate. I appreciate everything all of you have done for me. Now that I'm back on my feet, you know I need to learn how this new world works. Could you find a suitable place for me?"

"I'd be happy to, Mr. Smith," Nelly Alvaris responded with a smile. "Let me look up available places. How many bedrooms would you like?"

"One will be plenty," Adam said, "but I need to ask for financial help too. Where do I go for that?"

"No worries, sir. Somebody from the housing agency will come here to advise you. I'm calling them right now." Nelly's reassuring voice was comforting. "Why don't you wait in the lounge, and somebody from the agency will be here soon – or maybe they'll send a representative from a place they've found for you."

There was an old-style television, may be from 2020, for those who liked to watch big screens. Most used their personal tablets or Universal Connector handsets. Adam decided to catch up with the news. "*The Resurgence at 40*" flashed on the screen. The anchorman, with a complicated name Adam could not pronounce, was announcing intra-Unit and inter-Unit competitions in music, dancing, singing, painting, and elocution. Most popular, he said, were competitions that awarded prizes in the form of the newest most innovative devices, such as the fondly named 'Angelic AI'.

"At the inauguration ceremony on Mani Dweep," said the anchorman, "nearly 200 flags of the 'old countries' will be unfurled by young boys and girls from each region. A statement of unified economic and political Global Units, with cultural variations according to the traditions of former countries, will be the primary theme of the event."

Adam closed his eyes and let his mind wander, pondering what he'd just heard. *I wonder where and what this Mani Dweep is. Maybe it's in old Switzerland, where they used to have Davos, and CERN, and all that.* Adam dozed off.

"Mr. Smith, sir?" A young man was speaking softly to him.

"Yes, I'm Smith, and you are?"

"I'm Romero from the Five Trees Complex, sir." The man extended his hand, and Adam responded groggily with a handshake.

"I understand you're considering relocating to Five Trees. I can fill you in on what's available. Our complex is fairly new, five years old. So all the amenities, decor and furniture are Global Mix Contemporary, new and fresh. A gym, spa, clinic, and meeting hall are available. You can eat in your room or use the dining hall. Here's the schedule for weekly events. They are world-culture mix, what's called Fusion-X, which is very popular."

Adam listened to the details, waiting for the connected dollar amount. When he didn't hear costs anywhere in Romero's presentation, he finally summoned the courage to ask. "And what is the cost, the dollar amount, for all these wonderful amenities?"

"Cost?" Romero was unsure what Adam was asking, so he proceeded carefully. "As usual, it will be covered by the governance stipend coming to you. I don't really know what you mean by 'dollar amount'." Young Romero waited to see if he'd understood, if he'd been understood.

Adam kept staring, wordless, at this man who did not know

what the dollar was. "You're sure this is not welfare?"

"The Global Union is looking after our welfare, our well-being, in all Units, including ours. You'll get a stipend every month, like everybody else in the world, from the local community governance office. They fix the amount based on each one's needs. The system's algorithms contain the data needed to calculate those needs. That's the system."

Romero was twenty, and a people person, who'd decided not to pursue advanced education. But this was basic information that *everybody in the world* knew. So he was trying, without being rude, to understand Adam's questions. By Adam's wrinkled forehead and blank look, Romero figured this very old man might not be quite together. Maybe he was 125 or had dementia.

"Sir, you too would get all facilities, including transportation, as well as the stipend every month, like everyone, everywhere. The Five Trees Complex has its drones, as well as old-style self-driven vans and cars, if you prefer those," said Romero, to build his slow client's confidence in the latest improvements.

"Suppose I'm not comfortable in either one – a drone or a self-driven car. Can I get somebody to drive me around?" Despite his recent recuperation, Adam was still uncomfortable with so many novelties.

With a polite smile, Romero said helpfully, "If that is what you'd like, I'll see what we can do. I may find someone in the 'honorable unit' – which is a gathering place for those who've attained the greatest seniority – who's looking for company."

"Well I'm eighty-four, and..." Adam was interrupted by Romero's outburst.

"What? Eighty-four? You're so *young!* Why would you want such an old-fashioned transport system, sir?"

"I've been in isolation for a long, long time," Adam explained. "I'm adjusting as fast as I can, but I can't do everything at once. It would be very helpful, as long as you're searching for resources, if you could find someone who can tell me more about the new world as well. By the way, do I have to continue to live in your complex? Suppose I don't like New York, but want to go to California, my old home state?"

"A change can be arranged easily," responded Romero, glad to be on familiar ground, his specialty. "Now you can go anywhere you like, sir, not only in America, but anywhere in the world. The same formula of stipend and living arrangement applies everywhere. You're free to go wherever." After a brief pause, he continued, "However, I'm afraid California may be a little problematic, sir. Like the New York region, much of the California region was disrupted by the earthquake of 2020, and completely sank in the floods around 2025. It did not recover the way New York has. Instead, out west, we have an alluring Arizona coastline. Actually, with the red rocks of famous Sedona, the deserts and mountains, that coastline has become an even more enchanted land." Romero was relieved to be able to add a little color to the sad news of a sunken California.

"Stay Awake" – the call floated above their heads, as Adam's mind was completely hushed by the mention of Sedona, the nonexistence of California.

That evening, Romero, exuding enthusiasm, took Adam to the Five Trees Complex. Romero hoped his buoyant attitude would inspire confidence in his client, who was obviously adjusting in fits and starts to what was for the newcomer a very, very intriguing, but exhausting, brave new world.

15 The Resurgence at 40

Mani Dweep was busier than usual. Representatives from all Global Units had assembled to plan a big event for the following year, 2085, the fortieth anniversary of the Resurgence.

"The Singularity is Near" had been the call of the Resurgence in 2045.

"The Singularity is Here" would be the theme of the 2085 celebration.

Topics suggested for the planning committee to consider included a near-universe of possibilities: Where to from here? What was achieved? What needs to be expanded? Special attention was given to new fields of integrated activity, which included robotics research, assistance for Global Units in need of cultural coordination in the development of artificial intelligence, the science-spirituality confluence, and many more, especially genetics.

Delegates from around the world were excited to bring the creative presentations their individual Units had finalized after months of preparation.

Their enthusiasm was palpable.

Mrs. Muriel Kanugo was the Chief Counselor, selected the previous year by the joint Global Union Council. The Chief Counselor was determined by secret write-in ballot, somewhat resembling the selection of a Pope in earlier times.

Muriel Kanugo's ancestral hometown in Myanmar had been

destroyed in a freak mountain storm generated by the climatic distortions of 2025, the year of her birth. Her family moved to India, where she grew up and completed her education. She specialized in AI technology and philosophy, which included metaphysics and religions, in the interdisciplinary program at Delhi University. The year of Resurgence, 2045, was the year she got her doctorate. Now she was somewhat the queen of the world, inhabiting the highest executive position in the GUC.

Mrs. Kanugo rang the little gong on her table to initiate the meeting. As the RU representatives settled in their chairs, she began her prepared remarks. "Welcome to the GU Council gathering to plan celebrations for our landmark event for the fortieth anniversary. You've already spent stupendous energy and time in your respective Units, over the past year, to send proposals to us. I commend you and your committees for your insightful research and valuable input. Above all, I commend the enthusiasm and creativity of all denizens. We have an extraordinary range of projects to consider – from AI research to Space travel, from musical concerts to drama, from art exhibits to engineering, and from architecture to acrobatics – with creative combinations of many of these disciplines. It's incredibly varied and promising. Congratulations for exemplary work." She paused to let the applause inspire them and gather them in.

"I think some perspective can help us feel our place in the accelerated trajectories of our times, to remind us of our shared experiences. In the beginning of our twenty-first century, the pace of technology increased the distance between our mechanical sophistication and our human social adjustment. But we know now, toward the end of our century, that the *combined force of humans and technology* has expedited our progress toward the much-awaited Singularity. *Homo sapiens* has finally arrived at the threshold of the next evolutionary stage. We have witnessed – and contributed to

– the ways that humans have recognized their innate divinity *with the help of* technology. The first-ever human technologies were the control of fire and the design of the wheel. The latest is artificial intelligence, with all the downstream inventions it makes possible, all the new streams it creates. It has been a miracle to watch the refinement of the programming, so that the highest human and spiritual ideals are intrinsic to this new capacity of the human race.

"All of you know that we're seeing a stunning quickening of AI development, which was initiated only about a century and a half ago. Some of you here, our most experienced denizens, personally remember the first huge expansion in the early part of this century. The Resurgence in 2045 was the beginning of what many in the tech community were already calling the Diamond Age, with near-infinite algorithms flowing through crystal-like structures and shaping all areas of life – even a possible shift to using actual diamonds. At this point, forty years on, we've nearly arrived at the core potential of Singularity: *superhumanness,* another stage in our evolutionary process, a *universal* reality, which we are now organized to support, from here on Mani Dweep.

"This afternoon, we'll be discussing the contest – part of our celebration program – to give an official name to this convergence of organic, inorganic, algorithmic, and transcendent existence. Some of you have been communicating about entries already made public. One of the current favorites is *Homo lumenomachina,* a blending of spiritual firelight and machine with human, a name that some have said is too difficult. I challenge all of you here – and all the denizens you represent – to come up with a new name for our new selves.

"Those of you in non-technical specialties, please know that my excitement about the technology in no way limits my tremendous appreciation for the subtler dimensions of our existence – which, as we're coming to understand with greater clarity, with each passing day, are the deeper foundations for all that we do. You delegates are experts in how all these dimensions work together, but since this talk will be distributed around the world, and is the theme-setter for our celebration, I'll be specific about the ways we're evolving within ourselves. We've all benefited from meditation to enhance our human experience, notably Vipassana meditation, cultivated since childhood as part of our educational system of Three Ms – Music, Meditation, and Math. This makes us aware of the human mega-story in our bodies, and many of your proposals for the final program mention performances and presentations by students dramatizing these stories.

"During and after lunch, we'll meet in breakout and plenary sessions to talk more about where the Singularity takes us in business, Space research, Earth enrichment, health and healthcare, and above all, our master tool, artificial intelligence.

"In these sessions, I would ask that you pay special attention to an aspect of AI that we've addressed in previous annual meetings. All of you are aware of the obvious challenges that AI can pose with each new advancement, beyond what all our systems have been accustomed to. I invite you to share problems and solutions based on your experience, your research, and the on-the-ground issues you face in your regions.

"Thank you, everyone, for coming to this important session. I trust you'll enjoy the special luncheon we've prepared."

Representatives chatted as they moved en masse to the glass-domed cafeteria. Tables were spread out over a finely maintained carpet-like indoor green lawn. Surrounding fruit trees, colorful flowers, and fountains created a charming Old World look of the late twentieth century.

Instead of the usual electronic menus in average restaurants everywhere, here in Mani Dweep they had retro decorative paper with calligraphic lettering and painted floral designs. The vegan menu highlighted exotic items from all over the world. By 2030, diets worldwide were plant-based. Eating any kind of animal meat, fish, or fowl was considered cannibalism.

Certainly the meat-eating practices still continued in isolated areas. But the vast majority of planetary denizens had gone vegan. Whether any of the delegates still enjoyed seafood at home, this was neither the time nor place to confess it.

16 We, Water, Wave

Jankima's voice was deep, her eyes gentle, a smile always lingering on her lips. Kumar was watching a video of Jankima's talk, one more gem from his father's treasure chest:

> *"Water: Symbol of Life" Janaki Pundit, NY, 1992.*
> *The title of our upcoming book is "Where the Waters Are Born."*
>
> *Water is the source of life. It constitutes the major part of our bodies. Ancient civilizations grew around water, along river banks. Water is used worldwide in almost all rites of passage ceremonies: birth, death, marriage, spiritual awakening.*
>
> *We recognize, in our ancient philosophies, that the waters carry the world, and the word, into existence, thus evoking the age-old concept of the power of literature. The water also suggests the distinctiveness and connectedness of diverse literatures. While most cultures, however disparate, perceive water as regenerative force, each body of water is peculiar to its native land, changing from well to well, river to river, and yet the waters gather in the oceans of the world.*
>
> *We maintain that these merging oceans support distinct land masses, connected in harmony, not necessarily in tedious homogeneity, or aggressive hegemony. Our*

guiding spirit is, in our own words, "Let's celebrate our differences, so we can enjoy our oneness." This is our vision for our world here and now, captured in our literature.

"Revelatory," Kumar said quietly to himself, noticing that the sound of the word, in his new state of mind, sounded like water rippling over stones in a brook. He made notes in his writing tab, then reached back into the treasure chest. "Wow! Here it is. Just the thing I need." Ella heard Kumar's elated cry way down in her ground-level office: "Some more from your dad's junk box?" followed by laughter. Kumar ignored Ella's reaction. "Ma, you don't know!"

He was already watching the next video, a swirl of moving colors and flashes of light emerging from a black background, with a voiceover soundtrack. This one was by grandma Sunita, Samir's mother – Jankima's daughter:

Kali also means "black." She is the uncanny dark matter, dark energy, full of tremendous ardor. Scientists maintain that before manifest reality emerged, only dark energy prevailed. It vibrated in waves and particles ... like strings weaving a web. Its humming created sound that was not yet heard. It flowed over the yet un-reckoned cosmos...

In her cosmic energy domain, endlessly vibrant, there is no sunrise or sunset; there are roaming suns and stars, moons and split rocks. Galaxies, stars, super novae yet unknown. Humans were not yet born.

Unfathomable was that connection for humans to grasp, except through math, music, dreams, or meditation.

The Force seems to laugh like a loving mother. Often as a furious and protective guardian. Always as One Element, because all is Her. She is the pervading feminine force in all, including all gods: of earth, fire, wind, water and space. She creates life, destroys the destroyers of life.

Rig Veda 10: 125, c 1700-1400 BCE

Kumar was excited by this new find. "This is TattvaShaki. Wow...." Sitting before the treasure chest in 2083, even 1977 was remote antiquity, a time even before cell phones. Something from thousands of years ago was inconceivable. He cracked up. How could that rishi see what the scientists had proven now? That there was only vibration in what is now called Space.

The cascade of wonders sent him back to the treasure chest to look for more. He noticed a magazine review of a performance by his maternal grandmother, Ella (affectionately known as "Grand Ella," since her daughter carried the same name). When grandma Ella had been sixteen years old, she'd designed and presented some sort of cosmic dance. The review captivated the young man, who was having a hard time imagining his grandmother ever being sixteen years old.

We gathered in the beautiful "Global Unity Hall," the auditorium named by the dancer's grandmother. The program noted that she would perform "The Digital Dance Drama of Our Global Future," integrating the newest technologies, cultural nuances, and philosophical perceptions of human destiny into song, music and movement. It wasn't something I could picture, until I saw it.

The backdrop for the performance was generated by electronic and laser devices, creating a magnificent image of the planet Earth viewed from space. Multicolored lights displayed fragments of the globe parting and uniting in a futuristic symphony.

From the wing, the young dancer, Ella, narrated the prologue, her voice surprisingly powerful as it reverberated through the surrounding speakers – almost embracing all of us in the audience, putting us into a sort of trance. I can't convey the power of the words without sharing them here:

"Call me illusion – fantasy – real though I be. More real than what you know as real. When matter turns dense, too dense for a transformation, you come to me. When chaos prevails, no end in sight, you come to me. Some invoke me as a miracle, an insight, a new discovery, a new religion, a new belief system, yet another savior – the list is endless. Only varied names for the same saving grace. I manifest in dreams, desires, sensitivities, the needs of all five billion and more. Therefore I am One, but have many forms and names. I am All."

Laser lights kept rolling these final words, on the stage and over our heads in the audience. It was enchanting, in the most direct sense. Slowly the sound and music receded. There was utter silence. For a long time. A spell had been cast. We all sensed it.

A thundering gong shattered the silence as Ella darted onto the stage. Her face was painted half male, half female, each of her hands and feet painted in colors of different races. Her heavily painted eyes expressed total joy – benediction, peace, and harmony. Her agile footwork expressed anger, assertion, and power, as did her graceful hand movements. Her feet barely touched the ground as she floated and then stamped the floor to assert, to prevail, to manifest.

In her hands she carried a hammer and chisel, in her belt a flute. She danced, in what we could discern, with a hammer in her hand, was destruction of the old dysfunctional traditions, carving new modalities and structures with the chisel. She gently drew the flute from her belly belt and seemed to tune in the creation melody of joy, trust, and celebration.

In the finale, the young dancer Ella stood center stage, her arms raised, glaring into space above us all. There was another extremely long moment of silence. And then we all exploded in a thunder of applause that went on and on. It was an evening none of us will ever forget.

After watching the video, seeing the dance in its astonishing colors and movements and meanings, Kumar sat silently for a long time, marveling at the family that had eventually created him. He marveled especially about the women, realizing he'd never really met them before.

17 Revolution?

Adam Smith in Cottage 32 became popular with residents at Five Trees Complex. His childlike curiosity, born of his total ignorance of sixty years of world events, endeared him to everybody. He did not mind asking, even when people could not control their laughter or smirking, or their wonderment.

The manager, Emily Briton, helped Adam order new clothes and grooming products online. He said he missed the excitement of going to the mall.

"What do people do in their free time, if they don't go to the mall or to a movie?" Adam had decided to ask Niru, a woman he'd met on his regular morning walk. She seemed to be more mature than the younger people he'd met, so her explanations carried a depth that allowed him to understand the present in terms of his own past.

"They socialize with others in their homes, or the community hall. They talk, or get involved in creative activities like painting, playing music, writing, whatever they're interested in." A faint smile came to Niru's lips when she remembered the town-sized malls her grandmother had been hooked on.

"That's interesting at first," Adam countered, "but it can be boring after a while, don't you think?"

"Many people travel around the world every year, see different lands, exchange stories. Some may even stay in another land for a few years and then move again," she said. Niru had lived for an extended time in six countries in the last twenty years.

"Could I ask you about safety? This is a nice-looking neighborhood. Are other areas in New York City safe? What about crime? Guns?"

"If you asked twenty-year-olds that question today, they'd be surprised. They wouldn't know anything about guns, except from history lessons. I remember many things from my younger days of activism against guns, and of course many similar projects, like women's rights, gay rights, immigration, poverty, sex crimes. They were challenging issues during the dark ages of our civilization. Now that I'm almost ninety…" she said, laughing.

"*You,* ninety!?" Adam was astonished. "You don't look a day over sixty."

"Thank you. Since the Resurgence and the Calamity/Compassion agreement of 2045, all violence *worldwide* has dissolved. It's a form of evolutionary ascension, if you will."

"You mean masses of people rose to a higher level of thinking?" A note of skepticism in Adam's voice was loud and clear.

An emphatic smiling "Yes" burst from Niru, and she continued. "Communications and computing technologies, coordinated through artificial intelligence, and genetic engineering, were among many innovations. They infused an unprecedented avalanche, as it were, of *awareness* into all humans – the awareness that earlier visionaries and Einsteins of the world had experienced and shared."

Adam was adjusting his mind to Niru's passionate outburst. "So, if I understand you correctly, ancient philosophies and science were joining hands in human evolution?"

"Absolutely," Niru said, happy to still have the verve to feel so enthusiastic, to be articulate enough to share the excitement with someone else.

Adam wanted to continue. "If you'll bear with me, Niru, while

I adjust to all this, it'll help me to get the sequence in mind. Somebody else, over at Shanti Lodge, told me that guns were abandoned by 2022 in the US, the last country to fully implement the controls. Others had gun-control laws a long time before that. You're telling me that violence abated completely around 2045. Am I right so far?"

Niru laughed aloud. "Adam, don't hold me to exact dates. I'm giving you a quick synopsis of sixty-some years that you missed."

"Sure, I get it," Adam laughed. "I won't take you to court for misinformation. I remember the wave of 'marches for life' and the 'meToo' movement of 2018. I was eighteen myself."

"Well, I'd been an activist since 2010."

"Did it work? Usually such movements become tempests in a teapot, don't they?"

"What was different this time was that the voice of the common people – ninety-nine percent of the population as they were called – spread around the world through social media. In earlier times, politicians in power everywhere, including here, tried to penalize them. Many lost their lives."

"That's what I mean." Adam's cynicism intensified his voice.

"Yes, but by 2030, thanks to electronic interconnectedness and expanding intuitive capabilities, people's responses to violence and bigotry were revolutionized. It became possible for people's best instincts to emerge and find communion. Cooperation and humanitarian programs abounded. Of course, there were isolated pockets of prejudice and violence. But they were exceptions. Formerly they were the rule, as you and I witnessed. They were all part of a system based on predatory economics. You probably remember those times, when disparities in income and opportunity became extreme, when people began talking about reforming capitalism to make it more universally fruitful."

"That's why you call it a 'reformation', an evolutionary change from capitalism, to be free of domination by the one percent?" Adam had completely engaged with the conversation and hoped Niru would be willing to offer more clarifications.

"Certainly. But I'm not for any '-ism'. Capitalism is good, if it remains checked. Many in former communist nations created their own kind of capitalism and cruelty. Dominion over others is wrong, whatever the format. Real reform has to be a shift from self-interest to community interest. From 'me' to 'us'."

"That's very difficult to sustain, isn't it? Humans are naturally guided by self-preservation."

"True," she said, and paused to think. "But self-preservation and communal well-being are not opposites. They don't exclude each other. That was one of the misperceptions that got cleared up by the widespread use of social media. In the past we often lost sight of our history. For instance, I'm sure you remember that many white Americans refused to remember that majority America was a nation of immigrants, that they themselves were immigrants or descendants of immigrants. The Native populations who were here first didn't have a concept of land ownership, much less owning water or air. So they were cheated by white immigrants who 'stole' or 'captured' the Natives' resources, driving them to largely barren reservations."

"So how did hundreds, even thousands, of years of old domi-nator thinking change?"

"We were talking about Change, then, with a capital C. For in-stance, do you remember the nineteen sixties, when people de-manded change to end racial discrimination? Remember when the war in Vietnam ended after nearly two decades, when people pressured the government? When people demand with marches and strikes, occupying and rallying in town squares, governments have to listen. Similar calls, demands of various peoples, mush-roomed all over the world with the help of growing technology."

"The counselor over at the school was trying to tell me, when I first got here, about how all these demands, after the disasters, had resulted in a Global Union, with a Council that rewrote everything, to fit the new reality."

"The new GUC call of 2045 was for peace and harmony. Any local laws and practices of former nations that violated peace were eliminated." Niru's voice became more serene as she felt Adam was finally starting to understand. "Violators of any GUC regulations were committed to accelerated-evolution programs. No jails, no murders, no punitive measures. Only development. Now, forty years later, there are no violators of peace and harmony, the basic principles."

Something snapped in Adam. "*That* is hard to believe, Niru. *Really*!?" His traditional thinking, separated from the world for sixty years, was incapable of envisioning such a fairytale. Humans cannot change that fast, certainly not en masse. Individuals? Maybe. "How could it happen?"

"Because of their new magic, real magic. Artificial intelligence became real magic, thanks to new technology. Genetic repair, cell research, physiological and psychological programs, the Fetal Gene Enhancement initiative – above all, technology's probe into consciousness." Niru could have said this in her sleep – she lived and breathed these ideas. She had for more than fifty years. "People finally learned that for narrow-minded *nationalistic* thinking they were paying an extremely heavy price in human displacement and death. Too high a price for the nominal 'freedom'. If you ask me, in those days only one percent of people in the so-called *free* world really reaped the benefits of freedom – not just in the US, everywhere. The expansion of communications technology burst the bubble of so-called freedom for all. Now everybody has this power, not to vanquish the other, but to facilitate measures against whatever pockets might arise that tend to operate by injustice and persecution.

"What you might be having trouble wrapping your mind around is that the *operators* of the AI systems – the communications and robotics, the programmers – were, and are, also people who were part of the monumental evolutionary shift in 2045, or are descendants of that transformational generation. I understand it took them another ten or fifteen years to get all the bugs out, to get the algorithms rewritten, to develop new materials for manufacturing the devices that didn't destroy the Earth, to get all the communications transferred to frequency bands that didn't harm organisms ..." Niru sighed and took a deep breath to keep going ... "and to make all the implants compatible with the electrical systems of plants and animals and the atmosphere, but they did it. It was a miracle." Her shoulders dropped as she exhaled with a beatific smile, and she waited happily for Adam to absorb it all. Knowing him, it could take a few minutes.

"You're passionate about it, I take it?" Adam smiled kindly at her, enjoying being able to be the ironic one, for once.

"Were you in the country when people 'woke up' after President Trump's election of 2016?"

"I was. But politics didn't interest me. Both parties, for me, were the same. Their interest was their personal power – money and positions gained by money, if you ask me. Nobody really seemed to care for people."

"There you are. You agree with me. You ignored politics. I resisted. We took the country by storm in the 2020s. By 2025, the time of the rising oceans and floods, much was accomplished. Thanks to social media – trillions of views of TED talks, youtube presentations, twitter and the like – communication bloomed all over the world. With those tools and AI, medical, biotech, environmental, social, psychological, and political reform movements exploded in each nation. We were in a sort of global frenzy. A real ideological revolution. A revolution in *education*. Each one was unique in its mission and methods, but nurtured by the ideology of compassion and love."

"Impressive. It sounds like a brave new world, not of 1984, but 2084. What about religion? You haven't spoken of that." Adam's curiosity had kept running in the background, ever since Julia had told him the churches he'd known had disappeared.

"Well that's another walk. Maybe tomorrow?" Niru laughed as she turned off to the path leading to her home.

"I'd like that very much," Adam called out to her, and he kept walking.

18 A Day at Three 'M's

At the age of four, Anton felt like an elder in the kindergarten, where the oldest was four – especially now that he had an entire year's experience under his belt. He'd arrived early, thanks to Kumar's schedule, and sat to wait, leaned up against the wall with all the musical instruments. Eyes half closed, he breathed softly and surveyed the scene, other students arriving, and remembered how surprised the teacher had been when he'd announced his views on artificial intelligence – views he'd admittedly gotten from his brother, but which he sensed were true enough to repeat as if they were his own.

He'd said something about artificial intelligence not being artificial at all – that creativity like that was part of human nature, how humans evolve. He'd noticed that Ma Sophie turned and looked more carefully at him, as if he'd known something he couldn't know. She'd already told him earlier that his memory and diction were much in advance of other children his age. He'd talked about being homeschooled, which seemed to matter to her, but he'd never mentioned he was FGE, and she seemed not to know. He wondered if what his parents called FGE consciousness enhancement was giving him an unusual degree of detail about Ma Sophie's reaction to him.

‒͚‒

On this bright sunny morning, children walked through the doors of Three Ms with their escorts – at this age, still their family members and not yet a robot Philip or Kelley – looking happy to be there. Mostly. One-year-old Tim, his head resting on his father's shoulder as he was carried into the room, was a new entrant. He darted his eyes at the unfamiliar surroundings with an expression that asked Why am I here? As his father tried to put him down, Tim clung harder, tense with anxiety.

Sophie, mother incarnate, was ready. Her nurturing trait had a great deal to do with her appointment as a teacher at Three Ms. With extended arms and a loving smile she reached for Tim and gently lifted him away from Mr. Ainsley. "Hello, Tim. Look, what do we have here?" She took him to a toy chest where three other one-year-olds were deliberating which toy to pick for the day. It was important: they knew they were allowed to keep that one toy for the day. The next day it had to be another, not the same. Li Ting, Sophie's assistant for looking after the youngest, took Tim from Sophie's arms.

"What would you like as your friend for the day, Tim?" Li Ting asked.

Tim looked at a girl and two boys around the toy chest. Li Ting said, "This is Sonia, here is Kishan, and this is Roy. Tim and the children on the floor glanced at each other – a silent recognition. Slowly relaxing as Li Ting lowered him to the floor, Tim approached the toy chest, looking at the new classmates and piled toys.

Sophie began, "Children, time to start meditation, Sonia, Kishan, Roy, Tim, please come to your mats." Led by Li Ting, the four youngest went to cushioned mats on which they could lie down, if they wanted. Older children sat on their cushions.

When all were settled, Sophie said, "Say hello to Tim, our new classmate." All of them said "Hi," which made Tim more uncertain.

He was the first-born, one year old, so he had a lot to learn about adjusting to a group of fifteen in a room. Being in a new reality was challenging. All he wanted to do was cry. Lying on his mat, he stared at the ceiling. He saw, painted on the ceiling, families of giraffes, camels, elephants, and rabbits among green and yellow trees. He felt a bit relieved seeing those friendly animals.

Sophie asked, "Who will lead meditation today?"

Several tiny eager hands were raised. Sophie called on the quiet three-year-old. "Will you begin today, Patrick?"

"Yes, Ma Sophie," Patrick said softly. He began the usual practice. "Close your eyes. Take a deep breath in. O..o..o...o...m. Breathe out. Watch the air coming out of your nose, touching your lips. Breathe in. O...o...o...m." Thus began the morning meditation session. All fifteen were in deep silence.

After five minutes, Sophie rang a small bell.

⋅⋅⋅

For the previous thirty-some years, since the 2050s, around the world almost all children had basic life-information operating in their epigenetic fields, improving the expression of their intrinsic genetic structure: thanks to technological advancements in biology, psychology, and pre- and post-natal care, the intellectual and emotional levels of children were heightened, sharpened, deepened. And the FGE procedures had been around for at least ten years, since the 2070s.

While the one-year-olds napped after lunch, Sophie opened a teaching session for the older children. She raised a picture of a lion pouncing on a deer. "Why is it okay for a lion to kill a deer, but not right for humans to kill and eat a deer or any animal?"

Three-year-old Maria piped up. "My grandmother says when

she was my age it was okay to kill chickens, cows, pigs, fish. She loved fish the most."

Sophie, "That was true, Maria, then. But today, why is it not okay for humans, but okay for animals, to eat other animals?"

"Is it because people can cook vegetables and rice and all, but animals cannot?" Peter guessed.

"They don't have to cook. They can eat raw vegetables, like we eat salads," Shiraz suggested.

Melanie added, "My brother told me that big animals like giraffes and elephants don't eat other animals. Weren't dinosaurs vegetarians, Ma Sophie?"

Amber had been silent, seemingly lost in thought. "Ma Sophie, once you said we, people, developed fire and created the wheel. That started this world. I forget the word you used, 'ci….'"

"Civilization?" Sophie helped.

"Yes, that. And you said dolphins have big brains like ours. So why didn't they create ci..vi..li..zation? They are so intelligent."

Shiraz was concentrating hard. "Did you say, Ma Sophie, it was because humans have *better* brains? We have neo-corts so we can think, be better, and change our world?"

"Not neocorts, it's neo-cortex," Anton piped in. "My mother says the neo-cortex was very important. But so was the thumb. Humans can bend thumbs and hold things. Other animals can't. With a bigger brain and a magic thumb, we can create new things. I don't quite understand why it matters, though." Anton smiled and shrugged his shoulders.

Sophie said, "Yes, Anton your mother is right. When you grow up and go to school, you'll understand it even better." Anton, Shiraz, Amber, and Kimberly had that frustrated "not again" expression. They were sick of "Wait till you grow up" from elders and teachers. They wanted to know it now.

"I want to talk about honey bees too, Ma Sophie," Amber

urged, wanting to add to her inquiry list.

"We shall, another time. Now let's play some music. Who wants to lead? Melanie, would you?" Sophie knew that a bolder child sets the tone for the shy ones. Melanie had already retrieved her violin, her parents' gift for her first birthday. Being an FGE with music enhancement, Melanie's natural and cultivated talents were clear to her parents.

"Which song do you want to play?" Sophie asked.

"Let's play *Children of One World*," Melanie said as she walked to the center of the room. Other children went to pick up their favorite musical instruments from the collection laid against the wall. Anton pulled out his flute from his backpack. One-year-olds had tiny drums to beat and bells to ring. If a shy one-year-old wanted to be left alone, it was okay. Anyone older than one *had* to be an active part of the group.

Music, one of the three core components of basic education at Three Ms, in addition to mathematics and meditation, had to be *cultivated*. That was a prerequisite to enter school. Education was the number-one priority all over the world – on equal footing with food, shelter, and protection of life. Universal education had been generally practiced since 2030, but had been required by the GUC since 2045.

When each child was ready, Sophie whistled and children started playing. They had no written score. Sophie's hand and body movements, basic and simple, directed each player. On the big screen the words rolled across:

> *Children of One World*
> *We sing and dance*
> *Play and care*
> *With one and all*
> *Children of One World.*

Hey... hey ... hey
Hey... hey ... hey

After repeating the verse three times, a few youngsters got up and started dancing in a circle. It was all impromptu. The tune just wafted from the screen; children sang, or played the unwritten score on their instruments, or danced, each following his or her own inspiration.

A floating "Stay Awake" sounded, ending the session.

Sophie spun around to connect with each one in turn. "That was wonderful. Did you all enjoy it?" A vigorous "Yes!" widened her smile even more.

"Time for snacks and potty break. Tim, Ma Li Ting will take you to the breakfast room and show you."

Kishan interrupted proudly. "I will take Tim," he said, reaching out to his new companion. Tim was smiling.

19 World Wisdom Arising

Niru had encouraged Adam to attend this event, the annual celebration of "World Wisdom Arising" at New York City Central. It happened every January 1st. "Dr. Bradley," Niru had said, "is an eminent astrophysicist-philosopher from George Washington University in DC, where I teach. She'll be speaking, and she is very good." Adam, now in the audience, remembering what had brought him there, was getting ready to be further awakened to the new reality.

⹁⸜⹁

A few days after the Winter Solstice festival, on New Year's Day, Adam was flying. "New York City Central is the architectural showpiece of the sixties." Adam's drone operator, Tracy, was introducing this masterpiece with a New Yorker's pride. Some things apparently had *not* changed.

"I thought the Empire State Building was the landmark – again, that is, after the World Trade Center disappeared in 2001. And it was built long before the sixties."

Tracy, twenty-one years old, was puzzled. "Are you talking about the Empire State Building in the amusement park? The original *was* ancient. Back in the 2060s, New York City Central was built to resemble the GUC of Mani Dweep, a kind of replica.

If you've seen pictures of Mani Dweep, you'll recognize the transparent curved domes supported by slanted triangular pillars. Look, here it is." Tracy pointed at the view at ten o'clock.

"It is gorgeous," Adam marveled, enjoying the aerial view of the new New York City emblem.

When the drone landed, he said, "I'll find my way, thank you for the ride, young lady." He descended near the main entrance of center. A self-operated monorail chair arrived to take him to the hall.

In the surrounding lush garden, Adam noticed groups of people, fruit juice cups in hand, talking, laughing, waiting for the doors to open. Many of them were very young, in their late teens, he thought, from universities, or early twenties, coming from work, perhaps? Niru had said that this Dr. Bradley was popular for her scholarship, style, and succinct presentations, but Adam still was not accustomed to so many young people appreciating such things.

Adam walked through the corridors of the structure, admiring its transparent "walls" with laser art decorations that seemed to be hanging in the air. At the entrance, he heard "Welcome, sir, may I show you to your seat?" Adam looked around, saw no one – he expected the usual robotic being. A voice "walked" next to him. A laser person?!

"This is your seat, sir. Enjoy the talk," said the voice, which instantly became a pocket of silence where the sound had been.

Before Adam settled into his seat, he heard "How are you? I'm Demetrius." The person sitting next to him was extending his hand, apparently more than a laser voice.

"Hello, I'm Adam Smith," he said, glad to shake a physical hand.

"Have you heard the speaker before? I'm visiting from Greece. Heard of the speaker's reputation. So here I am."

"Well I'm kind of new here, too, following a friend's recommendation."

The audience fell silent. A man walked onto the stage and began speaking. "I'm Thomas More, Chair of the Annual Celebration Committee. With immense pleasure I welcome you all. I'm to introduce Dr. Julia Bradley, who needs no introduction. Here she is." He waved his hand toward the wing. In came Dr. Julia Bradley.

Adam's eyes lit up. "That's her! I met her at the first guest house the day I arrived in New York a few months ago!" Adam said in an excited soft whisper to Demetrius, who was appropriately impressed with a "You don't say" look.

"Thank you, Thomas," Dr. Bradley began. "As always, I will be brief. I have always responded, every year, to the title of this conference, World Wisdom Arising, as if it were new. And it is. Our shared wisdom expands with every moment.

"We're here to bear witness to the inconceivable moment after the formation of the Global Union, in the wake of the nuclear disaster, when humanity woke up. Some of us here personally remember that the destruction and pain had reached a limit beyond human endurance. What we recognize and celebrate today is that the *dead* awakened the *living*. The entire world woke up from centuries of slumber, from the building of empires, the accretion of colonial powers through wars, exploitation, and control. This was the time when humanitarian goals first fully replaced the industrial decimation of Earth, and, since then, our technologies have repaired the damage and created a new universe of communication and vibrant living. Thus, out of the ravages of 2045 was born the Resurgence. Next year we'll have a global celebration of its fortieth anniversary, a fact that still creates wonder in me.

"As most of you remember or have learned, and I welcome this opportunity to say again, it was a compounded nuclear *accident*, not a deliberate act of violence. Millions died. Those who did not die, *awoke*, some instantly, some in stages, as if arising from a trance.

I say again that I believe *the dead awakened the living*. Their death was the ultimate wake-up call.

"In that time of new wisdom, worldwide, each of the survivors recognized that not one of them could continue without the other. They realized that the 'other', whom they had denounced and destroyed for millennia, was a part of them. One of the traditions I've studied said it had been like cutting up legs because they were not like hands. Legs looked different, behaved funny, dressed crazy, or went naked, and lived in shacks. The thinking of hands, from ancient times till the Resurgence, was 'We are respectable, intelligent, powerful, rich hands, they are those ignoble feet.'

"The nuclear disaster awakened all, hands and legs alike. They recognized how foolishly they had lived for centuries, desecrating the Earth and humanity. Hands and legs finally realized neither could survive without the other. They were part of one body, *One Self.* That is the essence of the World Wisdom we're celebrating today.

"Many of you are adding every day to our understanding, deepening our wisdom, with your expanding sensitivities and creativity, your publications and artwork, your advanced AI programming.

"Many of you are great scholars of the world's ancient religious and philosophical systems. Expertise of this sort makes the current interweaving of biology-based wisdom with technological intelligence particularly startling, even after all these years of developing it. We humans, on our evolutionary path, have invented technologies of unprecedented intelligence. My focus is on how our technical advancements are impacting and mixing with the human mind and consciousness, expanding world wisdom, eventually affecting all of us."

Julia took a sip of water. "The great evolutionary leap was the rise of awareness in 2045. That's why we celebrate it as the *foun-*

dation of wisdom around world. It was not defined by or restricted to any *one* philosophy, tradition, religion, or spiritual or scientific practice. It was born of humanity's experience *deep down in the collective consciousness of pain*. Born of *collective suffering*, it contained the *collective wisdom*.

"Recently I was in the Iceland Region. The volcanic terrain and the images of the land's creation reminded me of new life's emergence from the mother's womb, full of agony, churning. Such is life's force, energizing, painful, leading to indescribable joy, the joy of creation.

"This new life, this new wisdom, was born of the commingling of our organic and inorganic potentials. Thus met *science* and *philosophy,* in the crucible, to embrace natal *consciousness*. Some called it 'magic', a 'miracle', or as the ancients called it, unnamable 'That'.

"*That* was it. Finally, all paradoxes were harmonized: the mind-body divide, the science-spirituality divide, the creator-created divide, even the so-called good-evil divide. All were churned in the *crucible of humanness.*" Julia Bradley's voice filled the vaulted room.

"That was the wisdom, *human* wisdom, already known by different names and forms in all traditions and religions around the world. Now it was felt in the bones of all beings." Another sip of water gave her audience a moment to absorb her words.

"As we all became more *conscious* Earthlings, soon our gaze was focused on intergalactic universes, launching further explorations of the Moon, Mars, Venus ... and beyond. Even the sky was not the limit anymore. In fact, we learned there was no sky. Sky is an illusion." Dr. Bradley's sly smile and a wink evoked loud laughter. "And yet we celebrate the fact that wisdom has become the Earth's predominant feature, worthy of venturing into other worlds and encountering other beings.

"Let me end by wishing you a Happy New Year for more ventures *out there* and *deep within.*"

After loud applause from the audience, Thomas More stood up, still clapping. "Thank you, Dr. Bradley, for connecting past, present, and future for us in such a vivid way. Our journeys continue. We are perpetually evolving. Our downward slides, as you said, become the ropes for upward moves. Sorry, I should have said 'chips' – 'rope' is so yesterday!" When the audience laughter subsided, he turned to the crowd. "Now let's have questions. Anybody?" Many hands were raised. More recognized one hand in the front row.

A huge woman, with a red flower in her hair, asked, "Dr. Bradley, can you tell us how the new thinking drew people away from religious and political prejudices? Weren't religions the prime cause of conflict and destruction in the early part of our century, the terrorism, racial prejudice, gender prejudice, wars, all of that?"

"Very good question. It's common knowledge that like hunger and sex, humans are hard-wired for spirituality. In fact, the 'wiring' for spirituality was the origin of all religions. That was good. But the *institutional hold* over spirituality became a religious noose for humanity. Many left the traditional fold, seeking spirituality outside the fold. In turn, the new seekers created more institutions. This perpetual circle broke in 2045. Thanks to the progress of AI, which in combination with human consciousness gives us access to the essential truth, we arrived at the 'Essence Energy' that we uphold today. It can never be *institutionalized*. It cannot be restricted. It always grows as people advance. Scientists, thinkers, writers, and philosophers have been phenomenally busy since our massive disasters. AI provided tools for inner development and outer communication to everyone: politician, scientist, activist, vegetable vendor, or student. That is what *awakening* was. Most of you have heard of, or even remember, the Arab Spring of 2010." The audience nodded, some rolling their eyes with an 'oh, that old story' look. "It remains one of the early harbingers of the changes we were to experience later, though there were interruptions in the process." Julia scanned the audience for the next question.

Adam raised his hand. When recognized, he started speaking into his admission ticket, which contained a built-in microphone. "Nice to see you again, Dr. Bradley. Perhaps you remember meeting me at the Shanti Lodge dining hall a while back."

Looking carefully at the man in the audience, she lit up. "Oh, yes, I remember. You're the wayfarer I met a few months back. You were lost in time, at the time, as I recall," she said, smiling. I'm glad to see you. You seem altogether present now." She laughed aloud. "So, what would you like to know … today?"

Adam spoke confidently. "Yes, Dr. Bradley, I've learned a great deal in recent days, but I'm still trying to fit what I know from history with what I'm experiencing in the world today. You mentioned 'interruptions'. Would I be correct in understanding you were referring to resistance against the radical thinking of those times? If I remember correctly, fundamentalist resistance, sometimes violent, became commonplace in some Muslim countries after nine-eleven. Even in the West, some traditional churches rejected new peace-oriented approaches as 'New Age' fads. Even Pope Francis, a Catholic 'liberal', couldn't implement his 'corrective' vision without resistance from within his own domain."

Many in the audience turned to see who this man was, invoking such outdated stories. Adam felt their stares and continued, "People can't just wake up and say the day after the 2045 nuclear disaster, 'I see the truth, and no Jesus or Yahweh or Allah for me … they all are One.' A loud roar of laughter swelled in the audience upon hearing this ignorant questioner, wondering where he was coming from. Some remembered Dr. Bradley's description of this man being "lost in time." Maybe she was right.

"I'm so glad you raise this question," Dr. Bradley said. "Much of what you say was true before 2020. Today we can review that past with greater clarity. With increased acts of violence, pandemics, natural disasters, and a collapsed kind of apathy, humans all over the globe from the 2020s through the 2040s were exhausted. What we're celebrating here today is the pivot point, after which social and religious leaders accelerated the development and dissemination of advanced technologies to 'revolutionize' the human psyche. As I said before, to achieve that, they spread new thinking through social networking, workshops, webinars, interactive video apps, and so on. Religious *stories,* which many had believed as literal truths, came to be understood for their inherent 'spiritual' meanings, for the subtle wisdom inside them. Masses finally recognized that all humans, in fact all living beings, were connected, whether we know it or not, like it or not." She continued looking at Adam while she paused for breath, for the next thought.

"Many awakened people," she said, "though a minority, had *known* the spiritual aspect of what they called 'religions' since the late nineteenth century in the Western world. But it was different in most Asian nations and Native communities. The *majority* in the West had not recognized it. Thanks to the spirit workers of religious traditions around the world, all that started changing perceptibly in the late twentieth and early twenty-first centuries. As a result, we've been able, with the help of distributive technology, to express these deeper truths even to our youngest. This is what you've seen in the Three Ms pre-schools – Meditation, Music, and Math. Social media helped the new awareness grow 'like wildfire,' as they say, among all generations. People did not *abandon* but *expanded* and *deepened* religious beliefs. They readjusted their traditional perceptions."

Adam smiled back to her and nodded deeply in thanks.

After great applause from the audience, Thomas More returned to the stage, saying, "Thank you, Dr. Bradley." The crowd rose and began chatting. Adam was too full of new information to respond to his seatmate Demetrius with more than a vague smile as they turned toward the aisle to leave.

20 Turning Wheels

On a bright beautiful spring day, Adam Smith felt light, bright, warm, "mimicking the sun in the sky," he said to himself, his lips parted in a faint smile. Perfect time for a walk.

Little swallows in a tall tree greeted him with shrill chirping. He couldn't remember the names of trees and birds, and his new malady of forgetting irritated him. "Who cares?" he whispered with a new nonchalance, and walked on.

"Nothing matters" was the message he'd begun to receive from his mind. His nudging heart kept asking "What is it? And why?" Encountering the new world was not easy, mentally that is. In all other respects it was a comfortable life, for which he had not worked. And that was okay too! It was not charity, or welfare, or insurance, or a family trust ... nothing from his earlier known world. Sustenance and work were not related, as before. Nor were politics, religion, and life, the way they used to be. All were transformed during the sixty-four years of his "sleep." The world had transformed and was displaying a new phase, an ascent from its former existence.

He saw Niru leaving her cottage, "Good morning, Niru. Care to talk? Another lesson in the march of civilization?" Adam asked, beaming.

"Good morning, Adam. Sure, if I'm not boring you with my long stories." Niru joined him and they proceeded along the landscaped serpentine path.

"When do you think America became a radically progressive nation?"

"Whoa. You just jump right in, don't you? Okay. My quick reaction, since you hit a nerve from my past, is to say" – and her tone shifted into an edgy kind of irony that unnerved Adam a bit – 'Wasn't it always radically progressive?' You're reminding me of battles fought long ago, pleasantly forgotten. But maybe hearing a discomfort I haven't felt in a long time will help you make the transition yourself. What I would say about all that is that many Americans thought they were exceptional, progressive, till the world around them started challenging it, often surpassing them with technologies that made their advancements seem obsolete. As you know, Adam, it's a process. Americans were ahead in new inventions. Others, especially the Chinese and Japanese, used new knowledge to create new technologies and then surpassed us in productivity and price. Our mindless consumption of their goods made us lose sight of depleting Earth's resources.

"Our country was only a part, albeit a significant part, of a bigger global picture. The entire world was interconnected. No country had an option to remain isolated – neutral Switzerland or communist China, authoritarian North Korea, or power-crazed Syria, manipulative Russia or efficient Singapore. Now you know how the floods and nuclear disaster turned the page of history, generated a new tide of compassion, everywhere."

"So now we have arrived," Adam posed, trying to complete the picture and shift into a more comfortable zone with his new friend.

Niru burst into laughter. "No, no, no. It's the journey, not the destination. Certainly we've come a long way, created a new world after almost unimaginable suffering. But the journey continues, into a perpetually new future. We're beginning again, with a new version of the ancient fire at the core of the first civilizations: technology and its ever-expanding inventions, including nuclear energy."

"Nuclear energy? When did *that* become a positive force?" Adam, like most in his generation, had been frightened by the word *nuclear,* as a sort of ultimate demon. Nuclear energy and weapon had been the same in most minds.

"Well, by now you've heard, probably from others as well as from me, that AI technology made great strides in that field. A few bright millennials, even before you left, though you probably weren't focusing on it then, developed ways to reuse nuclear waste and generate new energy that bypassed even wind and solar energy. Certainly the use of coal, oil, and gas had already begun to be abandoned whenever possible, since they'd created climatic disaster. You remember the havoc created by fossil fuels, right?"

"Sure. I hate to bring back an unpleasant topic I thought we'd finished with, but memories are popping back up about that time. Wasn't the 2016 president still supporting the old energy sources? Didn't he back out of international climate change agreements?"

"Well, it certainly was one more backward policy of his presidency." Niru's wish to restore some positive diplomacy to the subject was palpable. "After 2020, new startups in nuclear energy soared. You and I, and the whole world, would not be living the life we do, were it not for this *new version of our ancient fire.* Niru's enthusiasm was contagious. Adam looked at her admiringly.

21 Evil? What Is It?

In Cordoba, Argentina, in an old Jesuit Center that had been the home of the oldest university in South America, a seminar of scholars of ancient religions and philosophies from around the world convened to discuss the age-old issue of the *Origin and Nature of Evil*. They all knew, from their varying perspectives, that this issue had seemed unresolvable and had raised its head in every age since antiquity. In this new time, the usual worldwide specialty scholars were joined by poets, artists, and scientists from all seven Global Units. The aim was to generate a deeper coherence across history, so that emerging new concepts would not be separated from those developed during humanity's origins.

In preparation for the seminar, discussion papers had been distributed to all participants, to focus the topics, based on ancient languages of divinity that appeared in their scholarly works:

> *Who and what is Evil? If God created the world, why did He create Evil? If He did not create Evil, how did it manifest? How do we handle Evil? Can Evil ever be eradicated, or is it inherent to human nature? Who and where is God — is there one, two, many? Male, Female, Child, Androgynous? — and how is Evil being addressed thereby?*

The topics had been arrived at by a planning committee, who

had devoted several sessions to debating the dilemmas they faced. Most of the issues arose in interfacing with the traditions of all the spiritually autonomous Regional Units, issues they'd sought to clarify somewhat by studying the history of the controversy.

They considered that some believed humans created God, not the other way round. Still others maintained that we ourselves are gods. In some cases, scientists, atheists, agnostics, and metaphysicians converged on varied forms of nebulous theories about the "ground of Being."

The planning sessions had provided a preview of what the seminar would look like. In both cases – whether God created humans or humans created God – questions were discussed by philosophers and academics from the *former* religious traditions of the world. With Jewish, Christian, and Islamic representatives were Hindu, Buddhist, Jain, and Sikh scholars, mystics, yogis, and swamis. Also prominent were visionary Taoist and Shinto practitioners and Confucian scholars. A few Zoroastrians – Dastoors from Iranian and Indian territories – had been part of the planning and would attend the seminar. They were clear about pointing out that Zoroaster had been the original thinker regarding twin adversarial forces, Good and Evil, characterized by Ahura Mazda and Ahriman – a duality that impacted dualism in Judeo Christian theology. Many Native shamans from the Americas, Asia, Africa, and Australia also helped plan and then traveled to Cordoba.

So much had been endured in the nightmarish twenty-first century, by all populations of the world, the question of evil was still on everyone's mind, even if not everyone *called* it that.

To the divergent beliefs and theologies were added a profusion of colors, races, genders, and most importantly, recent scientific research results on consciousness. A veritable cacophony of nonconformity.

Cordoba was humming with words of the world's best minds

and hearts. Their eagerness electrified the atmosphere. In fact, many had communed on the internet and some had even communicated telepathically – these were frequently the quiet ones.

Among many theoretical issues, the gathering was to deliberate on *how to educate the masses* and teach them to address the issue of what various cultures called "evil" or variants of it.

The president of the conference, Dr. Yakamoto of Japan, began his opening statement. "We all feel the grip of what we call evil when it clutches our hearts, minds, and bodies. Those of us who believe that the goodness of the universal Force is the ultimate are unable to reconcile the simultaneous existence of an omnipotent creator God and an ever-present Devil. Let's begin our discussion. You have your tablets. Go." Participants began typing silently, watching the exchange unfold, responding to it:

> *"Evil is inevitable in our dual world. It is the antithesis of Good. Where there is Good, the other side of the coin is Evil. One cannot exist without the other."*
>
> *"I agree. The confusion starts when we use the **value laden** terms, good and evil. Instead if we use 'light' and 'darkness,' it is like day and night. Neither is good or bad. It just is."*
>
> *"That is the nature of universal Consciousness, the Big-C that pervades in each one of us as small-c. The Big-C is easy to comprehend as God, though many of us are not able to envision, much less experience, the Oneness of the two. So they divide the C, and make two Cs, when there is only One."*
>
> *"Once we know that truth, it can be explained to the masses. Many have done that."*
>
> *"THAT is the point. Our ancient visionaries, scholars and mystics have elaborated their vision of Oneness*

for several millennia through stories and other familiar images. Their followers mistook stories to be infallible truths, limiting them. Thus universal visions were compromised."

"The believers equipped with their limited knowledge, calling it faith, fought religious wars, each bragging his truth was the only truth."

"Fortunately in our times we have moved from such antiquated thinking."

"Now in our times we have our AI and procedures to transform human consciousness, to provide the Big-C for us all."

"Stay Awake!" Dr. Yakamoto roared in his sonorous voice, as he rose to address them all. "May all of you be awake!" After a pause, to let everyone adjust to the in-person format, he shifted into the seminar's mission. "Let's focus on how to awaken all our Regional Units. Some are trailing behind in each region."

"You're not suggesting old-style brainwashing are you, Dr. Yakamoto?" a shrill woman from Ghana shouted.

Waves of booing washed over the vast audience. It was a long-abandoned view, certainly out of place among advanced telepathic leaders at this world council.

"You know better than that, Miss Manigu." Dr. Yakamoto's voice was firm but not angry. "People gathered at this conference know we've moved far beyond those ideas of the early twenty-first century. At that time, each region, country, and individual was driven by self-oriented compulsions – killings, wars, domination, and destruction – all of which contributed to a more or less legitimate general paranoia, fears of being overtaken in one way or another, which in turn led to hostile, rude behaviors in all sectors of society. It looked like *evil*, in the terms of that time. Now it's a time of awakening. Let's focus on how the new-born Singularity awakens everyone around the globe.

"I'll conclude where I began: Stay Awake! We have no time to waste."

Thunderous applause completed the morning session.

22 Healing Center

It was a beautiful morning. But for her cat's purring, Niru would have remained snuggled in bed on this March morning. "It's Good Friday," she said softly aloud, getting out of bed. She liked to remember what her late husband had told her – that it was a half-solar, half-lunar tradition, the Friday before the first Sunday after the first Full Moon after the spring equinox. Her Buddhist in-laws had called it Impermanence Day, since it was about tran-sitory physical death. The tender memories lightened her sense of the day, sparked an appreciation for the ways the old traditions kept evolving, to become more and more universal, more attuned to a lighter spirit. Spring in the air danced in her body, and she thought of her own matrilineal ancestry's seasonal celebration – the colorful Holi festival of her Indian heritage. It was communal fun, throwing colored powder on each other, singing, dancing, joking, breaking the usual social norms for a few days.

A few minutes later, with agile movements she stepped out of her cottage for her daily walk. Walking serenely along the well-trodden path around her complex, inwardly she was soaring in the universe, traversing galaxies. As a child, she'd wanted to be an as-tronaut, an explorer. Well, Niru thought, she'd become an explorer of the interior universe, the human body, instead. A physician, a neurologist, to be precise. Not bad, exploration of the inner world! After all, she mused, the two are connected – the outer and inner universes. The trick is to *feel* the connectedness, the oneness. She very softly chanted her usual mantra, passed down from generations, communing with all of them in the repetition: "*Om Purnam-Adah Purnam-Idam Purnat-Purnam-Udacyate, Purnasya Purnam-Aadaya Purnam-Eva-Avasisyate, Om Shantih Shantih Shantih.*" Now that she had a new friend, an elderly student trying to catch up with sixty years of reality that he'd missed, and maybe thousands of years of inner insight he'd missed, she rehearsed what she could tell him in English, if he cared to hear. "The outer world is full with divine consciousness, the inner world is also full with divine consciousness. From the fullness of divine consciousness the world is manifested, because divine consciousness is non-dual and infinite. Peace, Peace, Peace." Would Adam be open to this, able to receive it?

"Why are his drapes not open?" she wondered aloud, passing by Adam Smith's cottage. She rang the doorbell. No response.

"Mr. Smith, are you in there? Adam, are you okay?" No response.

On the system chip on her wrist, Niru called local health center for an emergency crew and waited on the porch.

"Good morning, Niru." She heard Adam's gruff voice from the house.

Niru went to the window where the sound came through. "Good morning, Adam. How *are* you?"

"Not too well," came a faint voice, ending in a cough.

"Don't worry. I'm calling the cottage service desk. They'll let me in. Stay in bed and breathe deep, Adam." Ninety-year-old Niru sounded as alert as a twenty-five-year-old expert neurologist, a part of her that had remained since her first year of practice.

Soon Ms. Stenigraf from the desk service – a human, not a robot – arrived. "What seems to be the problem, Dr. Vyas?" she asked, punching numbers on the entrance pad to open Adam's cottage.

"We'll find out. I've already called the emergency crew," Niru said, entering the house.

"Hello, Adam. How do you feel? Breathing okay?" Niru the physician held Adam's wrist to feel his pulse. Adam felt relieved, and with a grateful smile looked up at her.

They heard the ambulance drone landing outside the cottage.

⟶🟎⟵

At noon, Dr. Sam Macintosh, standing by Adam's bed in the emergency division at Sakhem Healing Center, asked the patient, "Do you feel comfortable? Is your breathing easier now?"

Adam was all smiles. "Oh, I feel normal, a hundred percent okay. What was the problem … Doctor Mac?" He was reading the name tag on Sam's lapel.

"Well, you know, sometimes breathing issues arise with aging. Just an alarm, for now. We gave you a thorough checkup," Dr. Sam said, peering into Adam's eyes. Then he asked a question that had intrigued the whole department. "When did you have your last checkup, Mr. Smith?" There was no record of Adam Smith in their system. No name, age, address, records of work, hobbies, travels, residency. Certainly no health record. Adam Smith, it seemed, had dropped into their health center from nowhere.

It was not unusual, it was not rare, it was *impossible*. Everybody's records, worldwide, were in The System. Dr. Sam was concerned about some technical goof that would result in a long search. He didn't want it to spoil his planned spring break with his family, starting the next day. His ten-year-old, Natasha, was eager to go to Easter Island, ever since she'd seen videos of the statues there, which the old documentaries had said were extraterrestrial, a word she now understood as part of the universe beyond Earth, filled with Space Companions.

"My last checkup?" Adam tried to remember. "I guess it was … and I'm guessing, before I went on the research trip to Mongolia in early 2020. So my last checkup must have been in mid-2019."

It was a moment of stark disbelief, amazement, and jubilation for Dr. Sam Mac! He had a rare dinosaur on hand. In 2084, he had a patient, born in 2000, who had no chips or implants, no genetic manipulation, either in him or in any of his ancestors. Perfect specimen for medical research!

Dr. Sam could not hide his excitement. "You're amazing, Mr. Smith."

"Am I? I thought you'd be upset for my negligence, missing all my checkups."

"You're fine, Mr. Smith. I could release you now. But could you do me a favor? Could you stay in over the weekend?" Dr. Sam, in the back of his mind, was struggling with the idea that he was about to sacrifice his Easter trip to Easter Island with his darling daughter, a fanatic for anything Space-related, and his wife, Mary, a spiritual coach. For no apparent reason, except that Adam's existence was so preposterous, he was concerned his rare find might disappear if released from Sakhem.

"Stay here for the weekend?" Adam was intrigued. He looked around. The center was delightful. He remembered the sprawling gardens and health spas that he'd read about in the center's magazine while waiting for a doctor. He had no plans for the weekend. "Yes, if you wish. But why would you want me here, may I ask?"

"Oh, I'd like my superior, Dr. Mukherji, and other specialists in healing research to meet you, and I'd like to confer with them." Dr. Sam tried to make it sound casual, not the thrilling treat it would be for the specialists. Adam simply smiled and nodded.

"Well, then it's settled. I'll arrange for you to be moved to the refresher division for the weekend. It's comfortable, kind of a vacation spot. You'll like it. Thank you for extending your stay. I really appreciate it," said Dr. Sam, holding Adam's hand warmly, his face glowing with joy.

⁓⁍⁓

Adam was basking in the warm sun on the terrace of the refresher division, in front of his "vacation" unit, when his new handset rang. It was Niru asking about his discharge from the health center.

"Well, it seems I got rewarded for falling ill. I'm spending the weekend in their refresher division," Adam said with a chuckle. "Why don't you come over? We can walk here, if you wish."

"Well well well. Good for you. I was thinking of checking into the refresher div myself, one of these days. It's open for everybody, which you may've found out, in case you want to go back and you think you have to get sick to do it or come through Sakhem. People go for a sort of reboot, physical and spiritual. In case you've been lounging around and not exploring, you should probably know there's a meditation hall, a spa, and an exercise place. Tennis courts, swimming pools, mini golf, and all that. Even a theater for videos – and a large collection of them!" Niru was getting excited about visiting.

"My word! That is very good news, Niru," he said, graciously pretending he hadn't known all about the amenities. Will I see you soon?" Adam was happy to be the host, for once, in the new world.

"Let me call a drone," Niru said. "I'll see you within an hour or so." Spring fever was such a great pleasure.

23 Algorithms Galore

Over the spring break, Kumar Pundit, excited by his new discoveries in cosmology and ancient scriptures, thanks to his father's treasure chest, decided to stay on campus to use the lab and talk with the techies. He'd launched an entire new series of studies – mostly about DNA and all the phenomena it interacts with, the vibrations of it, the way it changes epigenetically through experience, through reproduction, through enhancement techniques.

"Hey Ted, what's the latest connection you guys have made between human DNA and the astral world?" Kumar caught up with Ted Mesquit, who was on his way home to collapse.

"Kumar, I don't think I can talk sense. I'm completely drained, super tired," Ted begged, forcing a smile, continuing to walk toward his drone.

Kumar fell into step with him and started chatting. "But listen, in my research I found that even before 2020, there were all kinds of weird blends of organism and computer. AI facial recognition was universally applied in China and increasingly in the entire industrialized world. People everywhere thought China's 'Big Brother' was trying to control everybody. And that it was only a matter of time before the AI could reach and read the phenomena people experienced in the astral realm – and beyond that, even people's subtle selves and realities would be controlled by the equipment, which would be controlled by somebody who didn't have their best interests at heart. They were always quoting Huxley's Brave New World and Orwell's 1984. My question is why people always think that the worst, the dark side of humans, will prevail? What's in the DNA?"

"Look, Kumar, I'm a tech guy with math as my specialty. But I can tell you this. It's the fear of the unknown that overpowered humans' higher consciousness for thousands of years – and once in a while still does. DNA was involved early on, in the sense that people who were instinctively cautious, you can say fearful if you want, tended to survive better, and produce more offspring. The vibrations of DNA were used later in some of the brain-mind interface programs, some of the very subtle algorithms. There were still people, for a long time, who got the creeps about that level of machine intimacy."

"That is what I'm after, Ted. Human reactions to every new AI development were fraught with fear. The more I study it, the better insight I get into the beginnings of the technology, and it's unnerving how many people did use it to control others, for self-preservation, self-interest, or greed, even for violent domination. But even as I keep gathering facts about the history of it, I keep finding myself asking why this was so. Why did it take so long, so many disasters, for it to be used for general well-being?"

No matter how tired Ted was, he couldn't walk away from Kumar, his childhood friend, his "twin" as their mothers had often joked. "DNA issues, in every part of our experience, are different now from what they were then. My great-grandmother, for example, in Australia," he said, turning to Kumar, "as I may've told you at some point, used to tell us about her childhood best friend, who had Aborigine heritage, and how the differences between them had effects on their social interactions that weren't always easy to deal with. Now, sixty years later, we don't even notice our racial or cultural differences. Even our teachers in pre-school called you and me twins, despite your Indian and my Australian ancestry." Ted was laughing, relaxing into his fatigue.

"Yes! Technology of all kinds," Kumar said excitedly, "made people totally, unrecognizably, different, especially genetic enhancement and the new chip implants."

"Different? How do you mean?" Ted was part of the great wheel of change in technology, one of its spokes. He turned and turned, conscious only of turning, and sometimes missed noticing the general change in one area or another.

"Man, you're the one turning the whole cartwheel of human evolution, Ted. Don't you see?" They sat on a bench to relax. The campus grounds were beautiful with the pink and white foliage of plum and apple trees.

"Our great-grandparents must have been impressed, and confused, by new technologies taking over every aspect of life on a global scale," Kumar said, looking at the blue sky, "so I can see why it was scary before the great worldwide change in consciousness, after the global disasters. I can see why their earlier experiences had made them distrustful, before the Asibot software patches made all the AI and robotics software safe to let operate, with no harm to nature. Now I'm feeling even more grateful that we live now, when it's all been transformed." Then he fell silent, meditating, eyes open, staring at an undefined point.

Ted, lost in thought, also stared into blue emptiness. They sat silently, stretched out, arms resting on the bench, watching the trees, hearing birds chirping, savoring the fragrance of the reborn spring. Their meditative trance, ingrained since preschool, was now a habit.

Ted broke the long silence. "You know, I'm enjoying this family memory. I think tonight I'll paint a picture of great-grandma with her Aborigine friend. Let me find out if Mom or Dad remembers her name." Ted's voice had lost its tiredness. He sounded inspired.

Painting was the other passion he poured his soul into.

"I'm fascinated by this flow of the past – your ancestry – into this moment on the bench, and into the future, in new forms." Kumar intuitively warmed to the flow-of-time. "You know my father's passion for collecting old family tidbits, his treasure trove? I guess I have my father's genes. I need to connect past, present, future – the process, the evolution, it's all about connectedness."

Ted followed up: "Now that you've got me thinking about the history of these things I work on, and take for granted, I'm remembering something about AI and all its algorithms moving faster than economies and political realities – around the turn of the millennium I guess. Maybe that's what freaked people out. All the civilizational controls they'd depended on started to come undone, and they felt vulnerable – they were vulnerable."

Kumar nodded. "That's always been the human story. Social and psychological realities always change more slowly than technology, ever since the capacity to manage fire. In fact, technology created most of the changes. AI technology in the mid-twenty-first helped all knowledge spread everywhere, and knowledge changes things." Kumar paused to take a couple of deep breaths and think.

Ted jumped in. "It wasn't just knowledge either, although it was – what did our teacher call it, the algorithm explosion? – oh yeah, conditional truth, or conditioned truth, one of those. People were starting to figure out that the designers of the algorithms were setting conditions on what people could know, and thus what it was possible for them to believe. I mean, that's what an algorithm is – a programmed set of decisions about how any piece of information will be handled. I can see that as a freak-out, if only a tiny number of people were designing the information conditions for the whole of humanity, based on low-level data-gathering and misdirected code. That's the way it was going, before it was decentralized after all the disasters, before everything went open source and the data-share program went global, before all the people running the systems had had awakening experiences.

The transformation is what made it obvious and natural for them to program everything for the common good. Did I tell you that one of my teachers was on the original design team that created the Asibots? Technology itself made it possible to make real the Asimov three-rule fantasy about robotics not harming humans – and they extended it to all of nature. I've been at this for so long, have been so deep inside it, I'd forgotten how exciting it was to first figure it out."

"Ted, this is helping. I've been looking at the history of when the AI tech had first moved inside the human brain. What still amazes me is how it's deepened and expanded human consciousness. When we – I mean people in general – reached some kind of awareness of interconnectedness, that's what helped get rid of the old tribal barriers – first among individuals, then in the minds of philosophers and researchers, then the kinds of social activists they had back then, even politicians. Humans were becoming more compassionate. Their next step, which created the world that you and I are living in now, was to develop more efficient interactive social programs. Something that had never happened before at a global level. The other thing that created our world was the effect on individual consciousness at higher levels. That is why most of the highly accomplished, cultivated beings in our lives are now telepathic, why our schools have programs to scan and develop the inner being of each pupil. One of the authors I was reading said that we, as human beings, had reached a new threshold of evolution in an infinitesimally short time." Kumar finally ran out of breath, but Ted could tell he had more to say, and waited.

"Listen," Kumar finally said. "What I want to know. Where are the inventions headed now?"

"We're moving a lot faster, exponentially faster than in our grandparents' time. And of course I'm being pulled into the consciousness issues more than I ever have been, into this or that cultural milieu, to fine-tune the AI responsiveness to all the acquired human patterns. Can you guess where the most resistance comes from today, for advancing into the unified field?" Ted asked with an ironic smile.

Kumar guessed. "From eastern Units in Asia and Africa, with comparatively more traditional populations?"

"Wrong. It's from the former supposedly more educated western Regional Units – European and American. A great many of them are still tied to binary thinking, a Cartesian mindset of either-or, a deeply embedded dualism, even if they're participating in the worldwide compassion energy. They have hard time reconciling their traditions that include an adversarial God-Devil or Good-Evil dichotomy. Even atheists have a problem. They may not care for God, but their minds still cannot easily reconcile the either-or divide. Most Units of Asia, Africa, even Australia and South America, with their ancient cultural heritage of communion with nature – meaning they never lost awareness of the astral dimensions, which is what you initially asked me about – adapted to the inclusive 'oneness' algorithms with ease. It's the so-called 'progressive' West that couldn't easily transform the science-spirituality or mind-body divide. It wasn't ever a technology issue before, but it is now."

"Strange, isn't it?" Kumar had mentally noted one more connection. "With its totalitarian political and cultural history, the 'non-West' could accept the new thinking more easily, because it resonated with their ancient teachings?"

"Absolutely, that's why China, the Eastern Unit, led the march in the early decades of the century. Its authoritarian political setup, ironically, moved faster and became more creative. It became a leader in the AI technological and ideological revolution. The so-called advanced West followed the Eastern Unit. Funny, isn't it?"

"And awesome. That's what I wanted to know from you, o tech master." Kumar was elated, "Go home, man, and rest. Thanks. I owe you one. Coming for our tea-time next Friday?" Kumar and Ted were members of the Tech-Philosophy Club.

"Most likely. I wonder why we still skip today, Good Friday," Ted mused. "I guess some of the old forms will stay active a while longer."

Kumar enjoyed the history of everything. "You know it's Easter weekend, Ted. The Greek goddess of spring, Eostre, was worshipped in England in the seventh century. It was adopted by the church as a holiday to celebrate resurrection, like the rebirth of plant life, baby animals and so on. So it's a spring thing, no matter what your family tradition is." Kumar headed toward his drone. Ted waved goodbye, and went to his.

Kumar sat in the drone and pulled out his tablet to make notes while he flew – follow-ups to their conversation, things he wanted to research further and maybe ask Ted about later: He completed his notes before arriving home and jumping out of his drone.

24 Compassion and Commerce

Niru had talked with Adam's doctors and knew how eager they were to learn from Adam's "natural" physique – unsullied by chips, neuron implants, biotech and such. She was actually a little curious herself, since Adam was the first person she'd talked with in decades who hadn't been "altered." Meeting him at the refresher would be even more expansive than the invigorating boost she expected from her week-long stay.

"Niru, let me ask you this." Adam was pouring tea for her. "It's a delicate question. I'll understand if you don't want to answer it."

Picking up her teacup, Niru smiled, wondering what he could possibly ask. "You're like a little babe lost in the jungle, Adam. Ask anything. If I know the answer, I'll share. If not, we have Alissa-10." Her eyes reflected the gentle rays of the afternoon sun.

"How are facilities like this one funded? Ever since I came to New York, penniless, I've been taken care of. Housing, food, healthcare. But I haven't received a single bill." Adam's concern shadowed his face. "I've asked a couple of people, but they just announce how things are different now, with no details on how it all changed." He paused, then smiled. "Maybe they just didn't have the benefit of your long-range perspective."

Niru grinned back at him, knowing that Adam had not yet grasped the full picture of the transformed world. How compassion and commerce, the two major global driving forces, intertwined. It was time to introduce him to the new concepts of money, once the overlord of the world, and the ways it now shared power with the spiritual lord, compassion.

"I don't know where to begin, Adam. But let me tell you up front. These people are telling you the truth: you don't have to worry about paying for your living facilities or treatments at the healing center or the refresher div. There is no monetary obligation. In the language you and I used to share way back when, the almighty dollar is dead, if you can believe it." Niru laughed aloud.

"What do you mean the dollar is dead?" Adam's vacant look had real pathos in it. He was not only confused, but mildly irritated by Niru's seemingly carefree attitude toward some very weighty matters.

"You and I have talked about the Resurgence before, and it's relevant to this topic too. The most fundamental thing that happened in the shift, at the root of humanity's experience of being alive, was the way the worldwide suffering generated an evolutionary leap into a universal awareness, and state of being, completely pervaded by compassion. At the level of logic, this translated into new insights about the material world. Wise world leaders, men and women, saw the destruction wrought by self-interest. They saw that nations, tribes, communities, corporations, and even families had wreaked havoc on others because of money."

"Everybody knows that. It's an old story. Gaining power over others ruled civilizations for millennia, since humans started walking on two feet instead of four. Actually before that – in the most basic animal instincts."

Niru was staring at the floating clouds up in the sky. "Control is the negative side of humans. What about the noble side, the creative, idealistic, compassionate, devotional?"

"So what happened next?" Adam's pragmatic side was wearying of the high-flown platitudes.

"One commentator put it – that early in the twenty-first century, trade, terror, and technology had tied the entire world together for the first time in human history. Unscrupulous money power, called dark money, ruled in rich countries. The same was called 'corruption' in poor countries. They were ugly times, remember? All that changed." Niru took a deep breath.

"So the old pattern shifted?" Adam was relieved to have arrived at a state of open curiosity, not quite belief but better than agitation.

"Every act of devastation has a hidden companion, compassionate action." Niru paused. "Everything in the universe moves in spirals, moving higher. Starting from a point we've talked about before, so you can feel the sequence of it, the compounded nuclear accident in the Middle East in 2045 became the inadvertent catalyst for all this. The Middle East, ancient cradle of human civilization, once again became the birthing point of the next turning for humanity. The only way for humanity to survive was through compassion. Conscientious people all over the planet had spoken of it for at least a century – truly for millennia in some places. But it had no aggregate effect: governmental and commercial interests, if they gave lip service to it at all, tended to view it as weak-willed emotional indulgence."

"I remember those days," Adam said softly, his eyes now turned up toward the floating clouds. "Those were dark days ... a very dark side of humanity."

"Adam, my dear student, you've been hearing the story everywhere, but it may help to repeat it in this context. In the twenty years between the floods and the nuclear disaster, compassion started to seep through rapidly in the human psyche, individually and collectively, with the help of high-tech communications and social media. Compassionate hearts and minds could activate humanity on a larger scale. Scientific inventions and new technologies – and complete redesigns of old systems – literally and figuratively changed human minds, which led to the transformation of currencies, which became globally shared instruments traded on decentralized networks." Niru looked at Adam to see if he "got" it.

"That's the hardest part for me to absorb," Adam sighed. He pondered, eyes still gazing up in the sky. "Economics, the power of money, controls humanity. That was the one incontrovertible historical truth I believed in. This turn, away from money, is the hardest for me to swallow." Adam was glad, if he was going to have to hear that his certainties had dissolved, to be hearing it from Niru. He was grateful to be able to be honest with her about his disorientation.

Niru reckoned this was the moment to turn the direction to another of their shared times, so long ago, when they hadn't met but occupied the same reality. "Remember there were so many shootings in early decades of this century? School shootings of innocent children, young adults? Shootings in public gatherings like in the Las Vegas crowd? In theaters? In each such incident there were people who tried to save others, even at the cost of their own lives. The shooters planned and acted from animal instinct, and the protectors reacted and responded intuitively. That is being human. Evil action becomes a catalyst for nobility, instantly. No thinking, just doing. Instantaneously, naturally, humans respond to cruelty, to mindless killing, with noble sacrifice. They don't think. They just act. They sacrifice themselves to save others. There is no logic. It is being true humans."

"You're saying that that's how global devastation became a catalyst for compassion?"

"Exactly. Adam, THAT was how the turning point in human history happened." Niru's eyes sparkled, her voice deepened. "The global sweep of unspeakable desolation and despondency was personified in the dance of Death, in many cultural languages. In my own tradition, it was like Shiva's Tandava of destruction evoking Shakti, energy, Shiva's other half, dancing. She is the creative force. It's simultaneous. From the god of terror arises the goddess of compassion, his other half. They are not separate, they are two sides of the same reality." Niru looked at Adam to see if he was with her so far.

"Let me get this straight. Shiva and Shakti are two halves of the same Force, like the Chinese Yin and Yang? It must've taken a while for everyone to understand philosophies like that, if they'd been immersed in other cultures."

"Had you ever heard of the hundredth-monkey theory?" Niru shifted in her chair.

"I heard people using it in conversation, but never quite understood its implications," Adam said, remembering it very well but wanting to hear Niru's spin on it. Her spin usually went in interesting directions.

"Even though the science of actual monkeys was supposedly refuted, it's still a good way to say, in visible terms, that morphic resonance works."

"Morphic resonance?" Adam's eyebrows lifted.

"It's a whole field of study showing how vibrations change the shape of things – morph them – in harmony with the surrounding resonance." Adam's quizzical look brought a smile to her face.

"That's why it helps to talk about monkeys. In simple words, say a monkey learns a new trick to get a coconut more easily, or starts to wash the bananas he gathers, and his family and friends learn it from him. Soon, more in the tribe follow this practice. Eventually, when a hundred monkeys start using this newly acquired skill, all monkeys all over the world, automatically, do it. It was known as morphogenic transformation."

Adam kept staring at his fingernails, thinking. "So how does that apply to humans? If a certain percentage of humans adopt a new 'habit' it becomes universal? Everyone in the world acts the same way?"

"Yes, you got it," Niru beamed. "And that habit of thinking became the way to describe the Force, the energy, that pervades the universe, that pervades Space, which is Essence, which is Tattva. And that is how TattvaShakti became the universally accepted Force" – which many call EE, Energy Essence. Same thing."

"Soooo…" Adam hesitated, then cautiously offered, "that's what the 'Aye, TS' greeting is all about. It's the Force within each that connects them all simultaneously with each other and the universe." Adam's eyes lit up, hoping.

Niru knew Adam was ready.

"That is how the Resurgence was born forty years ago. Compassion and cooperation reoriented the world, creating the Global Union and cryptocurrency. Initially the new global currency was misused like all power had been, before the systemic decentralization. But with the rise of the new consciousness, the shared currency's driving force was not commerce, but self-expression. Old trading relations gave way to a barter system. Greed gave in to sharing. With the grease of inner awakening, which is spiritual awareness, compassionate sharing became standard."

She kept staring at the deep-orange-red sky after sunset. The sound of Niru's words came from deep within her heart, "Our world donned a new face, Adam."

25 Friendly Friday

L ooking at himself in the mirror, Adam was lost in thought. In the six months since his arrival at Five Trees, he had learned so much about the new world, he seemed to be a new person. As he peered at himself, trimming his gray mustache and whiskers, he recalled his thick hair had been a joy for his mother. She always ruffled his hair to tease him, an image he remembered in combing his hair. In the countryside of Mongolia for sixty-four years, he'd hardly ever looked in a mirror. He'd had none. He chuckled at the change.

It was about 5:00, time to get to Friendly Friday at the clubhouse. His new wardrobe had the latest designs. What should he wear today? He pulled out a rich mauve shirt with a galactic design. It was classy. Dark gray trousers with gold trim would be perfect, he thought. Thinking of the non-existent wardrobe in his backpack for six decades, he laughed aloud.

"Hello, Adam." Bob Strange gave him a big hug as he entered the meeting hall, which for some reason was called the Sleeping Lizard.

"Hey, Bob, how've you been?" Adam hugged back, saying, "EE to you."

"You're becoming a natural. What is it? Are you six months old again?" Bob's constant teasing had become comfortable to Adam over time.

"Do I look okay?" Adam continued in a similar vein.

"More than, okay, friend. Let me introduce you to a few new-comers." Bob led Adam to a newly arrived couple, Dr. Amobi and Mrs. Ifedayo Olatunji. "Here is our retuned prodigal, Adam Smith," he announced.

Dr. Olatunji, who'd been a Christian minister way back in 2010, perked up. "Why prodigal? Has he been wasting resources, now a repentant returning to father's house?'

"More like a reincarnated lost son," said Fatima, a slender woman, laughing, holding a glass of pineapple juice. "EE, Adam," she said. He returned the greeting, shaking her hand, saying "EE" and touching his chest, a newly learned gesture befitting the welcome.

"You'll have to be more specific about the prodigal son's story," said Ifedayo Olatunji. "We are new here, and we don't want to inadvertently insult anyone."

Niru joined the group with a glass of mango smoothie. "There are a great many newcomers here, so you're in good company. We're all learning one another's stories as we go along." She, Bob, and Adam smiled hello, and the men indicated they were ready to head to the food display.

The central table was loaded with colorful fruits, juices, pastries, non-alcoholic and regular wines. At one corner of the room were alcoholic and Soma drinks. Another table had soups and main courses: pasta, vegetables, beans, breads and such. Typical Friendly Friday fare. Centerpieces on the buffet tables were colorful sculptures produced by Three Ms students.

Gentle music filled the hall, but became less audible as more people walked in. Bob and Adam, with full plates, chose a table by the window. The music changed, able to be heard only in that corner: each corner had an independent built-in music control system.

"Are you trying to hide, Adam?" Sandra Attenborough approached, and Adam was moved once again by the faint trace of a limp still present in her gait, knowing how she'd broken her ankle so very long ago.

"Is hiding possible in this place?" Adam smiled. "EE, Sandra."

"EE to you. I see you're adapting to the new world fast." Sandra's face reflected her admiration of Adam's adjustment.

"Do I have a choice?" Adam sighed, happily, feeling relaxed at last in the familiar Five Trees environment. He rose and pulled out a chair at the table. "Please, Sandra, do sit with us. I always enjoy your company, but you just now made the very pleasant mistake of noticing I've been dealing with adjustment issues. It just so happens that I do have a question, and I trust your knowledge about such things." When Sandra had sat in the chair next to his, he sat back down and continued. "Although most of my own inheritance sank into the Pacific a long time ago, and my own siblings died in the disaster, I keep encountering people who are dealing with all kinds of material things left over from earlier generations, and I don't know what the world today looks like, in that regard. I'm worried I'll say the wrong thing. So my question is about what happens if there's a dispute about inheritance. Say two siblings inherit property from deceased parents, but can't agree on the division."

"What do you mean? That they don't know where to cut the house in half?" Bob jovially retorted.

"Umm … something like that," Adam replied patiently.

Sandra said, "Adam, it's irrelevant. Whoever wants to live in the house, gets it. They decide it together. All the siblings take whatever they like or can use."

"So, if one wants the house, another gets silverware or artistic pieces, paintings of equal value?" Adam leaned into his question.

"Value is in one's mind," chimed in Dr. Olatunji, who had approached the table with his wife to join the group. "I'm still adjusting," he said, as he pulled a bordering table over and pulled out chairs for themselves, "to the idea that there's no monetary value, as in the old days."

An Aha came over Adam's face and he nodded as he remembered. He continued, "I'm wondering if people go to court for disputes about inheritance, divorce, child custody, business dissolution – you know what I am talking about." He looked at the Olatunjis and said, "I'm glad to see you're fitting right into the Friday pattern. These things have been a huge help to me, trying to catch up, with a mindset that was stuck in a pre-2020 time frame." Others from their initial group of greeters began bringing more tables and chairs to join the gathering.

Mrs. Olatunji, now more directly aware of Adam's missing years, said in her soft voice, "Our son, who recently retired as a judge in Memphis, says he didn't need to make too many changes in the basic structure between when he started, in 2025, and now, even if the structure is much more rarely used. As a social worker since 2000, I understand the way things evolved, though it's new for many. Disputed areas for inheritance have reduced drastically since you were familiar with the way the world worked."

Sandra laughed aloud. "Young judges today in 2084 work only half a day, Adam. Then they pursue their hobbies – music, painting, sports, whatever."

Adam gaped at both women with total disbelief. "Let me get this straight. The lack of a monetary system makes civil court issues, like ownership of the house, irrelevant? What about divorce, business contracts, and such? No courts are necessary?"

Everybody nodded Yes in emphatic unison.

"What about criminal cases? Theft, murder, rape, and all those? You need judges for those!" Adam thought he asked a pertinent question, not so easy to shove aside.

The circle had widened as more people joined the group and

brought more tables and chairs to make a growing constellation. Teng Chi, a former lawyer, said, "Adam, our old world before 2020 had those issues. These started decreasing very fast, once advanced technology could sort everything out. Prison rehab programs, and all kinds of social and developmental interventions, decreased the rate of heinous crimes worldwide. I expect you've heard about some of these developments. Judges of criminal cases became freer too."

Adam looked closely at Teng Chi. "Weren't you a lawyer before retirement? So your work diminished too."

"True. But that was no loss. I found my passion in music. Today my son is a lawyer. But he skis during most of the winter months, and sails in the summer. His online office is available to access, in case somebody needs his services." Teng Chi was obviously happy his son was enjoying life.

Bob, who'd been holding his remarks till Adam had absorbed the last jolt, expanded on the topic. "Adam, m'man, not only lawyers, even psychiatrists and social workers don't have much of the pre-2045 work anymore."

"You're not telling me, Bob, that nobody needs psychological help or counseling?" Adam was incredulous.

"Yes, often people do need help," Sandra said in her calmly confident voice. "All of us need help from time to time, especially in such a fast-changing world. Perhaps, since 2055" – she looked around for confirmation of the year and saw heads nodding – "the family structure started changing. With advanced tech, communication started improving, going from no contact to constant contact."

Adam responded, "But wasn't that initially with friends, not family?"

Fatima, thus far silent, spoke. "But that changed after the disasters of 2025 and especially of 2045. Families became more bonded, caring, contacting one another more frequently."

Sandra added, "Family integrity and support made psychological counseling redundant. Not that people became wiser overnight, but they had software and tech support available, and the areas of conflict decreased drastically. That was true for circles of genuine in-person friends as well as for blood-tie families."

Adam was digesting a new perspective, fast.

"But families can't prevent violent crimes. What about the police force?"

Bob's loud laughter pervaded the entire hall. "Adam, Adam, Adam … I have to take you to the New York police station. The entire unit is busy with community activities: creating neighborhood programs for adults and children. Some police units have their own orchestra. Some are ballgame coaches. The New York Blues have a different hue." Others in the group laughed softly at Adam's vacant gaze, comfortable that he was accustomed to being a font of friendly entertainment during his learning process.

Adam got up. "When I get back, I want somebody to tell me about the military. I keep hearing wild stories on that subject. Can I get you some Soma, Bob? Anybody else?" He looked around.

"Let's go," said Bob, getting up. A couple of others joined them.

"Adam is such an adorable guy," said Mrs. Olatunji when the Soma seekers left, her wide African eyes opening even wider to match her smile. "What happened to him? Why was he lost for six decades?"

Niru filled her in.

The Soma seekers were returning, already sounding passionate as they approached the cluster of tables. Adam's voice reached the group: "Now that is absolutely absurd. Unbelievable. Dissolution of the military? Give me a break."

Philip Appleton, who'd joined Adam's contingent at the Soma corner, was speaking in his determined, loud military voice as he and Adam and Bob got closer and closer to the group. "You have to take my word, Adam. As a former five-star general, I can say that in 2045, at the Resurgence, when I was forty, I celebrated the day of dissolution of the Army, Navy, Air Force, and Marines with great enthusiasm, even greater than at my daughter's wedding four years later."

Adam struggled, again, to imagine a world so different from what he'd known. They sat back down with the group. Adam's voice dropped, still incredulous. "Tell me more about what happened, and how it happened."

The former general was still directing his responses to Adam but spoke loudly enough for others to hear. "Military dissolution was an integral part of the formulation of the Global Union. With the dissolution of nations went their military organizations. All in one stroke of the pen."

"Phil, I would've thought you would've been dejected. You just said a few minutes ago you're from three generations of military family."

"Yes," Appleton said, his eyes searing Adam's, "Yes. But you know such a heritage allows us to see all aspects of it. We are painfully aware of the dark, unjust, inhuman history of our profession. With nobility, service, and idealistic aims were intertwined irrational, cruel forms of authoritarianism. But as soldiers we could not question them. We adhered to them. It was do-or-die loyalty. We did it, but often it seared our souls."

Everyone in the group knew the facts. But all were listening to this eighty-five-year-old general baring his heart. He still looked young, energetic, sure of his perceptions. His voice carried a unique passion that touched everyone listening.

The general continued, "That day in 2045, I was reborn, my America was reborn, humanity was reborn. And I am proud of it. The former military, everywhere, is renamed the Regeneration

Force. They use their rigorous training for all Regional Units that need help. It can be in education, natural calamities relief, agriculture, or anything else that the receiving RUs need. And you know our formerly armed forces can do anything."

Adam stood up, clicked his Soma glass with Gen. Appleton's, and kept looking at him, eyes sparkling, perhaps teary.

26 Telepathy

"" "He smiles in sleep. Maybe he's dreaming," Pa Soham said to the class, as he stood to one side of the painting he'd mounted on the classroom wall. Hafiza was the title of the painting, one of many by this title, the one he'd chosen specifically for this class.

Soham wondered how his telepathically advanced students would respond to it. Would they be able to see, to feel the reality, the source, of this painting from the long-ago past? What else might they find? Soham was sure each one of them would have a unique response – which would lead him deeper into his ongoing research on consciousness.

Camille spoke first. "The painting depicts an admiring mother musing over the sleeping baby in her lap. Her eyes are focused on the infant's face with such intensity."

"She seems oblivious of her ravaged surroundings," Nathan added. "That's so striking, even strange."

Asimov challenged, "What's strange? It's been like that every day, forever. That is life. Nothing new there. Her baby is her focus. It's palpably realistic, with shelled buildings, steel hanging from the roofs, shattered balconies. Look at those ruptured walls."

Teng surprised himself with his new sensitivity to color. "I love how the artist has captured devastation through colors, shades of browns, grays, and blacks. It's deep. I can actually breathe that heat, the shattered dreams in the broken walls of the homes, just through the menacing colors." His voice trailed off in reverie.

Kavita said with tears in her eyes, "I love the way the artist high-lights the central image with different colors. The only green is Hafiza's scarf, covering her head, hiding all traces of hair. Her smile, on pale cheeks and lips, is highlighted with shiny beige mixed with brown. And look at her intense eyes, glaring at her sleeping baby wrapped in deep blue cloth with yellow embroidered flowers. We cannot not notice...."

Nathan, who'd been intensely brooding over the painting, raised his hand, the other hand still on his chin. "Didn't ancient visionaries establish that we experience reality in four stages: waking, dreaming, dreamless sleep and turiya – meaning literally beyond these three? Hafiza seems to experience all four in her mind. Not that she has any knowledge of philosophy or sciences. Maybe she doesn't even know what the words meant. But she is experiencing reality. That's what her expression suggests to me."

Soham looked carefully at him. "Do you want to elaborate your observation, Nathan?"

"The more I gaze at the painting," Nathan said quietly, "the deeper my awareness. Hafiza's gaze sees right through me. Look at the slanting sunrays reflected in her dark eyes – two golden spots – radiating light to her son. He's asleep in the midst of chaos, undisturbed, peaceful. I see a flickering peaceful smile. It reminds me of Buddha's smile."

Randy jumped in. "That's going too far. We know your wild imagination. But this is too much."

Soham knew it was time to shift gears. "Why don't we sit silently and focus on this picture, telepathically reading all our responses."

Everyone in class knew it was time to go deeper. All sat on their cushions. When they were quiet, Soham rang the little silver bell, as always. In meditation they read each other's thoughts, agreed, disagreed, commented, moved on – inside themselves, silently. All was felt, experienced, but was unnamable, indescribable, like Hafiza's stare, and her infant's smile.

Soham was content with his new experiment in pure awareness. Neither higher nor lower. Not here, there, or beyond. It is such. Tat sat.

⁓⋇⁓

Dream Day had come. Graduation was getting close for this class of advanced telepaths. It was a ceremonial inquiry for all graduating classes – looking into what everyone wanted to pursue in life.

"O..o..o..o..m…" Soham started the usual chant from behind the eighth-graders, ten girls and ten boys ages thirteen and fourteen. Exuding energy and excitement on this special day, they hadn't noticed Soham entering the classroom.

Hearing Pa Soham's chant, they quickly settled on meditation mats, closed their eyes, breathed deeply, and began chanting, "O..o..o..o…m." – a habit they'd cultivated since before they learned to walk.

After three chants, they were silent. Deep breathing from top to toe and back continued till they heard Pa Soham's prayer bell. During the silence, some heard ethereal sound, some saw blazing light, some felt energizing vibration – and some experienced all three – and some none, except absorbing silence. But all were at peace, in deep one-pointed meditative dhyan state.

Dream Day was a highlight of the educational process because the purpose of education was to follow one's passion, and this was the day to cohere the passion into a plan. It could be art, politics, finance, spiritual practice, painting, music, dancing, art, architecture,

Space research, AI, healing, inner enhancement, sports – in any combination. Everyone in this class would soon go to universities for advanced special research. Learning was for advancement, both personal and public. Their approach to their studies was thus free of economic considerations, since every individual around the world had universal income, sufficient for a comfortable living.

Most of Soham's students in this advanced class were products of Fetal Gene Enhancement, each with his or her special talent and inclination. After graduation they would have ample choices to follow their dreams. Most teachers and researchers were advanced telepaths, and a minimum level of telepathy was a requirement for any research, so many of the students here might incline in that direction.

"So, Teng, what is your passion? Could you share your thoughts?" Soham asked.

Kavita raised her hand, "Pa Soham, I have a suggestion. Could we telepath? Let's read each other's mind and share."

"Great idea," said Asimov, all smiles, ear to ear. "We can test our ability to read each other's dreams."

"What about privacy?" Nathan was habitually cautious, about most things.

"That is so yesterday!" Camille snickered. "Who cares? In this day and age of AI and telepathy, our life is an open book. What does it matter if people know what direction you want to take?"

"Camille is right." Abdul's voice raised in pitch. "This privacy business is ridiculous. Back in the first two dark decades of our century, when people did everything online and then attacked the service providers for privacy violations…."

"Let's not get side-tracked," Soham intervened. "It was a different cultural world, a different technical world. People were new to the system and didn't understand, and there were some bad actors involved, before the Resurgence. But back to today: yes, I like

Kavita's suggestion. Who wants to telepath Teng's plan after graduation?"

The class focused on Teng. A couple of minutes later, Randy spoke. "Teng wants to go to the Philippines to dig into his ancestral roots. Is that right?"

"Gee ... you're right, Randy. If I find something of my heritage that's valuable for us all, I want to explore that. One more knot in our multicolor tapestry." Teng's eyes shone with joy in the fulfillment he dreamed of. The class sat for a few moments, savoring the experience with him.

These students lived in a universe unimaginable to long-ago generations. In the new times, all FGE children's ability to communicate thought from a distance was enhanced in their mother's womb. Soham, born in 2046, the year after the Resurgence, was among the first of the new generations. His parents, products of the post-2020 shift into AI and singularity, had been the avant-garde generation. Now at thirty-eight, their son Soham was training the newest generations in raising consciousness. It was the call of the time.

Kavita felt the moment shift and asked a question about one of her passions. "Pa Soham, I'm considering specializing in consciousness research. You told us one time about supramental consciousness. I'm remembering you told us about an Indian mystic and his partner, who experimented on transforming cells in the second half of the twentieth century. Have our improvements in technology in the last fifty years brought us closer to higher consciousness than they were?"

"Sure, genetic engineering has contributed a great deal. In the beginning, like in any experimentation, the results were not encouraging. But since 2035, remarkable strides have been made in that field. That would indeed be an excellent field of study."

"Pa Soham, I too want to know about Sri Aurobindo and

supramental consciousness," Teng said, his hand in the air.

"Well, his major work was titled The Life Divine. The title says it. He maintained that human evolution did not end with us, Homo sapiens. We continue to evolve. We reach divinity. Arriving at that superconscious state is the goal of human awareness, it is divine awareness. You can access this info online, as some of you have. We'll practice it in class and at home." A few raised eyebrows did not go unnoticed. "Yes, I guess that's not everybody's favorite homework," Soham smiled, "but you signed up for this advanced class!"

Randy confessed to being among the disappointed. "But much of The Life Divine is very dense. I tried reading a few chapters but got lost in the long, long, long paragraphs," he complained. He had thought of dropping this class.

"That's why you have quite a few other sites for simplified summaries by his advanced followers. You need to get that help. Did anyone else have success with it?" Soham scanned the class.

"I found the followers' writings very helpful," said Abdul. "Some of them speak of Savitri. Could you tell us some more about that work?"

"Is that connected with consciousness?" Kavita wondered.

Soham had been waiting for this moment – students' inquiring minds leading the learning process. Kavita continued, "Savitri was a princess who brought her dead husband from the god of Death back to life. She is the incarnate goddess Shakti. Her persistence, determination, fierce energy, immense love and dedication are captured in one of my favorite poems."

Several students reacted almost simultaneously: "Is she the goddess TattvaShakti?" "I didn't know we followed a Hindu religious track." "Our tech-lady, TattvaShakti, was once human?" "Is Savitri a techno-myth?" "How is consciousness related to her?"

Soham's uproarious laughter surprised everyone. Nobody

thought they were asking anything funny; they were all dead serious.

"Listen, hopeful telepaths, here is your exercise for today. Sit quietly. Focus on me, read my mind. I'm thinking of Savitri's story as it was told in the Mahabharata, the world's longest epic. You write down my thoughts. This is your practice in telepathy."

The class was intrigued. They were accustomed to Soham's ways of teaching, glad that he was not only brilliant but funny. With unblinking eyes they all stared at their teacher. A few seconds later, their fingers on their notepads started moving, recording the reading of Soham's mind.

27 Adam Smith's New Economics

Adam had come to look forward to his tea sessions with Niru, even though each "awakening" left him disoriented for days. He was glad to be at the refresher, where he could adjust all his physical systems to accommodate his ever-adjusting mind.

Teacup in hand, he returned to his most challenging topic, his mind still whirling after Niru's comments from the day before. "So tell me, Niru, what actually happened after the dollar was dead? Was it the Chinese yuan that prevailed before Bitcoin and the other digital instruments took over?"

"Oh no, Adam. It was a gradual death of all traditional currencies, the end of the times when the international monetary markets fluctuated each day, each instant. After the initial confusion, for about five years I guess, up to 2024 or so − I wasn't keeping historical track, just adapting to the effects − there was no traditional money of any kind at all. Only virtual currency. It had no national mark of any country."

Adam's skepticism furrowed his brow. "How could a millennia-old global structure, with deep roots in the human psyche, be eliminated? It's incredible." "It was the power of technology," she began.

"AI was the primary driver. At first, businesses and economists were dubious about cryptocurrency. There was no central organization controlling it. Some called it self-governing, others derided it as 'anarchical'. But it persisted and was adopted. Let me give you a parallel example. Remember how emailing practically eliminated postal service in our time? Even Fed-Ex and UPS impacted traditional postal deliveries. Something similar happened with traditional currency – worldwide. It was a gradual change over several years, less than a decade." Niru knew she was simplifying, but she had to start somewhere.

"That's a mighty short time to dissolve old, old traditions," Adam mumbled.

"After 2020, the year you 'disappeared' in Mongolia, Bitcoins and other cryptocurrencies became widespread, though traditional currencies still predominated. But by 2030 it was all digital crypto, nothing else, and the blockchain system underneath it made it safe." Niru was gently enjoying Adam's consternation, as well as his courage to imagine a world in which he had no experience whatsoever. "At first, the financial experts were all over the place. Some saw it as investment. Others as virtual money. Some thought it was worthless. Others saw an opportunity to make more money."

"So, initially, do you buy cryptocurrency with real money – Euros, yen, dollars, pounds?" Adam's eyes narrowed to a concentrated stare.

"Yes, at first it was like that. A commodity. But it soon changed." Niru paused, listening for the most helpful terms. "Let me explain it another way. Instead of gold coins in ancient times, when humans started using paper money, would you say the paper money was a 'token' currency for gold? I'm going to stick with gold, for the purpose of our conversation, and not get tangled up in issues about silver. Just use gold metaphorically to mean all hard metal with a declared value. So. Paper money was a token for gold?"

"Yes, I would say so," Adam said cautiously.

"Later we eliminated even the gold standard. A million dollar paper bills were considered a real million dollars, without equivalent gold bars. Weren't they?" Adam nodded, so she continued.

"Cryptocurrency is just like that – symbolic digital money replacing old symbolic paper bills that symbolized gold."

Adam stared at Niru, wondering where she would take him next.

"As humans moved through the twenty-first century, even paper money became a myth. People did all monetary transactions online. Your money was simply numbers on your computer screen. And you carried it in your plastic cards."

"So my money was not even in the bank," Adam agreed, sighing. "You're right. We've used symbolic money for a long long time."

"Now cryptocurrency is the next stage in the same game. When paper is gone, values are represented by digits known by different names, known as crypto." Niru was happy her student finally seemed to be getting a handle on the evolution of wealth.

"Tell me, how does it translate today, in the 2084 world economy?" When Niru looked unsure where to begin, he added, "How do you explain everything being free? I don't have any financial resources, no Bitcoins or other cyber-instruments. And I've now heard, a hundred times, that the free services I've been receiving are available all around the world. That to me sounds like a fairytale, Niru." She just smiled at him, waiting for a good moment to start responding. So he kept talking. "I'm confused. Even if you and I don't pay for buildings and services and supplies, somebody has to. Where does the money come from? Who builds the buildings, for instance? Or how are food and medicine produced? Who pays for them? How are the producers paid? By whom?" Adam's distress at feeling lost in an alien world clarified an opening for Niru.

She thought deeply for a moment, again listening for the most appropriate expression. Finally she asked, "Do you remember the ancient barter system, Adam? Crypto's rise was similar to that. Once the digital system replaced 'real' money, people could do away with banks. No banks. Crypto gave rise to a global system of exchange comparable to the old barter system. It soon became a global barter system."

"That is what baffles me, Niru. Let's go to basics. Everyone works at what he or she is good at, and enjoys doing it. Some become expert bakers, philosophers, farmers, singers, AI techies, artists, astrophysicists. They could be teachers, scientists, doctors, administrators, comedians, whatever. But how are they paid for it? With what? By whom? How do they pay to be an astronaut for instance? How do they pay for their training?" Adam felt energized by this target topic.

"They exchange cryptocurrency," Niru said with a lingering smile, staring at him.

"So they just transfer these bits on their U-set or their wrist-tab and it's done? But I still don't understand. Where do you get your crypto units?"

"Listen, Adam. I don't fully understand it either, any more than in 2020, when I was thirty, I understood how the Federal Reserve or banks, or Wall Street worked. But I did banking and investing, and paid for my education with student loans, all on the internet."

Adam broke into hearty laughter, happy to be relieved for the moment from the arduous task of absorbing all the details at once. He resolved to consult someone else later, since this was a primary interest of his. From Niru, he could get a finely developed picture of how it worked for the people who used the system, day to day. He wondered where the gnomes were, operating the system. With a slight chill, he remembered that even before he left for Mongolia, a high percentage of the gnomes were algorithms operating as part of AI. Were there any human gnomes left? Niru had already said she didn't care to know, so he decided to let the issue rest for the moment. He shifted back to the societal effects of the new system.

"Every single individual on Earth," he continued, "gets adequate provisions for life, like a universal salary. If you don't want to do anything, but just roam around, you'd still have enough for food, a dwelling, and the basic amenities of life. Isn't that encouraging dependency, laziness?"

"That's old thinking," she responded kindly. "When you raise children, don't you provide them with facilities to learn, grow, be educated, without asking to get paid for parenting?"

"Sure, you're the parent, they're your responsibility. You give them a chance to grow, and then they're supposed to look after you." Adam did not see the relevance.

"What did poor parents do then, if they didn't have the means to support their children?"

"Well, the kids in third-world countries had to work. Child labor was a curse for those people. I saw that in China," Adam said, wondering.

"In nineteenth-century Europe, the same situation predominated. However, the technological revolution was different from the industrial revolution. When globalization developed cryptocurrency, the entire world underwent an economic transformation about the same time – within ten years or so – compared with millennia of economic power controlled by monarchs, churches, governments, corporations – structures humans had lived with and thought were permanent."

"Technology hastened the change, because there was no centralized control?" Adam sat up straighter.

"Of course. Did you not see that the economic or environmental reality in Mongolia was impacting Austria or Canada or any other part of the world?"

"So, what you're pointing to as a sort of interdependency helped create – what did they use to call it? – a new paradigm?"

"They still call it a new paradigm," Niru smiled. "And you're exactly right. It was a combined effect that accelerated, when all the factors reacted with each other – new interdependency, new technological tools, and above all, the disappearance of centralized monetary control. Such moves had already begun in the beginning of this century. Initially of course, as you, I mean you personally, might expect, the old habits of corruption and self-interest plagued the system. But all the changes happened so fast that often people couldn't keep pace with its total impact on their lives. Often they were confused and misread the signs."

"What about different countries and regions? Political units as well as individuals always work for self-interest." Adam wanted very much to be clear on this point.

"Sure. At first, much blood and sweat flowed in pursuit of political self-interest, as it always had." Niru felt the sadness coming back, remembering those old days of strife, climate change, human migration, all the political and economic nonsense of the first two decades of the twenty-first century.

"So, I think you're saying – and dear Niru," he said, smiling, "I'm sure you'll correct me if I'm wrong – that's how the floods and the nuclear accident played a part in global monetary transformation."

"Yes, but it's important to remember that it had started before that. By 2023, cryptocurrency had already replaced the major world currencies. That allowed the universal income to be put in place around the time of the Resurgence in 2045. We the people of the world were ready for the new barter system, which was based on two major principles: one, contribution by each individual according to one's ability, and two, provision to each according to one's need." These words were etched in Niru's being. She had been one of the activists in those days.

"Wasn't it feared as a communist principle? It could even sound like anarchy, the way you said some people said cryptocurrency itself was a form of anarchy." Adam argued, he realized, as a means to open up more pathways to hearing more details.

"Yes, at first it was, by some, in a few power-based societies like ours. But some kind of shared wisdom finally pervaded consciousness everywhere. The old story of having to work in order to make a living, to survive, disappeared. In the new time, which we're occupying now, you follow your passion. Go cycling, singing, or telling stories, raising a family. Or be an astronaut, or a research scientist to explore black holes. You help the disabled, the slow, the less gifted, so we all rise. You live, you grow, for yourself, your family, and the community."

Adam was still not satisfied with an understanding of how this was possible. He pressed forward. "So virtual money was at the core, is still at the core. People exchanged what they had – steel, oil, buses, drones, food, talents, teaching, music and ... anything?" He stretched his imagination to accommodate such a complex exchange, operating not just in a small community, village, city, county or country, but worldwide in all Global Units.

"I'm happy to see that for you, it's not so difficult to comprehend, after all. You knew of billionaires' children living for generations without working for money. Some became artists, musicians, or astronauts. Not working for money or upkeep is not always demoralizing, it doesn't always make you lazy, as some people still believe, if less so now than before." Niru rose from her chair, preparing to leave.

Adam Smith could not argue with history, however incredible. He was finally starting to understand the new economy – always the inevitable manager of material life – which had now transformed human nature from the lust for control to an active engagement in cooperation.

And technology helped. Immensely.

It was certainly a giant step forward in human evolution.

Niru walked over to check the plants on the patio. Little pink and blue flowers, in pots against the green lawn behind, seemed to smile. Life is so wonderfully pretty, she murmured to herself, and left.

Adam sat on the patio, staring at the sky for hours till it got dark. He saw the lonely evening star smiling. And soon more and more stars tumbled in bunches into his waiting eyes.

28 Student Resurgence Projects

Susan Tee's fifth-graders were noisy this morning. It was the due date for their project for the "Resurgence at 40" celebrations.

Susan rang the "attention" key on her wrist clip. All students settled on their meditation pillows.

"O...o...o...o...m" filled the space. Then silence. Three minutes. The peaceful faces of ten-year-olds glowed.

To signal the end of meditation, Susan called out, "All awake. TattvaShakti!" The class responded, "TattvaShakti!"

"You all look happy this morning. All ready with your project proposals?" Susan looked around. "Who wants to go first?"

Susan had no idea what might come up next. Topics could range from home life to governance, military and money to climate healing or child rearing or flower arrangement, Space research to animal rescue, entertainment to ecology to philosophy. Fifth-graders were asked to examine the impact of AI in the area of their choice, since no activity was separate from the technology empowerments that characterized the new times. "Who wants to start?"

Nye was getting eager, but looked around to see if anyone else was ready. Having mom as class teacher had its pluses and minuses. He had to help mom not look partial. If he had to, he'd wait till the next day.

Carmelita, holding her dark hair up above her head to cool down a little, raised her other hand. "Ma Susan," she said, "I can go next. Gee, it's so hot in here. I don't have my thesis written out yet, but I have a topic. I was thrilled by the info I found about the Global Union governance center on the Mani Dweep, atop the old Maldives Islands. My sister, the geology nut, says its position makes Maldives the vital energy field, the most suitable location for TattvaShakti."

Many eyebrows raised. They obviously were impressed, which pleased Carmelita. She let her hair fall. "I'm working on the structure of the GU Center."

Zak exclaimed in his shrill voice: "I've heard people calling the GU Central the all-time wonder of the world!" Laughter erupted all around him.

Susan said an intense "Quiet" and shifted into the next question. "Who goes next?"

Nye thought this might be his moment. "I'm still working on my summary, but I want to invite everybody today to a separate project. Plus, I want to enter that contest the Global Union is sponsoring, to name this new lifeform. I'm already tired of the first one I thought of – *Homo lumenomachina* – too complicated. So anybody who wants to brainstorm this with me is welcome."

"Thank you, Nye. Good idea. Who goes next? Zak, are you ready?" Susan looked at her wrist read-out, wondering how many more topics they could hear about before the alert sounded.

"Yes, Ma Susan." Zak opened his tablet. "My original title was 'Money down the Toilet'...." He froze, seeing Susan's stern stare, then rushed ahead. "But I'm thinking of changing it, for the competition. The most important AI achievement has been the elimination of the monetary system."

"That is so obvious and so old," freckled Gloria piped in, inadvertently mimicking Zak. "What are you focusing on?"

Zak sat up tall, courageous. "Money was a force that created terrible things: greed, cruelty, wars, murder, stealing, personal exploitation, murder, suicide. It was AI that created the blockchain and cryptocurrency, which led to the barter system. Our generation is so familiar with this system that working to make a living seems strange to us."

"Yes, Zak, but what would be your *focus*?" Susan's voice was insistent.

"My new title for my thesis will probably be 'The Human Shift from Cruelty to Compassion through Monetary Management.' *That's* the focus."

"That's great, Zak," Susan acknowledged, pleased. "We all look forward to your presentation."

Ivo raised his hand. "Ma Susan, I was looking for some shining spots in the first two dark decades of this century. I found the International Science and Engineering Fair, founded in 1998. It was a competition for what they then called 'high-school' kids, ages fourteen to eighteen."

Always impatient, Maloney spoke up: "What's so shiny about it? They seem slow to me, if they were still in school. That's college age for us!"

"Calm down, Maloney," Susan said firmly. "You know Ivo is speaking about another time, another age."

Ivo continued, "In that world when there were different nations, these young boys and girls from eighty-plus countries participated in annual scientific research competitions. It was rigorous. Often many top winners came from what they used to call 'developing countries.' It was heartening, to me, to see how the competitions revealed the human strength despite the fractured political, racial, religious, and climatic issues in each region, I mean country. I consider these young scientists as real torch bearers for the one world we enjoy now."

Susan responded, "That is an astute observation, Ivo. But you have to be specific. Emphasize why you call them 'shining spots.'

Good topic. Who goes next?"

Abhishek sat up straight, unready to leave the topic. "I want to know," he said, "if Ivo is addressing the science-spirituality divide of the dark decades."

Ivo's guttural voice was loud when he turned slightly toward Abhishek, still directing his comments to the teacher: "*That* is my focus. They were our scientist pioneers with sensitive hearts. They were called Millennials then, during rapidly changing times, with uncertain resources, and political, social, and racial upheavals. They were *trying* things, when all around them people were becoming blind-folded in all kinds of panic. That's what drew me to the Science Fair. Were it not for those young scientists, always *testing* their intelligence, courage, and tenacity – fighting all odds, going beyond their own limited selves – we would not have arrived where we are. I see them as pioneers, using their talents and strength under tremendous threat and pressure. And mind you, out of a thousand-plus competitors, only a fraction would get a scholarship prize. The rest knew they would simply go home and continue their journeys." Ivo's passion had silenced the room for a moment.

Susan let the powerful vibration hum, then added softly. "Yes. That was the transformational period in the human journey, when our darkest and brightest urges struggled with each other." She paused, knowing they were listening intently, then went on. "That was the dawn, when technology began dancing with consciousness." She smiled at Ivo. "Good theme. Dig deeper, Ivo."

"Is anyone else ready? Cecilia, you mentioned something to me yesterday. It sounded very ambitious. Are you ready to present it?"

"Almost, Ma Susan. You're right. It's ambitious. The deeper I get into it, the more I wonder … well, it *is* what I want to do in philosophy—to celebrate how the Resurgence brought all the world's religions together and actually shifted the *nature* of the traditions. When they all encountered each other, with a new awareness, they found many of the energies the same—and many obstacles to awareness to be similar."

"That's indeed the case, Cecilia, and worth celebrating. If you haven't summarized yet, could you at least share some of your discoveries? We're almost out of time for today, but I want to give you a chance to get started."

"Thank you, Ma Susan. I got fascinated by a number of religious traditions. Jews were waiting for the Messiah, Muslims waiting for the hidden Imam. For some Jews, Jesus was the Messiah. My dad said that was one of the ideas that had an essence underneath the stories, an essence that was shared, and that the Resurgence had helped people go deeper and find their shared faith, but he said I should look into the old differences. So I looked up articles by historians about *faith* being personal, but getting institutionalized into *religions*. One of them wrote something I may include in my celebration project. It seemed important because so many in our region came from the Christian tradition, and we still acknowledge a lot of the holidays." Cecilia lifted up her tablet and read from it:

> *The Christian faith never had a chance to be a personal faith. After the 325 CE Nicene council, followers of Jesus had to obey the established religion. Other prevalent gospels, the Gnostic, were rejected as invalid. But they, in fact, were real faith documents. They were still taboo as late as 2020—after being dug up in the 1940s—because the only Christianity known for almost 1600 years was the politicized version, not what historical Jesus taught. Protestants with the help of the printing press— the new technology then—helped challenge the established church. But their hands were tied. It wasn't till the*

Resurgence that the majority of people came to understand the similarities among their innermost faiths.

Silence enveloped the room. Many young eyebrows were raised. Susan let the feeling shimmer for a moment, then said, "Thank you, Cecilia. That will be a very important project, indeed. I'm sure your classmates will help, bringing you insight from all their traditions, and I certainly will help." Surveying the class, Susan closed with the necessary reminders: "Please remember, all entries will be submitted for our local competition first. As you know, the winners' entries will go to the GU Regional office. Do your best."

"Stay Awake" floated around them, alongside the signal for the end of the class.

Saying "TattvaShakti," they all stood up, joined hands and bowed, then grabbed their backpacks to hurry to their next class.

29 Family of Explorers

Every Full Moon night, the Five Trees Complex produced an event. It could be a talk or debate by scientists, inventors, poets, or philosophers, or a performance by a singer, dancer, or comedian. Often there would be a group presentation by residents. Sometimes they'd arrange a debate on a topic of local or global interest. Occasionally there would be a dramatic event, a play by residents of the complex. After the presentations, residents enjoyed dinner and dancing.

It was an eclectic mixture of fun, information, intellectual curiosity, new inventions, and anything that caught people's hearts and minds. Most of the permanent residents had retired from active membership in society at large, but their advice was often sought by many young creators. Since the aging process had perceptibly slowed since the 2030s, most residents, at over ninety, were still considered young centurions. In essence, the elderly experts were constantly keeping their minds and bodies actively involved in mixed socio-politico-spiritual community events. The club was appropriately called "Sparkling Super Novae" – honoring the elder "stars" that may die.

Adam Smith was contemplating his first party of this kind at the complex.

"I hope you're coming to the Full Moon monthly tomorrow, Adam," Niru mentioned over their afternoon tea on the terrace.

She'd become adviser-in-residence for him about practically everything. He hoped she was genuinely enjoying bringing him up to speed. At least she smiled a lot. He was almost convinced that he'd adapted smoothly to her eruptions of laughter whenever he expressed some supremely uninformed viewpoint.

"Sure," he said enthusiastically. "I have to make up for my sixty-four-year-long sleep. The 'Stay Awake' reminder seems made especially for me." Adam chuckled at his own joke.

"Well, I'm glad to hear it. You'll meet my grandchildren, too."

"Your grandson is here in New York, isn't he?"

"Yes, his name is Soham. He's a seeker. His sister Lizzy is a Space explorer," Niru said, with unabashed grandmotherly pride.

"What do you mean by seeker? Is Soham a philosopher?"

"No, a neurologist. He teaches eighth grade at the academy. His focus is on telepathy, consciousness, science of the brain and such – so he's a seeker of the nature of mind. We're science-struck family: my mother, Gita, was an astronaut. My father, Tim O'Hare, was a geologist of Irish descent. My husband, Hal, was an astrophysicist from Indonesia, I worked as a medical doctor. My daughter, also named Gita, after my mother, was a medical engineer. My granddaughter Lizzy, like her brother, is a product of Fetal Gene Enhancement. She's in the Galactic Research program." Niru had mentioned her grandchildren many times, but this was the first time Adam had heard so many details.

"It will be delightful to connect faces with names," Adam said, and took another sip of tea.

"Perhaps you'll do more than that. Lizzy is the speaker tomorrow, so you'll have a voice and a mind to add to the face!" Niru said with a twinkle in her eyes.

"Really? Your granddaughter is speaking tomorrow? You must be a proud grandma." Adam, looking impressed, followed up, "What's she going to talk about?"

"Her specialty is outermost Space. Having spent a few years on Mars research, which included a two-year stay on the red planet, Lizzy is now searching for 'greener pastures' as they say. In fact, it's not green at all, it's the darker world, dark, dark, dark infinite space," Niru said dreamily, seeming to be exploring black holes herself.

They heard footsteps. Niru turned. "Here he is. Hi, Beta Soham." Niru started getting up. Soham reached out to stop her, then bent low to touch Niru's feet to show respect, following the ancestral Indian tradition. "Namaskar, Nani."

Soham looked his usual relaxed self. "Good afternoon, sir," he said, extending his hand to Adam.

"Hello, young man, I'm Adam Smith," he smiled in response, with a warm handshake.

Soham pulled out a chair and reached to pour tea. "More tea, Nani?"

"I'm fine, Beta, thanks." Niru smiled at Adam politely and helped him out once again: "Adam, I'm sure you're smart enough to figure out that Beta means son and Nani means maternal grand-mother. But I'm so in the habit of cluing you in, I can't stop my-self." Turning to Soham, she asked, "So how is your new class this semester?"

"They are gifted kids. It's a nice geographic mix too. More global diversity this term. You know it's an advanced class. All of them are 'enhanced chips' as we call them, so they are telepathically advanced. In the past they were predominantly from America and Europe, of mixed heritage. But this time I have students from China, the Middle East, Chile, India, Vietnam, and Africa – still with the mixed heritage that's come to be the norm. I'm looking forward to making significant strides in consciousness research with such a mix of multiple traditions. I'm really excited about what we're doing."

"So what about consciousness, young man?" Adam asked, intently attentive. "This isn't about the physical brain, is it, even though you're a neurologist?"

"Correct." Soham relaxed into his teaching mode, already knowing he was going to elaborate more than was maybe necessary. "The exclusively physical emphasis was dropped way back in the early decades of our century. Today it's about integration of physical, psychological and spiritual phenomena, to enhance our awareness. Neurons are activated through technology. In that way, AI has advanced awareness tremendously. All the kids in my class have had some chips implanted in them after their birth, as well as before. Even my sister and I had them almost forty years ago. But they were basic. Now they're more refined. The technology has increased our ability to perceive reality at a much deeper level than many could do simply with their own effort. Of course, with exception of the Buddhas and such, in all traditions."

Niru added, "Soham's father's parents are deeply involved in advanced group consciousness. They're now in their seventies, vigorously active in running a community home in Wisconsin."

"What's that? Like a rescue center for the needy?" Adam asked innocently.

Soham suppressed his smile out of politeness. Niru, after all her time with Adam, laughed aloud and explained. "No, no, no. Once again, no one is needy for food and shelter any more, worldwide, remember? Tom and Elisa are passionate about communities, extremely social and generous. They are people persons. Elisa's family came from South Africa two generations ago, I think. Am I right, Soham?" When Soham nodded yes, she continued, "Tom was part of a Buddhist sangha community in Japan for a few years. He met Elisa in Japan, perhaps in 2004?" Niru looked again at Soham for confirmation of details.

"Let me get this straight," Adam intervened, before he got lost in this global family genealogy. "Your grandson Soham has an Indian maternal grandmother – you, and your Indonesian husband was his maternal grandfather. Soham's mother, your daughter, is also a physician and married Keith, a writer of repute, whose parents are Tom and Elisa. Elisa is from South Africa, of black heritage, I presume?"

"Yes, and Tom has Russian heritage and met Elisa in Japan," Niru added.

"My oh my. How do you tie these multiple cultural knots?" Adam had never before encountered such multicultural, multicolored, multitalented family strands.

"Quite easily," Soham responded, still relaxed and natural in teaching mode. "My sister and I grew up not knowing any cultural differences. We were a family of loving and smart parents, grandparents on both sides, and like in any other family they had their special qualities, likes, dislikes, preferences and expectations. We all loved each other, honored each other's peculiarities, like in other families. And there were many holidays that included vigorous talks among us all." Soham noticed that this fact of his own daily life still seemed odd to Adam.

"So what happens," his elderly student asked, "if one in the family wants to celebrate Christmas, another Diwali, a third Eid, or a fourth Hanukkah?"

"Well, in fact, we celebrated all of them. That was the fun part for me and Lizzy." Soham laughed aloud, remembering those bright holidays full of colorful clothes, gifts, toys, firecrackers, and sweets all year round, not to mention new tech- gadgets.

Niru offered some context. "You may remember, Adam, that time I tried to clarify that these are social traditions. Religion, as you and I understood it in the early part of the century, has undergone a spiritual reincarnation. It had actually started way back in mid-twentieth, after World War II. By the 2020s, around eighty years later, the world had changed, drastically, as you well know. Cultural fusion was accelerating, soaring. Even in those days, I'd picked up a mantra that was starting to be heard everywhere: 'Let's celebrate our differences so we can enjoy our oneness.'"

Soham entered back in. "That fusion evolved, around the mid-2030s, into a universal mantra, part of our everyday life – I'm sure you've heard people saying TattvaShakti. Maybe some have already defined it for you. They may've said it's a scientific-spiritual construct, which it is, or they may've said it honors a shared sense of global oneness, which it does, but I expect you'll come to sense the depth of it if you keep hanging out with my grandmother."

Niru smiled and reminded Adam, "Do you recall the shift in consciousness I mentioned before?"

"Thank you, Niru, for weaving the pieces together," Adam said softly. Then, turning to Soham, he expanded the classroom atmosphere: "So, Soham, you train these thirteen-year-old boys and girls in deep telepathic communication? So how is that practiced? Is it for their personal advancement? Or do they use it in their work situations?"

"They are only teenagers now. This awareness opens up new fields of perception, beyond what their pre- and post-birth chips gave them. They can use it in any area of life – their work, their search for self. No matter which field, they can utilize this talent, this awareness, for greater insights, research, inventions, or spiritual advancement. They can use it to create new forms of dance, music, theater – whatever inspires them. Or for better interactions with people. My sister went into Space research, and I became a teacher. It's a matter of personal choice."

Adam, so receptive that he allowed his old conditioning to arise, asked, "Isn't being an astronaut more lucrative than being a teacher?"

"Remember? Money and economics are redundant in our times, Adam Smith." Niru's words were nearly swallowed by her loud laughter. "Once, money was everything. I say again, now nobody works for money. Work is for self-fulfillment. Nobody gets paid for it, period."

Soham spoke with a polite smile, "Work is not connected with money, but with dharma. I'm sure you've heard the word, but maybe it would help to hear the definition that many in our current culture use. Dharma means 'that which holds one together.' Each one of us finds our essence, our dharma, and follows it. So we call it the rule of dharma."

"Wow. That is certainly new. To me. One more perspective, for being fully part of this re-formed world. I hope you won't be offended if I don't completely understand it yet. I promise to spend more time with the idea." And then Adam burst into laughter too.

᠆᠊ᴟᵢᴟ᠊᠆

Staring at the Full Moon on the autumn evening, Adam lounged on his deck, comfortable to be back at his cottage – familiar now, unlike the rest of the world.

Such enormous changes in every aspect of life in sixty plus years while he was "asleep." What a strange waking up. His archeologist mind was slow to assimilate the fast and furious changes in such a short time. Before, he was viewing the past; now he was the past, an archeological relic, a novelty. People watched him with curiosity and compassion as he struggled to be in the present, in the Now.

Up in the sky the magical Full Moon was healing, familiar. Adam felt connected to it. The silent night, twinkling stars, a solitary cloud drifting gently over the Moon, vibrated his heart strings. Only he could hear the silent music as a violin player does, in his heart, even before the strings quiver. He floated into memories of those solitary days in the Mongolian wilderness.

Now in the world around him, he knew he was still a solitary stranger in many ways, even in companionship. Brilliant autumn-colored trees in the courtyard donned peculiar hues in the moon-light — yellows, greens, deep violet and orange, shimmering, ethereal. Like heavenly damsels, their branches were moving, danc-ing in the gentle breeze, leaves showing their silvery backs. Adam smiled. "You show-offs," he grinned, as he reclined a little in the lounge chair, fell asleep, and soon began dreaming.

"Day and night, light and shade, good and evil. Why are there always twos?" He asked.

"Can you have one without the other?" She asked.

"No. Each is meaningless without the other. But why is it so?"

"Because"—She pouted—"every question does not have an answer."

"But why not?"

Endless, even purposeless, words continued.

He and She saw the Moon descending. It came closer, closer. The two stared at it unblinking. The Moon sat on the cushioned chair in between the two. Dazzled He and fathomless She kept staring at the Moon.

"Am I up there or down here?" Moon asked.

The two looked up. "Up there," He said. "Down here, too!" She said.

In that instant the Moon dissolved. The Moon knew they un-derstood — that "up there" and "down here" is one reality, per-ceived as two.

Disbelief and doubt disappeared. So did endless arguments. He and She sat silently staring into the dark abyss of space. The dazzling Moon and twinkling Stars kept laughing – silently.

If reality "up there" is a construct of individual consciousness, then it must be true that explaining the universe entails explaining consciousness.

Adam was awakened from this dream by Megh, the neighbor's dog, sniffing his ear. In the wee hours of the dawn, Adam was still on the sandalwood swing on his deck. Rubbing the dog's neck he whispered, "What lesson do you have for me, buddy?"

꠸

"Good morning, Adam." Niru was knocking at his door. "Ready for the walk?"

"Good morning, Niru. I'll be out in a minute. Woke up late. Enjoy the patio swing a good friend lent me," Adam said, peeking through the kitchen window. In fact it was Niru's swing, made in India perhaps more than a century ago, an antique Maharajah swing that had been collecting dust in her storage area.

Niru sat on the swing, relaxing her head on the intricately hand-carved backrest. She gently caressed the fine woodwork, breathing in the faint aroma of sandalwood, and perhaps of forgotten years. Memories of the past enveloped her. She was the queen. By her side stood a maid pushing her swing. Cool breeze tickled her cheeks. Niru was in another time, another life. Hers? Someone else's? The antique wood frame had stored countless memories of generations.

"TattvaShakti, Niru." Adam felt and sounded glad to use the newly learned greeting as he stepped out onto the patio.

"TS, Adam. Ready?" Niru gently touched the woodwork of the swing, looking at it wistfully, her voice still distant, before getting up for their routine morning walk.

After a few minutes of silent walking, Adam said, "It seems you're in another world, Niru."

In fact, inwardly both were somewhere else in time and place. Adam was still in his Moon dream, Niru was caught up in the swing's memory of generations of people who'd sat on its lap. From royal couples' romantic moments to a Maharajah's political ploys. But who knows whose experience she witnessed.

Niru sounded suddenly serious. "Our consciousness uses our brain as a tool, Adam. I've concluded we can indulge in outward activity, but our consciousness is aware of another reality, which I can only call the 'inherent inner vital force'. Everything one experiences is a construct of one's own consciousness. Unique. Unduplicated." Her voice had the ring of absolute conviction – rooted in conscious, diligent awareness, not just "faith."

TattvaShakti, for Niru, was not merely a greeting. It was voicing the ultimate awareness of one "Energy of the Essence" – one Consciousness conscious of itself in the many.

30 The Student Club

Eva Rosenstein from Kentucky had been elected President of the Student Club at New York University. She was conducting their final meeting before graduation – an event that echoed earlier graduations, when the students had announced their dreams of the future, before moving on from school to come to the university.

While the club members chatted and began to sit in the assembly, Eva, on stage, wondered how many dreams had changed, from then to now – how many dreams that she heard today would be fulfilled when they went their separate ways. Although she'd grown up during the transformed times, she'd included history in her specialty – so she had a sense of how far humanity in general, and individual students in particular, had come, since the dark decades. The breathtaking advancement of AI, the shift of so many life functions to the zone of algorithms, the use of specialized chip implants and biotech in almost everyone – all of this painted a radically new picture of the university itself and the students who attended. This was their third year in college, the launch point for everyone to go into a field of special interest. Every year the list of interdisciplinary research was expanding, along with the AI-assisted advance in understanding of how everything is connected.

She looked out at the crowd and marveled at the extraordinary beings gathering in the hall. Genetic enhancement was the force, the core of all thinking. Before her were future academics and researchers who'd be participating, all over the globe, in telepathic discourses.

Dream Day for the university group had an impact far beyond individual plans and imaginations, an impact that had expanded since the 2030s. The graduation ritual, followed in most universities worldwide, reflected each institution's unique programs, which reflected the student body, its aspirations and achievements, its identity. All data from the convocation was made available online for all who had "eyes to see," or "minds to expand," or in the words of Arthur, the Comedy Club president, the "nose to follow the shit."

The crowd was still chatting and cruising the room greeting each other. Eva was disinclined to put a stop to this part of the celebration. Besides, she was enjoying her own contemplations. She surveyed the hall, mentally writing out recommendations to improve the acoustics and décor. She'd been the architect and engineer for the residential complex, which had all the latest facilities. Each house, besides being eco-friendly – a universally accepted building code – had a unique form, its individuality reflecting the designer's and occupiers' special preferences. Eva had shared her plan for a music house, her latest design, at the previous meeting.

Finally the crowd settled into chairs and turned toward her. She had prepared remarks, but on this special day, knowing everyone so well, she just grinned at them and looked around, intuitively waiting for the students themselves to start the action.

Michael Santos did not disappoint. "Why do we need plans? Life unfolds as we move along." His full lips, fair complexion, and curly brown hair had earned him the nickname Cupid. "Cupid without arrows," his roommate Terry Windham often added, emphasizing Michael's reclusive behavior when they were freshmen. Now Michael's name was Natural Visionary – NV for short – for his impromptu remarks.

"That's right," Eva called out brightly. "That's precisely why I needed to plan the music house I showed you last time. The father of a musical prodigy wanted his house built so there would be a constant humming of his favorite symphonies in various rooms, so that the family could live naturally, spontaneously." Eva's voice shifted into that tone she used when she meant for people to retain what she was getting ready to say. "Planning and spontaneity for individual and collective fulfillment may seem opposites, but they are connected." She waited a moment for it to sink in, then continued, "Michael, each one of us has unique needs and abilities. Collectively we create that which others can appreciate. That makes both of them fulfilled. Remember the ancient image of Indra's net? We're like multifaceted crystals on each knot of that net, reflecting our specificities! Facets of crystals project our uniqueness as well as our connectedness."

Terry's voice had an ecstasy in it. "That is so beautiful, Eva. I'm working on creating something similar for astronauts cooped up on space stations or in flight for years and years. Maybe a chat with family or friends as if they were sitting in the same room with them would help."

"You mean sort of a fourth-generation Zappe?" Nishi asked.

"Probably. Earth contact with the launch station is normal. But I'm trying to match live contact with family and friends anywhere on Earth," Terry said dreamily, letting her imagination float into generation upon generation of technologies to open visual and auditory connections among people across the far-flung universe.

Another voice chimed in. "I want to go deeper into consciousness, famously the last human frontier." Shashi echoed a widely shared metaphor, to connect with her listeners.

"That's a big undertaking," said an enthusiastic Terry. "So much had been done since the dark decades, but much still remains obscure."

Michael the natural visionary pressed on. "Can you be specific? What interests you? Consciousness is all there is. For the last thirty years we've probed into it. It's pervasive and yet so elusive, which I would think makes it hard to separate anything out and study it in isolation."

"Precisely. That's why I'm snooping around. Gently, slowly. Not much progress yet," Shashi answered, looking at him with moist eyes and a gentle smile.

Michael encouraged her. "I've been going over some ancient texts, and it seems the ancients did experience cosmic reality. They tried to express it in words, which were meaningful for a small group. Then those stories got made into religions, strangling the unique individual consciousness in the process."

"You're right, Michael. I know. My family says this awareness is in my genes because of my ancestral heritage. I don't understand it fully, the epigenetics of it. Not in my head, but I do in my heart." She still spoke softly, but now with conviction.

"So, you think your project will take you to the mission to harness deep consciousness?" Eva asked.

"That's my hope. When we humans reach that awareness the ancients spoke of, we will be complete. Poorna, as they say, in a Vedic hymn, completion." In the hushed silence that filled the room, her eyes shone with a fuzzy radiance. Minutes passed. The subtle beauty in the atmosphere was palpable.

Finally, Michael felt the moment had come to resume. "Then humans," he said, "will be poorna, complete, and that is the divine ascent? Will artificial general intelligence enable us to reach some other kind of awareness? As organisms, we stop with our highest, our best, but what if evolution is endless? Maybe it's possible to go beyond the completed human." Michael's eyes were dreamy, intense, his voice elated, excited.

Dazed looks persisted on all faces in the room, in total silence.

31 Encounter in Mani Dweep

Traditionally the tropics of South Asia had two romantic seasons in their literature. One was spring, kicking off with splash of exotic multicolored flowers, fruit trees, and constantly chirping birds. Millions of people celebrated spring, mimicking nature by throwing colored powder on each other over the Holi festival in that region.

With different school years in north and south, and all management personnel coming for meetings, Mani Dweep was active year round. This spring, Mani Dweep was alive with visitors from all over the world during these festive months.

Zainab was home for Holi. "What are your plans for the spring break, Zainie?" asked Mandy, the ever-inquisitive mother. Her questions were only a formality. The anxious mother perpetually scanned her only child's mind, a skill Mandy had developed as a professional psychologist and neurologist at Central GU's research center. She was a *fanatical* psychologist, according to her husband, Amir Khan, the astronaut who worked at Space Research Central.

"Umm ... not far," Zainab replied wistfully, staring out the window. "In fact, I decided to spend time with you guys. Enjoy being home this spring. Mani Dweep is so beautiful and inspiring this time of year." Her eyes rested on the blue ocean surrounding them on the enchanting artificial island. As a totally designed structure and organization, Mani Dweep had a perfect balance of climate, technology, and culture.

"So … off to the German region after the break?" Mandy was pushing.

"TS, no!" Zainab splashed the typical teenage shorthand for TattvaShakti. "I think I need to spend some time in Auroville in India."

Mandy smiled, *knowing* Zainie had been thinking about the next stage in her research on consciousness. "Auroville? It's ancient now. Is it still active? Have you found a place yet?"

"Working on it."

Zainab looked at her wrist tablet. "*Here* he is! Kumar's coming from New York, Mom. I invited him for the spring break without asking you. Hope it's okay."

Mandy laughed. She'd adjusted to her daughter's spontaneity in everything. In fact, she often joked about Zainab to her colleagues at the Psychology Research Center where she was in charge: "Zainab is *unconsciously* following her search for superconsciousness."

"Of course. Kumar is always welcome. Your dad will be happy to hear about his parents. I know you know Samir and Ella are his old-time buddies." Like most mothers since the beginning of time, her major concern was her daughter's social life, even more than her daughter's pursuit of consciousness. Being a mother was … being human.

"Yes. He just texted. His uber-drone is here." Zainab rushed to the door, pushing a few buttons on her wrist tab.

Mandy cheerfully straightened the room and rushed to the kitchen to program robot Kelley, her cook. Next she texted Amir to come home soon. "This will be a fine romantic spring," she thought, smiling.

"Hello, Kumar," Mandy enthused. "Gee you're a grown man. Last time I saw you, you were this high," she said, pointing to her waist. "You do take after your father, handsome and proper."

Mandy's excitement was a little too much, Zainab thought.

"TattvaShakti, Mrs. Khan." Kumar greeted her with joined palms and then bowed to touch her feet. Mandy shook his hand, touching her chest with her other hand.

"TS, young man," she said, touching both his cheeks with hers.

"Mom, do you know off-hand the date of the spring concert at Maldives Auditorium?"

"Most likely it's March 17 to 23." Mandy heard Amir's drone landing on the roof terrace. "Here's Dad. Let me see how far along Kelley is," she said, heading for the kitchen.

Kumar noticed Zainab's rush to plan entertainments for him, wondering if she remembered the priorities they had discussed for things to do on the island. She knew his focus was to *feel* the energetic flow of Mani Dweep, so silence was primary for him, and now it seemed she wanted to race around. Nevertheless, he still felt the connectedness that the two of them had recognized three months ago, when totally out of the blue, Zainab had contacted him. And now here they were.

"TS, son," Amir Khan said as he entered with his arms extended toward Kumar. "You're the spitting image of your father. How is Samir? Ella traveling, as always?" Amir happily accepted the tight hug.

"They're both busy in the pursuit of happiness for all, I guess," Kumar said politely with a gentle smile, releasing the hug and touching Amir's feet.

Zainab was ready for dinner. "Let's eat, Papa." And so they went to the dining table, still chatting.

⌇★

"How is your 'linking' progressing, Kumar?" Zainab asked as they retired to her den after dinner. It was her refuge – to write, think, sing, go within, create, meditate or whatever inspired her in the moment. Her doting father, Amir, had used his creative skills as Space explorer to build a 'Space house' for her. It was an oblong transparent bubble in back of the main house, equipped with the latest techno-gadgets. Needless to say it was upgraded every so often with new devices and apps, months before they went public.

"What a view, Zain!" Kumar admired the magnificence of the starry expanse above, an exhilarating sight from inside the bubble house. "You watch the stars and constellation moving above your head every night while in bed! Wow!" He kept turning around, his gaze fixed in the sky.

"Yes, and many a sleepless night too," Zainab laughed. Kumar looked for a place to sit and she said, "Wait a sec," touching a button on her wrist pad. A luxuriously cushioned chair popped out of the floor. Kumar sank in the reclining chair, comfortably watching the sky.

"That's super." Kumar was impressed, but not surprised. His father had spoken highly of Amir's passion for creativity when they were in aeronautics school.

"Tell me about your 'linking'. I'm genuinely curious," Zainab pressed.

"Yes, okay. I'll repeat what you know, to get started. I feel there's an evolutionary process that links past, present, and future, not just individually, but collectively as well. Individually, at a molecular level, our ancestral connections are traceable. That's an old story. People were passionate about that in the early 2000s."

"What about the collective link?" Kumar's preamble was too slow for Zainab. "I'm super-curious about that."

"I've been looking at recent research in human development that describes many complex links between races. Our initial understanding of fight-or-flight for survival was simplistic. It turns out, each contact with 'other' humans resulted in some 'rubbing off' on each other, some kind of mutual developmental influence, possibly partially epigenetic. I'm still not clear about the patterning, if there *were* any patterns to it."

Zainab's eyes lit up. "Hmm ... *that* ... really is significant for *me*, I think, since I'm coming at it from the point of view of connections between individual and collective *consciousness."*

"Since the Resurgence, *intuitively* our leaders adopted the term TattvaShakti to depict the universal guiding Force, more subtle and more powerful than any of the measurable phenomena science had been looking at. Now we have the technology, the tools, to establish the scientific accuracy of TattvaShakti, at measurable levels, like genetics. That's the 'linking' I'm focusing on." There was a tone of trust in his voice, a confidence that this was the right path for him.

Zainab sat silently, looking at twinkling stars. Kumar too was lost in thought. Both relaxed back into the meditative habit they'd known since pre-school days. Kumar let his mind drift into the starry context for the search that had brought him to Mani Dweep, to the GU Center, with its vast records of the latest genetic research from around the world. Being here in the night with Zainab, he knew he'd made the right choice – showing up in person instead of depending on online resources. He wanted to connect with other researchers, on a human level.

"I want to *feel* the linking through personal contacts with advanced seekers and researchers," Kumar added after a long silence, "feel them to know the Force within."

"You've already begun, Kumar. You contacted me, without knowing if I was really interested in it. I was your link to the Island, I guess." Zainab smiled teasingly.

"True. Dad suggested contacting you. That's another link ... an esoteric one?"

"You're not kidding. It's spooky. This morning I was talking with Mom about possibly going to India. Supramental consciousness is my focus. So I'm looking for leads to be in Auroville. Maybe your dad with his Indian heritage and passion could be *my* link! My father calls your dad's passion 'dawdling in two zones, *particles* and *waves*,'" Zainab said gleefully, excited.

"Awesome. Really? You're interested in Sri Aurobindo's vision!?" Kumar was incredulous. "I want to trace my linking with India. Soon."

"You'll find relatives five times removed perhaps? Indians are exceptionally good with their records, especially in places of pilgrimage, I was told. Maybe those are digitized, now. Then of course there are the *akashic* records, the 'sky-texts'," she smiled, "the *ancient* 'digital' system. You might find a sweetheart there from another lifetime! Your *karmic* soul mate?" Zainab was in teasing mood.

Kumar burst into laughter. "You bet. Maybe I'll find the link, or mate … or maybe I already have," he winked.

The "Stay Awake" call floated above. Both smiled at the synchronicity of the call and Kumar's words. Another link? Neither said anything about that inner knowingness.

Mandy knocked on the bubble door. "Come in, Ma." Zainab touched her wrist pad to open the door.

"So, how do you like Zain's bubble pad, Kumar? Isn't it cute? I have an early morning appointment, guys, need to turn in. Will you show Kumar to his room, Zain?"

"I'll go with you, Mrs. Khan. I'm ready to rest after today's travel and all this excitement." Kumar rose and moved toward the door. "Good night, Zainie, happy star gazing!"

"See you in the morning. Good night, happy dreams, Kumar."

Zainab lay staring at the expanse above, penetrating into darkness, the deepest she could. Searching consciously … the next evolutionary stage….

32 Transformational Robots

Tr … Trr … Trrr. Mandy heard the alert in the upper part of her left arm, the ISC internal systemic chip. It was a signal of "immediate attention" coming from her office. As Assistant Chief at the GU Central Medical Lab, she got the first alert call, along with her boss, Dr. Sarika Menendiz – though, as usual with assistants, Mandy was required to check out the situation first and then call the Chief if necessary. Without wasting a second she got into her slippers and ran to her drone, still donning her night robe. The signal indicated, as usual, that the alert was from the Medical Lab, not her Psychology Research Center, which wasn't prone to emergencies – so far, though the overlap of medical and psychological phenomena was blending her responsibilities, more and more, into a single discipline.

The drone had been preprogrammed remotely by the Robotic Medical Help Division at GU Central, activated simultaneously with the alert delivered to Mandy. Since the mid-2030s, major hospitals and healthcare centers around the world had started using robots for all aspects of patient care, including transport of medical personnel when needed. Robotic nurses, fondly called Nurse Robs, were nurse's assistants. They had more information on the patients' medical history, problems and treatment than human nurses did. GU Central was the headquarters for research and development of robotic nurses, and Mandy enjoyed using her advanced AI engineering skills – required for all advanced research responsibilities – to develop psychology-related chips and software to install in the nurses.

Once in the drone, Mandy texted her personal emergency code to Amir. Since both were on call for emergencies at their offices – Amir having a "galactic occurrence" ISC in his arm – they had created a personal code to keep each other advised in chaotic circumstances.

Before the drone landed on the roof of the Medical Lab, Mandy had gathered more details about the emergency. The alert was from China, the Beijing Transformation Center, formerly known as a hospice.

Transformation Centers had emerged in the 2070s, when worldwide robotic research began to focus on creating robots that could induce *transformation*, not just aid patients in transition – robots that could stimulate *awakening* with technological devices.

Mandy's readout indicated that a ninety-nine-year-old woman in the Beijing Transformation Center had started dancing like a twenty-year-old. That was not news. There had been quite a few similar reports from around the world over at least the past ten years. The woman had started scribbling mathematical formulas while chanting mantras and dancing in a frenzy. Evidently the attending Nurse Rob, Lu Shin, had "triggered" the woman's deepest/highest awareness. This was a major breakthrough, signaling also the need for new modulating technologies to smooth the transitions for individuals going through a disorienting process. Mandy was very excited to help people experiencing a radical awakening.

She dashed into her office and started talking with Dr. Li Chun in Beijing on Zappe-6. "Show me the transcript, video, whatever, Dr. Chun," she nearly shouted.

"Will do better than that, Dr. Khan. Here is Mrs. Kim Chen." Dr. Li Chun could not hide his eagerness to share the miracle.

Kim Chen was still dancing, waving her arms, stepping lightly like a belly dancer, reciting mantras and writing formulas on the floor, walls, glass screens, patio floor. On her screen, Mandy was simultaneously observing the Nurse Rob's recordings of Kim Chen's neural circuits.

Mandy was elated. Finally, their research in consciousness had moved several notches up.

"Congratulations, Dr. Li Chun," Mandy said with a thrill in her voice. "Plan on coming to Maldives as soon as you can with the algorithms you used, the frequencies and imaging, and the data, to share with us at GU Central. This is a major breakthrough for all of us – for humankind. Let's share it – honor it – at our 2085 Resurgence celebrations. I can't wait to break the news to Sarika, Dr. Menendiz." Suddenly she realized she was in her night-gown in full view of the Chinese contingent on Zappe!

"Excuse me, folks," Mandy said, pulling her robe and gown close around her and shutting off the screen. "Dr. Li, we hope to hear from you when you can be here in Maldives, at your earli-est."

"Will do," said Dr. Li Chun.

Mandy sat in a dazed stupor. Or was it meditative silence?

⛬

When Mandy's drone landed on the home terrace, Amir and Zainab were in the kitchen struggling over making waffles. Instead of programming Kelley to prepare breakfast, they decided to have a father/daughter breakfast challenge. It involved elaborate plan-ning and execution: what to make, how to make it, and where to find the ingredients. Being herself a robotics engineer, Mandy's domestic robots were really advanced since she constantly improved their skills. The one major disadvantage was total dependence on Kelley.

"TS, guys. Good morning." Mandy's voice was cheerful, too cheerful.

"So what makes you so chirpy, darling, especially after an emergency call?" Amir looked sideways at his wife.

"Ma, you're in your nightgown!" Zainab stared, incredulous, at her normally elegant and refined mother, returning from the office in her night clothes.

"Guys ... the Singularity is *here!* The *real* Singularity! You won't *believe*. Humankind has taken the next step in ascension. In Beijing, a patient has changed the world. I hope I'll be allowed to show you a recording. Mrs. Kim Chen's *solitary* transformational dance has become a dance of *collective* humanity. *One small peek into Kim Chen's brain is a subliminal stare into human consciousness.*" Mandy's giggled words sounded like a teenager's babbling. She was dancing herself, arms aloft, disheveled hair, hands clapping.

"It sounds incomprehensible, Ma. Or is it prophetic? What *happened*?!" Zainab was laughing too, watching her seemingly insane mother.

"You look as pretty, lively, and exuberant as on our first date," said Amir, coming forward to give Mandy a hug. He sensed something truly stupendous had happened. Mandy had seen pretty much everything, so this must be cataclysmic.

Giving Amir a quick kiss, and slumping into a fluffy recliner, Mandy continued, "We have the *data* from Beijing. Mrs. Kim Chen's brain activity and configuration before, during, and after the intervention; before, during, and after her transformational dance. We'll see if this is the end of her life, a transition toward immortality, or a fusion into the cosmic energy soup! We'll help her prolong her life, if she so wishes. She's only ninety-nine. That's young. She can live at least thirty more years. What's important is that we have the chart of the *actual circuitry of her brain, and how it realigned with the healing interventions, how the brain's substructures shifted*. We now have the footprints of an awakening." Mandy trailed off but her family stayed with her, sensing she might resume her verbal ecstasy at any moment.

33 At the Pond

The pond between two buildings of the Five Trees Complex was ornately beautiful. Pink and violet lotuses with multicolored fish in clear water revived Niru, they were her favorites. Long-legged pink flamingos enchanted Adam.

They found a bench in the shade of a great sycamore.

"How do *you* deal with the inherent conflict between good and evil, now in 2084?" Adam asked.

"Perhaps we talked about it before, in another context. But genetic engineering and post-natal medical intervention have worked wonders in reducing or eradicating the so called evil tendencies." Niru knew she'd dropped another conversational bomb on her student, so she offered it up all at once. "We call it 'grin' – G-R-I-N – Genes, Robots, Innerdata, Neuroanatomy – and some people refer to it all as a class of biotech. The algorithms, weaving all these together, flung the world into a new reality, a sort of Singularity spin." Into the perplexed silence that followed this introduction, Niru added, "Noble genes, virtuous qualities are enhanced. Tendencies toward greed, vengeance, cruelty, anger, hatred are reduced. Just as tendencies for diseases were managed earlier. Deeper research in various fields have created new humans – loving, kind, inventive."

Adam pondered for a few seconds then courageously challenged her. As rude as it might've seemed to an earlier version of himself, he'd become comfortable in opening even the most controversial subjects with his teacher. "Is that not called 'playing God'? That's what I heard in the pre-2020 years."

"Oh Adam, don't get me started on that. We – I mean the whole culture that moved through the changes, while you were, uh, napping – we had enough of that argument. Wasted years and resources, above all, wasted lives. You know that I was an activist in those years. I was sick of illogical human opinions and double standards. You could install a new heart, brain, arm, leg, kidneys, eyes, in fact any part of the body. It could be a transplant or artificially created limbs. Were you not playing God then? You could prevent propensities for diseases like cancer by genetic treatment or manipulation. You were not playing God then? You gave shots to newborns against diseases like smallpox, polio, and so many more. You were not playing God then? You could meddle with sexual leanings and gender preferences. You were not playing God then?" Niru's passion made her voice increasingly high pitched.

She kept going. "But if you enhance the *natural* genes of a fetus for creativity and compassion, or decrease genes for evil inclinations, *that* is 'playing God' in an unacceptable way? And such manipulation is to be resented? Forbidden? Considered immoral? Give me a break. Where is the logic?" Niru was practically shouting. "Fetal Gene Enhancement, which you'll keep seeing referred to as FGE, is the most vital step in human evolution to *eradicate* cruelty, the senseless wars humans fought since the beginning of civilization, and all selfish motives associated with the power of money. FGE has been the best protection against the duality of good and evil, usually referred to as God and the devil in the West." Niru took a deep breath.

"Why the West?"

"The East in general, and indigenous traditions everywhere, had to struggle less with this eternal good-evil duality. They had a head start, so to say, with their balancing of duality: with yin and yang, or Mother-Father God, Earth and Sky, a protector mother goddess who was also a fierce destroyer. Vanquisher Kali is both protector Durga and nurturing mother Amba – all facets of the same *Energy Force*, Shakti."

"Ah. So that's what TattvaShakti is." Adam smiled.

"You got it. But it is more. Tattva is Essence, Shakti is Energy or Force." So it means Energy of the Essence. I expect you've been hearing people refer to EE, the way they refer to TS. It is *scientific*, not old-style religion." Niru seemed calmer. Adam still felt a wavering sensation, in this tale of resolving the seemingly unresolvable science-and-religion conflict.

"Back in 2018, when I was twenty-eight, I came across a verse in adoration of the feminine energy, from the *Rig Veda*, the oldest scripture of Hinduism. You know it's the world's oldest religion, and many of its aspects are currently intertwined with science, technology, and consciousness or spirituality. When I discovered this rather less well known verse, which seemed to reflect a powerful transcendent unity involving what was then known as the feminine force, I was ecstatic – especially since it was from a reputedly patriarchal tradition reflected in the *Rig Veda*. I learned it by heart."

Adam kept looking at her. He could only imagine what she might have been like as a soapbox orator in her twenties.

"Do you have any photos of your younger days as a radical revolutionary? Maybe in boxes in your storage unit?" Adam winked with a smile.

Niru laughed and gently hit Adam on the shoulder. "You make fun of me, Adam. But listen, it will help you to remove your blinders. In my talks in those days I used to speak of the 'intercultural bifocals' needed to view the emerging new global world. Today, global denizens have arrived at a different level of awareness. Yesterday's supposedly 'eccentric' or 'outlandish' views are now considered 'prophetic'. Yesteryear's so-called revolutionary views now *define* our everyday reality, our real world."

They reached Niru's home. "Well, now you're free. No more sermons. Still friends?" Niru extended her hand.

Adam held her shoulders, gave her a hug, and said, "This has been a great day. It started last night, in fact, with a heavenly visitation. I'm being blessed. Thank you for your friendship." He stared at Niru with moist eyes.

They stood silently gazing at each other.

It was Niru who broke the reverie. "My grandson is coming for dinner this evening, join us," she said. "We'll be sitting down at 6:00."

"Oh. Thank you, Niru. I would love to chat more with Soham. He's so bright, and so patient with me. Would you say astute awareness runs in your family?" Adam looked at Niru and laughed aloud. It seemed laughing was the only way he could handle brand-new ideas, situations, and people in this new world.

"See you later," he said, and kept walking.

34 Space Exploration Academy

Samir Pundit was lost in thought. Standing on the balcony of his home, staring at the clear dark star-studded sky, habitually he would envision the still-uncharted expanse of the universe. Today, intuitively, he wondered what Benedict, his childhood friend, might be doing right now. Benedict and his wife, Min Ting, had been living in a Martian cave since their first-born, Orpheus, was two. In fact, Min Ting and Ella had been in the same hospital birthing their first-borns, Orpheus and Kumar. Was that twenty years ago? Incredible.

Samir was the most popular professor in the Space Explorations division of the regional university consortium. While his leading-edge astrophysics expertise focused on the future, most admired was his fascinating ability to connect past, present, and future – a fascination he had bequeathed to his son. As he envisioned future explorations to other planets or galaxies, he never lost sight of where humans were in the 1500s, or even in 5,000-year-old antiquity. His co-researchers sought his feedback on their own findings to get a fuller perspective stretching over countless millennia. Fondly they called him "Magic Connector." His notes, videos, and other memorabilia enchanted his son Kumar who loved to explore the collection in the attic, which he called his father's "treasure chest."

"Ding, ding." Samir's wrist pad sounded, signaling a Zappe connection. "Hey, Samir, how are you, friend?"

"Good, good. Benedict, I swear I was just thinking of you."

"So was I."

"Well, there we go again, good old telepathy!"

"Listen, Samir, we're getting ready for our trip to the Moon, in your summer. In our Martian caves, it doesn't matter. No seasonal changes. So we can choose the time for some venture or other, every few years."

Over the previous five years Mars had become a launching site for all interplanetary explorations. Everybody on the Moon, on Mars, and in the new explorations on Venus kept track of Earth's calendar, even though they all had different scales of time. It was not only necessary for mission coordination, it was convenient for scattered friends to reconnect. Of course, the travel time from each location being different, all coordinated ventures needed advanced planning.

"Sure, I'll check with Ella and let you know. I'm also eager to discuss our Venus project. Our crystal planet. Any more findings, since we talked last time, was it '83?"

"What's brewing in your over-active brain?" Benedict gave a hearty laugh. He knew Samir's intuitive hunches too well, with memory tracks stretching over lifetimes and over vast arrays of people, planets, and stars.

"I'm not sure I ever shared this very early childhood vision I had." Samir's voice deepened into a reflective tone. "I was five, I guess. It was probably too silly to share when we met in college."

"Hey, man, I'm used to your silliness. You were still the same when we were fully grown." Being on different planets, Samir and Benedict aged differently, even though both were born in the same year on Earth.

With a smile Samir continued, "I was on Venus. I saw myself dancing in a circle with some other people around a sacred object. It looked like a huge quartz crystal. But even we, the people, were made of quartz crystal – kind of rubbery crystal. We could twist and turn – like those chewy gummies, I guess. The entire land was made of crystals of different colors and consistencies – the houses, trees, everything. The river was 'crystal clear' fluid." Samir trailed off, trying to remember more images.

"You didn't eat a crystal apple, did you?" Benedict's laughter filled the room. Then he added, with a growing urgency, "In fact, the latest data we got from Venus suggested a crystal layer on what seems to be dried fruit. We still don't have enough data to determine if it's mold or actual crystal fruit."

"Really?! With our Deep Mind-6 research project, perhaps my childhood vision can be scanned, inside my head, so I won't sound so foolish!" Samir's excitement sped up his words.

"Absolutely, man. Why don't we spend some time in the Moon Central Research division before our real vacation begins? Ella and Min Ting can catch up while we do the scans. Orpheus and Kumar will have a lot of life-history and research results to exchange."

"Sounds good. Let me check with Ella. I don't yet know what Kumar is planning. He may be back on Mani Dweep. But Anton can keep Orpheus busy, if Kumar's unavailable."

"Fabulous. Is Anton ten now?"

"Yes, going on twenty! He'll enjoy the Moon trip the most, I bet. He'll keep all of us on our toes with his questions, which get more uncanny as he grows." Samir's laughter was dipped in fatherly pride. "What is Orpheus busy with? Any plans to visit Mother Earth?"

"No way. His eyes are all set on Space Companions, now that he calls himself a 'naturalized Martian'," said Benedict, joking, but with admiration. "The closest he wants to get to Earth at the moment is the Moon. All his sights are set far beyond."

"I'm more and more keen to make it happen," said Samir Pundit with some intensity, in his element now. "Is Orpheus connecting with other galaxies and Space Companions?"

"That's the plan. I hope Kumar can come. There's a lot they can share with each other about the evolution of sentience, everywhere." Benedict was elated by the prospect of father-and-son pairs on exploratory journeys.

"Don't forget Min Ting and Ella will have a lot to exchange too. Ella's latest is a new venture in FGE, with even greater consciousness enhancements in fetal genetics. Every so often, I hear her mention Min Ting's research on Mars. What's her newest venture? I remember we used to talk about Martian rocks having unending geological research possibilities, even after years of robotic excavations."

"Believe me. Min has trained her Kelley to go dig rocks around Mars's surface. You know our Research Center routinely does robotic exploration. But this is her personal search," Benedict added, with affection and amusement.

"That's intriguing. What's she after?"

"That's the beauty. She doesn't know. All she does is leave her Kelley in areas where nobody explores anything. Her 'drifter-robot Kelley', that's her pet name, is unique, she says. Min trusts the guidance she receives in dreams and meditation ... and I believe her."

"This is all exhilarating. I imagine we'll have some quality family time – arguing, agreeing, learning, and growing." Samir's laughter didn't allow him to hear Ella come in.

"That sounds like genuine happiness laughter. Who are you talking with?" Ella asked, pressing Zappe-keys on her wrist pad. "Hello Benedict, what a joy to see you."

"Well, we'll see you soon, in person, on the Moon resort." Benedict waved goodbye.

$$\sim\!\!\iota\!\!\sim$$

Watching the harvest Full Moon in his glory from their bedroom window, Ella was ecstatic. Humming one of her own countless Moon-poems, she was literally dancing, which was her way around getting ready for bed. Dancer grandma Ella's genes were active tonight. Samir was already in bed, checking the latest Space news on his Universal Connector.

"It's heavenly time," she said, getting into bed, pulling up the covers.

Samir turned and drew her closer, saying softly, "And you shine like a heavenly star in the sky, dear."

Ella mused in his arms, "Why does the Moon look so dazzlingly bright tonight?"

"Are you asking the astrophysicist or your loving husband?"

"You mean the two are different?"

"Well, not really," Samir began slowly, listening for his favorite thoughts to flow, always some blend of science and myth, and in this intimate exchange, a touch of lover's insight. "The full glory of the Moon is because goddess Savitri, the Force of the solar orb, has inundated the Moon with her full force. The cluster of stars, with Venus in the lead, are celebrating."

"You clever one, I know why I married you." Ella kissed him and whispered, "Good night, darling." Soon both were asleep and dreaming.

─⟋⟍─

Wandering in the Himalayan terrain near Mt. Kailash, Ella and Samir were ecstatic. Can love ever be felt more deeply? No way.

Samir looked around – what a magic land it was. He felt the veins of the rugged terrain in his entire being. Gazing at the nearby snow-laden peak shimmering in the sunrise, he intuitively started reciting the Gayatri mantra to the effulgence of the Sun, savitur.

Aum bhur bhuvah svaha
Tat savitur varenyam
Bhargo devasya dhimahi
Dhiyo yo nah prachodayat

Samir held Ella close and pointed to the mountain, whispering, "In this glorious peak I see goddess Savitri. Look up, there. See the outline of the peak and a face?"

Focusing on the point, Ella was speechless. She kept staring.

Samir was overwhelmed as he saw Ella's face looming close to the peak, encircled in a halo. Out of it streamed words ... "wisdom ... strength ... loving energy of the heart." From the dream state, Samir fell into deep sleep.

⋅⋆⋅

On May 10 on Earth's calendar, Chandrayan, a self-driven Moon rocket, landed on the Moon's surface with the Pundit family.

Clad in their rocket suits, the family stepped out and saw the blue-green Earth shining in its glory, once again. A few years back, this splendor had vanished, and Earth had looked gray, dull, even dying, they knew. But that was the old story of the mid-21st century.

From the Moon, they saw the new Earth vividly. It was enlightened in every sense of the word: bright, shiny, and alive. The sight called up their deep knowing that it was also filled with awakened people. Much of this transformation had happened with the help of technology, which had heightened human awareness. Thanks to the Earth Charter, the research divisions on Mani

Dweep, and Space Exploration Academy programs in universities worldwide, planet Earth had regained, even surpassed, her old blue-green shine.

The Earth had been rescued by humans, the creators of new, advanced technology. Some called the evolved humans transhuman or post-human. Such labeling was a habit abandoned by the most aware: the much-derided Anthropocentrism, which human-centered civilization had come to be called, had evolved. In earlier centuries, it had minimized or destroyed other species – animal, mineral, vegetable – and Earth was darkened. But since Anthropocenes had evolved in awareness and revived the Earth wisely, with ever-more efficient technologies, reality was accelerating on the evolutionary curve. As the species evolved, new names were proposed for it with alarming frequency: the once-popular Homo lumenomachina was rumored to be almost outdated.

Samir of course was fascinated by the history, the progression of all these phenomena. He knew that many on Earth, especially in the Space Exploration Academy, continued to speculate about the possible role Space Companions had had, creatively and destructively, in the early part of the twenty-first century. Some believed that some of the satellite transmissions that kept parts of the internet working during the floods and after the nuclear accident were actually alien transmitters. As Academy personnel kept expanding their presence within the solar system and beyond, enhancing their technologies to discern more and more, the debates became more elaborate.

"There they are, the Pundits!" Min Ting waved from inside the Rocket Port. She'd spotted the visitors first, identifying them by their Moon-rocket Earth suits.

"Ma, that lady is waving. Do you know her?" Anton was the first to notice.

Ella saw Min Ting and waved back.

The Moon Rocket Port was a huge transparent bubble, with facilities suited for all kinds of travelers. Most were transit travelers on their way to orbiting space stations. A few were on their way to other planets or galaxies. But many came to vacation or visit friends and relatives living on the Moon. The Moon bubble port was a convenient meeting place, a sort of grand solar central, for travelers going in all directions.

The Pundits went to the rocket-suit disrobing unit.

Family hugs and cheerful laughter filled the bubble. Samir and Benedict, Ella and Min, Kumar and Orpheus, started chatting. As "you've grown some" or "how sweet" rose among them, Anton was left alone to observe the Rocket Port bubble. After all, this was his first physical visit to another world. For the rest of the families, it was routine, almost.

Anton looked out the windows at the Moon's land mass, trying to locate darker patches he'd seen from Earth. Not succeeding, he walked around inside the port to browse.

Seeing another rocket landing was a real treat. Excited, he returned to the family circle – easy to find, since all the wrist-pad connections made it difficult to get lost anywhere on Earth – or the Moon. All were connected all the time.

Orpheus saw Anton walking toward them. "Hey buddy, what are your plans for the future?"

"There are so many choices!" Anton called out as he approached. "It's hard to focus on just one. But I may want to follow up on connecting with Space Companions, and intergalactic connections, the new frontier." Ten-year-old Anton spoke with a certainty that surprised Orpheus.

"It is not so new, buddy," Orpheus chuckled. "I've been training in it for a few years now. My teachers have been investigating the field for at least ten. You know the ET theories are ancient, at least 200 years old." Assuming Anton was still hooked on childhood fantasies, Orpheus was referring to oldies about 'ancient aliens', his own favorite shows growing up.

"I know, I know. That's baby stuff. I want to work with Space Companions – on intergalactic systems. Communicate with them." Anton's gray eyes had gone dreamy, Orpheus noticed.

"Whoa," he said, paying closer attention and shifting his voice into a more collegial tone. "My Space Connector guides are deciphering messages now. I'm in training for a year. Next month, I'll be in charge of the interstellar communication division, which has Earth stations for communication. Maybe I can send you links and useful data. Algorithms. Whatever I can share."

Orpheus and Anton connected silently by eye contact, surprising both of them a little.

35 Under the Wisteria

"What an exhibit!" Kumar said as he and Zainab walked out of the museum.

"You'd already *seen* it, Kumar. '*Pre-Resurgence Evolution*' has been online for a while. What impressed you more this time?" Zainab's question sounded strange to Kumar. He looked at her to see if she was teasing him.

"Testing me, Zainie?"

"No, I am serious." She gently patted his shoulder. "I'm completely aware that you're passionate about this evolutionary process, the racial links, the ancient and modern technology. You're the expert. I'm curious to know what was new for you. I can learn something." Kumar noticed a gentler Zainab, not the challenging powerhouse that she always seemed to be.

He looked at her with his eyes staring into hers, smiled, drew her closer. "Let's find a place to sit. I promise I won't lecture."

They strolled through the famously eclectic surroundings of the Exhibit Hall, with its gardens modeled on historical European and Japanese styles. Kumar led her to the Japanese corner. "How's this?"

"Perfect." They sat by the pink-lotus pond on a low bench shaded by a deep purple vine of wisteria.

Staring at long-legged pink cranes and lotuses against the setting sun, Zainab exclaimed breathily, "Such beauty! What more does one need?"

"Mani Dweep has been so impressive. These few days of my wanderings on the Island have been a treat." Kumar put his arm across her shoulder, pulling her closer. "I wish I could explore more of its beauty. Our engineers and architects have blended nature and technology with such a gentle poetry. It's inspiring, transformative."

"So true. I grew up here and often took its magnificence for granted. In my younger days, exploring other places of the world was exciting. Today, now, I feel Mani Dweep truly is a jewel, the gem that its name describes."

"Isn't that the truth? Mani Dweep is the most precious creation of the human race. I'm glad I can still be amazed at this blend of science, technology, philosophy, arts, music, and nature. Earlier generations could not possibly have imagined how algorithms could've helped fuse inner awareness and outer reality, with such an astonishing aesthetic."

"I often wonder," Zainab said, "if we're ignoring the flip side of such a creation, so intertwined with technology?"

"Well, there's always been a flip side to scientific and technical advancements. We know it was part of being human. There was a choice: use the new power for the growth of all creation, or for personal gain or power over others. But, and I know you've looked into this, Zainie, so I know you can feel and appreciate it, in our time the positives have neutralized the usual negatives in behavior – the personal, social, political, and economic. In earlier times, which I've spent so much time investigating, the self, the small-s individual, was at the center of all thinking, oriented toward self-indulgence, selfishness. Even many spiritual seekers were focused on self-enhancement. Spiritual teachers spoke in adoration of Bodhisattvas, but most remained far from reaching that state of being. I've looked at the trajectory, and it looks like, since the 2040s, the aggregate shift was finally toward the ultimate Self –

capital S – in *practice*, not just in words." Kumar was staring at a crane, standing in meditation as it were, who had just caught a fish, a quick catch.

Zainab saw Kumar staring at the crane. "Would you call the crane self-centered?"

"Not unless it's on a suicide mission. The fish is its food, its source of survival. He needs the fish." Kumar stared mischievously at Zainab. "But humans didn't distinguish between 'need' and 'desire'. Cranes don't go beyond need." Zainab was leaning on Kumar's shoulder, staring at the sky lost in deep thought. Kumar's eyes turned to the rippling water. After several quiet moments, Zainab responded to the idea.

"What do you think, Kumar? Is my search for deeper awareness my 'need' or my 'desire'? Or yours for that matter? You're driven by this amalgam of science and spirituality. Is that your 'need' or 'desire'?" Her question intrigued her companion, who kept staring at the blue water down in front while she kept her gaze on the blue sky.

Kumar had *felt* this urge as his driving force. What was it *for*? Desire for name, fame, money, power and all those ancient compulsions? Certainly, none of those. Then what? Why was he *doing* it? What was 'it'? He confessed to himself that he didn't really know. It seemed he couldn't help doing it, whatever 'it' was. Like the rose could not but bloom, or a singer could not but sing, it was spontaneous. He reached tenderly for Zainab's face and turned it toward him. "It seems it is my need, not a desire. It's spontaneous." Kumar spoke with deliberate conviction while he stared into her gentle inquisitive eyes. "How about you? What do you feel?" Was he reading her face? Her expression? Admiring her beauty? Or did he know her answer, not yet uttered?

Turning her head to the blue sky strewn with white clouds, Zainab said, "See those crazy shapes of clouds? They have streaks spreading out like rays. So ... to go deeper, higher, be more aware, is the natural essence – of being human too. And it's a solitary search. Each unique in itself." Zainab paused. "Is that self-centeredness?" she asked.

"That's *your* specialty. You tell me. I *know* it when I *see* it," said Kumar.

"It is tricky," she said slowly. "Spirituality, inner awareness, manifests in human behavior, language, arts, music, compassion. Each 'expression is *unique*. Mine is not the same as yours, and yet is still connected." Her eyes kept tracing lines of cloudy craziness, unique connectedness. She leaned against the back of the low bench. "It is my *need*, not my *desire*, to do anything I can articulate as having caught my attention." She turned to Kumar and chuckled. "Of course that's what drives Ma crazy."

Pulling her closer, his eyes fixed on the undulations of the lake, Kumar spoke slowly, contemplatively. "The fruit of your need and mine will be a surprise for all."

"We shall see," Zainab said, touching the purple and violet petals of wisteria that had dropped into her lap. She looked up at the vine. Tenderly collecting the petals in her palms, she kissed them. Then turning to Kumar she held the petals close to his lips. Kumar leaned into the embrace.

The intertwined vine *felt* the passion of the embrace and the kiss. "It was deep, pure," the vines declared through their throbbing veins, a reminder of the Kabuki plays of love and sensuality in their homeland, Japan.

But above all, the abundant flowers kept laughing, gleefully, exuding expanded consciousness into the passionate kiss of young lovers.

36 Generational Exchange

At the simple vegan dinner, Adam turned to Soham. "Your grandmother gave me a major lesson on the evolution of consciousness this morning. Very revealing. You mentioned when we met before that you're teaching advanced students, and I'd really like to understand better. For example, what is your focus for your graduating thirteen- and fourteen-year-olds?'

The sunset cast colors in the sky. Under the awning on Niru's patio, candles in hurricane globes charmed the elegantly set table.

"I begin by identifying each student's unique talent, first on my own, without seeing their tech-data online," said the teacher, warming to the topic of his expertise. "I expect you've heard we coordinate data on their FGE records, chips, implants, shots, and so on. Most in my advanced class have strong telepathic traits – it's a requirement for that class. But everyone has different talents. Some tell stories, some sing, some want to create a new robot, or some are interested new sorts of flying machines, for Space exploration. One wants to be a social leader, another a business entrepreneur. One girl wants to be a comedian, another a spiritual adviser. In my classes, I share some of the ancient stories reflecting the higher/deeper awareness of the visionaries. I ask my class to bring their awareness to their *personal* experience, and to *feel* its relevance in their individual lives, their intcrests, passions, consciousness. In some ways, it's what you might call *philosophy and spirituality in action.*"

"So you direct them to connect their hearts and heads, so to say?" Adam was catching up.

Soham smiled and said, "That's a beautiful way to put it, Adam. And yet it's much more than that. It might sound strange, if you're not immersed in it, but the extraordinary technologies of recent times are helping a lot. Most of my advanced telepaths – the ATs – can shape-shift, scan the nearest planets. And the even more advanced can be in two places at the same time. All with what you used to call technology, now fully integrated into the human form. This new reality we call *enhanced awareness*. The nanotech and AI, the biotech of it, are probably too much for the dinner table, and it takes slides and videos. It's almost impossible to explain without pictures, and I doubt you've learned to use your UC handset to that extent yet, but I could create a mini-seminar if you like. You could both come, and bring friends if you like."

Niru burst out, smiling, "Oh Soham, you're too busy for that. We wouldn't dream of taking you away from your actual, official students."

"It would be my pleasure, Nani." Soham's affectionate admiration warmed everyone. "Plus, you could be resources for any of the kids who want to know more about what life was like *before* the great transformation. Some of them have trouble imagining it, even though their gifts allow them to transcend time."

Adam responded, "That must be a lot of work, each student with his or her own individual talent and degree of proficiency. How do you address it in one class?"

It was Soham's turn to laugh. "*That* is my self-fulfillment as their teacher, my life's purpose. It's not *work* anymore. It's *living* my '*self*'."

"When Soham was young, he used to call it his 'obligation'," Niru said with an amused smile on her lips.

"Yes. When we humans reach that awakened state the ancients

spoke of, we become complete, Poorna, as they say, in one of the ancient Vedic hymns."

Adam rested back in his chair, pondering, recalling all he'd heard in recent days, letting it flow together. "So humans are becoming complete, full, infinite. I am almost beginning to understand, thanks to my teachers, that that is the ascent to the next evolutionary stage." Soham and Niru glowed silently at their guest.

After a moment of resting in the beauty of it all, Niru said softly, "I call that *Poorna Manav*, the full, perfected, completed, human." Her eyes shone with a fuzzy radiance.

37 Space Companions

Kumar gathered his gadgets, reminiscing that little Anton had called them "tech toys" so long ago – twelve years ago now. Rushing, not to be late for the family dinner for his father's birthday, he mumbled aloud, "It *can't* be that long. Time itself must have crunched."

The Pundits were particular about observing traditions. Friends and relatives knew that, and joked about it too. Especially since none of them was invited. It was "significant time with Ella and the boys," Samir always emphasized.

It was family time, private, creative, connecting with traditions and creating and dreaming the future. Samir's passion to connect the past and the future, a passion he'd transmitted to his sons, largely through the treasure chest of memorabilia, was usually highlighted on his birthday. The boys had known and enjoyed it as a natural part of growing up.

As the dishes started making their way around the table, Anton launched the conversation. "Dada – or Pa, I keep shifting back into old patterns when we have these gatherings – I still have the Superman cape you gave me on my first day of school," he said. Now fifteen, and the tallest in the family, he chuckled and put his favorite onion pakora into his mouth. "I've been thinking about how our image of Superman has evolved. Do you think we're at the next stage in evolution of being *cosmic* humans?"

"Well, what do *you* think, Anton?" Samir asked.

Kumar was quick to interject. "Pa, you're violating your own rule: don't answer a question with a question – 'bad habit' you said. And I also have a question about the Superman evolution. How widely accepted do you think it is now – compared to what you saw in your early days at the Academy – that what we used to call ETs, extraterrestrials, are now known as what they are: SCs – Space Companions?"

Ella burst into laughter. "Boys, did you plan to give your father a hard time on his birthday?" All started laughing, reaching for extra helpings of their favorite dishes. Shreya had prepared everybody's most favorite savories and sweets with rice and roti.

"Ma, you can help Pa," suggested Anton, "Do *you* think humans have now evolved to be Space Companions, Supermen as we said for so long?"

"Yes, Mother, what do you think? Are humans Super-ready?" When Kumar addressed Ella as "Mother," not the usual "Ma," he was serious, even challenging.

"Ready for what?" Ella asked, reaching for penda, her favorite sweet.

"To commune with our Space Companions, Mother." Kumar was getting more intense.

Samir stepped in. "Yes, Kumar. Those of us in the astrophysics community are ready, and have been for at least three years. The beings identified as ETs, since the last century, were at last understood to be part of the cosmic movements influencing and interacting with everything – an endless galactic phenomenon. Now we're inventing instruments for deeper time travel and exploration of dark energy – which will enhance our capacity to connect with SCs." Ever-aware of his sense of continuity, he added, "Historically, humans, with their limited ability to perceive from Earth, called them '*extra*-terrestrial'. These days, we know we're all in the same cosmic, intergalactic energy soup. Connected. The ancients, as you know, described it as Indra jal. They knew it then. We've learned it with scientific equipment."

"Indra jal is basic knowledge," Anton interjected, "isn't it? We learned that in school."

Samir, Ella and Kumar all laughed aloud, and Kumar clarified the reason: "It was *you* who knew of that in school, not everybody," he said, reminding his little brother, for the millionth time, of his FGE status, which grasped reality differently, intuitively, naturally.

Ella smiled at the boys and turned toward her husband. "Samir, now that we scientifically know humans were connected with SCs, what's the next probability? What's new in your space exploration program?"

"We're hoping to connect with the Venusians. Now that we have our base on the dark side of the Moon – we're still in touch, by the way, with people who were around when the dark-side probes were first announced around 2019, I'm storing some clippings about it, Kumar – and with Martian underground habitats, the next frontier is to connect with the SCs using Venus crystal energy. Our instruments are advancing rapidly. Enhanced human awareness is the key. Our hope, mine in particular, is to scientifically reconnect the links we lost. Not only with Space Companions, but with deep-sea explorers, our aquanaut colleagues."

Kumar was elated. "EE, Pa. Zainab and I were arguing about that five days back. She brought up the joint ventures of astronauts and aquanauts. Their findings verify the origins of the creation stories of various cultures."

Anton chimed in, "Aquanauts have much shorter distances to go, deep under the sea, than astronauts, who've been traveling in space for countless years. Didn't the aquanauts have a late start?"

Samir enjoyed sharing his professional life with his sons. "In fact," he said, "aquanauts' first ventures were as early as the 1960s.

Their objective was to build undersea houses. Unfortunately, the loss of their major diver-scientist halted that program. Eventually, their explorations revived, and since around 2060 we've collaborated with them to build houses underwater as well as on Mars."

"Samir," offered Ella, "didn't the aquanauts' research scientifically support the creation stories of the Mayans? Their creators came from within the Earth, not from outer space, considered gods by Indians, Egyptians, Greeks, Chinese and many more."

Anton stopped sipping his cup of lassi. "Ma, I learned all those Mayan and Aztec stories in sixth grade. That's old news. What was Zainab's point, Kumar?"

"You know her driving force is supramental consciousness," Kumar said with a sly smile, knowing his family was familiar with Zainie's "obsession."

Undeterred, Ella elaborated: "It would be wonderful if she can connect new research and AI ventures with the old myths, to further consciousness research."

"Ma, do you know how many scientists and techies are FGEs worldwide?" Anton asked, posing a totally irrelevant question before putting a piece of roti dipped in sweet shikhand into his mouth.

"You mean you haven't checked it with Alissa-12 yet?" asked Kumar, laughing and taking a bite of sweet puran poli. Laughter went all around the table, since FGE was the new norm, and had been, since the late 2080s.

Ella turned toward her FGE child: "Why do you ask, Anton?"

"I've been wondering about the next level – where the dance of technology and consciousness will take us." Anton opened it all up to the grand vision: "Are we balancing the Force? Can we?"

Samir's response was confident. "I believe we can. We can, and will, evolve to the next level of conscious awareness, by commingling AI and biotech with human sensory capacity at ever-higher levels of sophistication. We've certainly sped up our progress in the last forty years. The next stage, as I said earlier, is to collaborate with our Space Companions. We'll continue the evolutionary process, accumulating knowledge and wisdom as we go."

"What about love and compassion, Pa?" Kumar asked. "At one time they were watchwords for people."

Samir and Ella looked at each other meaningfully. These were their own parents' watchwords. Samir responded, "When humans all over the world recognized their connectedness, late last century and in the early part of this one, as you well know, they evolved with love and compassion. Now love and compassion are part of our DNA. We don't need to inculcate it."

Ella added, her voice deepening, "It's different when you speak of individual love for one mate, family, and so on...." She looked at Samir with intent; they had noticed Kumar's growing friendship with Zainab.

Switching the subject, Anton burst out, "Let's have Dada's favorite creation." He got up, moved toward a wall switch, and clicked it. "Tah dah. Cosmic holographic Indra jal singing."

A giant screen, covering the entirety of one of the dining-room walls, emanated vivid light, colors, and music, and they all happily felt the vibrations in all dimensions.

38 Plato's Cave Revisited

On the circuitous path around Five Trees, Adam's old memories were awakening. He felt the old familiar sensations of searching … no, it was not searching, it was knowing. Knowingness that did not "know" but was felt.

He remembered. He was nine, or maybe eight.

His mother, Jessica, was holding a painting of a multicolored serpentine figure, showing it to Jesus, Adam's father. "These are the dream-people's images, the Australian Aborigines," she said.

Jesus touched the circuitous curves of the image. "They look like my didgeridoo, the way it connects magical sound, and color, and my heartbeat."

That image of his father and mother, standing close, holding that painting with its vivid resonant colors and sounds, stayed in his memory screen after the first flash.

Jesus from Guatemala and Jessica from California, both dreamers, had first met in magical Sedona, in 1996. Adam was their first-born, in 2000, whose birth certificate carried the name "Adam Smith," a symbol of primal connectivity, the dream child of the future. Neither Jessica nor Jesus was "Smith."

Adam kept walking, and another scene flashed on his memory path. He was a part of the Australian dream people walking the Earth to feel the unifying element of the opposites – the complementary polarity of night and day, dark and light, moist and dry, Earth and Sky, Yin and Yang. Adam savored the remembrance: one does not exist without the other. If there were no darkness, light would be unrecognized. Just as we do not notice the air we breathe, till we start suffocating without it. A faint smile came to his lips as he remembered the lines of Lao Tzu he'd often chanted softly to himself during his wanderings in Mongolia: "There are ways, but the Way is uncharted." His favorite, brought to mind by his dream-walking contemplation of opposites, was "These two come paired but distinct … the gate to the root of the world."

Yes, yes, the deepest pairing opens the gate to the root. This was Adam's moment. He imbibed, absorbed, became the perpetual dual, non-dual awareness of the one root, consciousness. He remembered his personal story of growing, evolving, now revealed to him through dreams, the same story of oneness prevalent in all human stories – Australian Dreamers or Indian Hindus, Buddha's birth stories or Greek and Egyptian myths, Shinto and Confucian aphorisms, or Wise Women's words that taught what they felt in their beings as they birthed new life.

With all these joyous memories flashing, his eyes squinted and created deeper wrinkles on his face. "It was my dream I was following in Mongolia, searching for those Deer Stones." What were they? Who erected them? What were they for? Did he ever find the answers? Certainly not as an archeologist. Today he felt they were dream-posts of people who'd walked those paths – earthly, or non-earthly, from other planets, other stars.

As Adam drifted deeper in his inner search, he sensed a huge gap in human memory. How had the rift between religion and spirituality surfaced? He continued walking, thinking, dreaming, listening. He had a vague feeling of having done this before. His breathing was calmer, almost blending with the surrounding air, which he'd been unaware of before. Now the two blended – his footsteps touching the ground melding energetically with the soil beneath his feet. One becoming the other? No, there was no 'other'. He vividly remembered the feeling he'd had every time he touched a Deer Stone in Mongolia. That's it. He was touching 'the root of the world' each time he sat gazing at a newfound stone.

He sat on his favorite bench by the pond, gazing at the sky reflected in its tiny calm blue waves.

He became aware in a new way that he was watching his past and present lives all at once. He was at a melting point, in an alchemical crucible, where he was one, the same, perfected, one manifesting as many, the other, and the same. There are no rifts, he realized, as he felt the rippling curves, mingling as a germinating mother principle. He felt the universal Force, the Essence. In it were the visionaries, scientists, scholars, writers, poets, artists, musicians, farmers, animal keepers, gardeners – women, men, and children – connected in this dream of the universal mind.

⚹

That evening, Adam sat next to Niru on the carved-back Indian swing on his porch and said, "Niru, I fully know now what you said yesterday – '*one consciousness conscious of itself in the many.*'"

This was their usual 'happy hour' on the swing every day, or every other day, with some fruit juice – pomegranate, apple, strawberry-banana, or a mixture of all flavors.

Breaking into a loud laugh, and coughing as the apple juice found its way into the wrong pipe, Niru said, "What do you mean?"

Undaunted, Adam continued in a serious voice, "It was a revealing walk this morning. I recalled a past life, my childhood in this life, dreams I've been having, my archeological ventures with the Deer Stones in Mongolia ... all of them blended into each other." Niru was about to say something, but Adam put his hand on his lips and continued. "This Indian swing has helped, and so has the neighbor's dog, old Megh, as well as these chirping birds. All our walks, sunsets and sunrises, the Moon's movements, observed or not, all have contributed to expand my universe. Your lessons on technological expansion, and my encounters with them, have been an explosion of understanding. At first I was a slow learner. You know that. But now I feel I've traversed back and forth, mingling this life and others. Most significant was my 'experienced' reality this morning. I have to thank you for your persistence in guiding my journey." Adam spoke passionately, and finally stopped, staring at Niru, locking his eyes into hers.

For the first time, Niru had no words. She kept looking deeply into Adam's eyes.

⌇

Dark clouds hung low against fluffy white ones, creating unusual patterns in the blue October desert sky. Against red rocks and the evergreen pine valley, the azure sky wearing gray-white attire was magical. Sitting on his deck, on that ancient Indian swing, Adam was lost, viewing another reality.

There was a cave. In it were seated a group of men, women and children – virtually tied to their seats – watching, on a huge wall, the shadow play of a live drama, which was being enacted behind them, in front of a fire that cast the shadows. Popularly known as Plato's Cave, this was not just an evening entertainment for people tied to the bench, it was their whole life. The only reality they had lived, known, even enjoyed. They were happy or sad vicariously experiencing the pleasures and pains of shadows. Much as people see movies these days. But when the movie is over they go home, or to bed if it is on TV or any other AI gadget. For the people in the cave, there was no 'other' real world, just these shadows.

Among the shadow viewers, Adam saw a restless woman leaning against the warm wall, looking around. She was agitated, trying again and again to unleash herself, unsuccessfully. She closed her eyes and sat quietly. Her deep breathing became a hummm.

Then, almost magically, Adam saw her easily untie her rope, get up, and walk out of the cave. Dazzled by the sunlight, the woman blinked. What was this? Where was she? She stumbled as she tried walking on her unsteady feet, from darkness into light.

Adam automatically extended his hand to help, then realized it was a dream. He woke up from a blend of sleeping and dreaming, not knowing what was real.

He opened his eyes. In the deep blue sky above hung white and dark clouds, now bordered with a golden lining. It was an unusual mix. Adam kept staring at this heavenly display of darkness, light, and bright lining around dark clouds.

A gentle wind caressed him. His lips quivered in a smile, his eyes closed. He lapsed into a dream.

The woman was standing on the edge of a cliff, viewing the deep green valley, surrounded by dark brown and red hills jutting out, under the shining sun. She tucked her hair, blown by the wind, behind her ears and turned around to grasp the entire view. An eagle flew above. She recognized the royal bird whose shadow she'd often seen on the wall. How alive, majestic, colorful he was. Not just a dark object with wings spread! She giggled like a child. Taking a long deep breath, she viewed the terrain again and kept walking. Her breathing became audible as she mindfully watched her steps. She arrived at the edge of the rock. Stopped. In front of her was the green valley. She could not walk any farther. But her eyes followed the upward curve of the valley. It rose to another peak, then another. She turned around 360 degrees, absorbing the surrounding grandeur. Unimagined, un-experienced, an explosion of wonder, beauty, a grand new vista, never before seen or heard of.

She stood there, for an eternity, it seemed, transformed.

She *needed* to walk back to the cave. She *felt* the need. She started walking back. At the mouth of the cave, she hesitated for a second and looked back at the valley. Did she want to go in? She wasn't sure. What if she never came out again?

Then, determined, she stood at the edge of the cave, one foot in, the other out.

"Awake!" she called out. "The Real is not here in the cave. It is out there." Her arm stretched out, pointing to the light and the valley outside.

Huge screams and loud voices of fear, curiosity, and denial echoed through the cave: "Where? What? Who? How? Why?" Some sat steadfast, some looked helpless, a few struggled to get free. Many were angry, fearful. Some sat silently, looking down at the floor.

After a noisy confusion, some men and a few women and children undid their bonding shackles, got up, and slowly walked purposefully to the cave's opening. A few more tumbled out, unthinking, dazzled. Some fell on the ground outside. The rest, frightened of the unknown, remained huddled in the cave.

The woman stood erect, steadfast, aware. Everyone was looking at her.

"I have seen!" she said in guttural voice that came from deep within. "*That* is the Truth."

She led them to the edge of the rock overlooking the distant horizon, the spot of her awakening.

With wobbly feet, squinting eyes, inquisitive minds, and hopeful hearts, some followed vigorously. Many, yet dazzled by light, fearing the unknown, dragged their feet. Some wondered if they should still get back to the familiar cave. And a few did. The young in the crowd were eager: with dreamy eyes and strong limbs they held older hands and helped the hesitant elders to the edge.

"Awake, arise, onward march to the future," one young voice implored, intuitively. Others picked up the call – some murmuring, a few younger voices singing. They all walked to the edge.

Scanning the stunning, never-before-seen terrain, all of them fell silent.

There was no sound, except the gentle westerly breeze.

After what seemed to be an eternity, they heard, "The Real is here. Look around, feel it, know it ... *consciously.*"

All eyes followed her outstretched hands.

"Masters can't be wrong." An old man's voice broke the silence.

"Masters have been waiting for us to wake up. From our blind faith. From our ignorance," the awakener woman declared.

A young male voice was heard: "Leave the cave, be in light."

A girl's singing voice floated in the air: "Be enlightened. Know the ideal and the real are one."

A young man, entranced by the enhanced reality, chanted, "I am the universe. Aham Brahmasmi."

"Tattvam Asi," said the woman who had led them. "You are That."

~\|/~

Tender early-morning sunrays touched Adam's hair, gliding over his forehead, touched his eyes.

A blue bird flew toward him, perched on the back of the swing, and began pecking ... tick ... tick ... tick...

Adam woke up.

39 The Universal Connector

The technology specialists – or tech-specs, or, privately among themselves, still the most honorable geeks, though now known publicly as techies – shared a great dream: to use the Universal Connector, the UC, as a tool to reach divinity. In the near future. By the 2060s, the later-generation UC, with its new dream-tracking tool, had become Mandy Khan's favorite, not only for her work unit at GU Research, but also to track her daughter Zainab's dreams. Her next product, the UC-7, was almost complete, with the conversion of Mrs. Kim Chen's brain data into algorithms now being finalized. Mandy was ecstatic.

The original UC handset had been very widely used, much like smartphones in the pre-2020 years. By the mid-2020s, people participating in the stimulation and coherence of global dreams were using UCs to share their dreams and even hold worldwide conferences. Like the old software for convening meetings remotely, they had a much more elaborate conventions app, with holograms for participants in earlier states of evolution, all in the service of saving the Earth by reducing the carbon footprint of gatherings, as well as serving human evolution. Operating on the subtler life-friendly frequencies of the new G-2 connectivity, these systems actually improved the health and focus of the users. All over the world by around 2040, annual conventions were attended by participants from home with the help of UCs.

Thus the 2045 Resurgence celebration became a global experience. Everybody in the world could participate in the celebration, sitting in their backyard. All were excited to be virtually in Mani Dweep.

Now, in the 2080s, the UC-7 would be a tool to evolve spiritually, raising universal awareness, creating the potential to evolve beyond the physical, beyond the denser subtle, into states of divinity – a unity of organic, inorganic, algorithmic, and transcendent, with no separation.

That was the objective. For Earth. Also on the table were plans to adapt future generations of the UC for advanced communication with the Space Companions in other galaxies.

What about Mandy Khan's surreptitious viewing of her daughter's dreams? Was it ethical? Was she excused because of her high position as a researcher in the field of consciousness? With her best intentions for her daughter, did she have a right to spy?

"Mother, why do you pry into my dreams?" Zainab asked one morning, walking into the kitchen.

Surprised, Mandy asked, "So, no 'TS, Ma'? You go straight to allegations? Did you have bad dreams, Zainie?"

"Don't avoid the question, Ma. You know my dreams, so why ask?" Zainab was really upset.

Mandy realized her motherly concern had crossed an ethical line. Her little girl was now a woman. She had been viewing her daughter's dreams since Zainab was a year old. Even though well intended, old habits died hard, especially since Mandy knew that her own professional expertise had contributed enormously to Zainab's exceptional achievements at a young age.

Mandy walked to Zainab. "Sorry, dear girl. You know I never ever intended to hurt your feelings." Holding her chin and caressing her head, Mandy said, "You're still my little girl, the closest to my heart, a part of me. I admit I failed to see you're grown up and are now apart from me. A big omission. But no excuses. My fault.

Can you forgive me?" Mandy's moist eyes were searching Zainab's, her hand still holding her daughter's chin.

Embracing her mother, Zainab burst into tears, "Mom, I love you. I didn't mean to yell. But your spying did hurt. I know you never pressured me to do or not do anything against my wishes. I know that I am what I am because of how you and Dad raised me. I'm not hurt in my heart, it was my head. Telepathically I've known you were prying. As a little girl, I thought that's what mothers did. But now, I resent the intrusion." Zainab's tone was conciliatory even if the words were abrupt.

At first Mandy had been stunned by the outburst her daughter had directed against her. She had always supported Zainab's outspokenness. But it had never been aimed at her, her mother! "You're right. I know you know that consciousness research has become my second nature. It blinds me. I automatically fall into this 'spying within' routine. She shook her head and added, "No excuses." Zainab hugged her mother.

"Let me have something to eat before I go. Kumar will be waiting for me at the museum."

"Anything special happening at the museum?" With her unpredictable, busy schedule, Mandy was out of the loop with events around town on Mani Dweep.

"Ma ... are you being funny? It's your department's exhibit, 'Universal Connectors, 2020 to 2090', the whole evolution of UC handsets. You and your division created the exhibit! And you're asking me what's happening at the museum?"

Both burst into loud laughter. "Yes, of course. The exhibit opened a month ago. I forgot all about it. These days, I'm totally gripped by Mrs. Chen's dance of consciousness." Mandy shook her head – she and her one-track mind. But it would be an overload for almost anyone: information from around the globe flowed into her office at GU Research, and she was expected –

especially by herself – to keep up with all of it.

"Why was the new generation of Universal Connectors named Hermes? What's the relevance, Ma?"

"He was the mythological Universal Connector of the ancient Greeks. Of all their gods, Hermes was the most humanlike, with his mix of good and less-than-good qualities." Mandy chose her words carefully. "According to legend, Hermes was the only god who was a go-between, between humans and gods, a kind of a messenger, mediator, and mischief-maker rolled into one. I wish more people would use the name, instead of just UC or U-set. But people get attached to what they've known – even after something's evolved beyond what they ever knew before."

"Interesting. I'm seeing the history now, which was hard to imagine, since the UC replaced universal smartphones sixty years ago. Our generation had barely heard of smartphones. But evidently they were the first major device to revolutionize people's lives all over the world. We did learn about all this in Three Ms classes, but Ma, I know you know I was always interested in now, and the next – the future – not so much in the past." Zainab sighed and added, "But Kumar is always connecting the past, present and future. He's looking forward to the exhibit. Perhaps I can tell him things about old good Hermes he may not know – my privilege as a daughter of one of the creators of the exhibit," Zainab said with the smile of a daughter proud of her mother's accomplishments.

"Well, that young man might surprise you," Mandy said with a twinkle in her eyes. "He is his father's son. He might provide some details that we might have missed. What do you want to eat, Zainie, before you leave?"

"Oh, I programmed Kelley to fix me a bowl of soup and a salad as I came in. Here she is. Thank you, Kelley." Kelley walked in, carefully set the tray on the table, and said with a smile on her shiny painted lips, "Here you are, Zainab. Enjoy your soup and salad. Would you like your latte, now?"

"Yes, thank you," said Zainab.

Kelley turned to Mandy. "Mrs. Khan, would you like your meal now?"

"Come, Ma, eat with me," Zainab urged.

"Okay. Kelley, bring me the same as Zainie's. Thank you." Mandy spoke hurriedly, her eyes already set on her wrist pad. She continued, "I'll have to rush soon. It seems some more reports are coming in from the Asian unit, Japan region. A Shinto elder has recorded some event. I need to know how it relates to the Chinese. Oh this is exciting."

"Do you expect them to be different, culturally diverse?"

"As far as I've discerned so far, only the words and symbols are varied, coming from different cultures. Essentially, it's balancing yin and yang, or spirit and matter, with varied names and symbols. We're very excited about the constant in all cultures. Some are more detailed, others seminal, but similar. For us, most significant are the personal data. It allows us to collect scientific evidence of spiritual experiences, bridging the artificial gap that we've agonized under for more than 400 years."

"To experience the scientific truth? Like waves in the ocean? Different forms of the same real?" Zainab clearly enjoyed the question.

"Yes, but to go beyond. To establish scientifically that they are all variations connected in one fluid entity."

Zainab smiled and nodded. "Which is why the old visionaries compared humans' oneness as drop of water in the ocean."

Mandy, staring out the window now, spoke dreamily. "It's more like the drop knowing it's the ocean. Each drop has its unique qualia, its qualities, each of which knows it is the whole. It is the oneness within. Drops keep their identities, but know they carry the ocean within."

"Ma," Zainab started, then paused, then found her words and pronounced them slowly as she stared at her mother, "that is the depth of sublime truth. Now I believe I have a deeper sense of what you mean when you say, 'Let's celebrate our differences, so we can enjoy our oneness.'"

They kept looking at each other for a while – bonding within.

40 Dancing Snowflakes

By late 2084, Adam Smith had become a regular denizen of the brave new world. At first totally lost, then bedazzled, then informed, then an integral part of new reality — a roller-coaster ride. Whoosh! Adam breathed a sigh of relief on January 1, 2085, his eighty-fifth birthday.

"What a life," he mumbled with mild, contented amazement as he sat by the window, looking at the glittering particles of the brand-new snow, piled six inches high overnight. He kept glaring at the sparkling snowflakes, as the Sun rose from behind the hills and gently spread colors over the fluffy white terrain. Snowflakes seemed to be talking to him.

"Look at us. We shine, we breathe, we melt. Be vapor, be clouds, be rain, be snowflakes, floating in the air. Then we settle. We live."

"Do you ever get bored?"

"What's 'bored'?

"Like there is no end, and no purpose in living and shining and melting."

"What's 'purpose'?

Adam gave up. Snowflakes were not human. They couldn't think. They were pretty, though, he had to admit. He laughed aloud, not knowing why.

"You sound happy this morning, Adam, are you ready?" Niru called through the door, knocking. It was time for their usual walk.

"Come in, Niru. It's time to enjoy the splendor of freshly laden snow, from inside where it's warm." He opened the door, waved toward the breakfast table, and closed the door again quickly.

"Gorgeous, peaceful, isn't it?" Niru said, pulling out a chair.

"Coffee?" Adam moved to the kitchen counter.

"Yes, sure."

"What is the life span of a snowflake?" Adam asked with a wink. He was being intentionally funny.

"From a few seconds to almost eternity," Niru responded, smiling, in the same vein.

"How? Explain," Adam urged, bringing the additional coffee mug.

"Some flakes melt upon reaching the ground, others freeze into solid ice, like in the Arctic for several millennia." Niru was not sure where Adam was going with his seemingly simple questions.

"No humans 'witnessed' the Earth being created with a big bang or any other way, or later being a freezing ball. But it did happen, even though nobody was there to 'see' it. So did it really happen?"

Niru heard echoes of the old conundrum of the tree falling in the forest, and whether it had fallen if no one had heard or seen it. "So?" she said, still totally lost as to where Adam was headed.

"No human being experienced the tree falling. But snowflakes were there! The tree fell right on a cushiony cold white blanket of them. Would you say the tree fell?" Adam was obviously going beyond his limited Anthropocentric perspective, and Niru struggled to adjust to this new person sitting across from her. She listened quietly as he resumed.

"How do you reconcile relativity, quantum physics, and the fallen tree that really did not fall because nobody experienced it falling?" Adam did his best to sum up what he was newly understanding to be the absurdity of human thinking. He let his mind wander in the silence, back to the original impression that had launched this reverie. Could he look at life as snowflakes did? The snowflakes just are. After a long silence, still staring out of the window, Adam spoke softly. "Can humans be like snowflakes? Without desire, or purpose? What keeps humans alive? What makes them wake up every morning?"

"For most younger generations, in these times, such questions are irrelevant, Adam. All our technologies have skyrocketed their evolutionary process, beyond such questions." After a brief pause she continued, "They truly are like snowflakes, which shine and be … they are aware of being their essence." Niru wanted to say more. Certainly her grandchildren, Soham and Lizzy, could remain active without any attachment to desire or purpose. Lizzy, the astronaut, repeatedly said, "My purpose is no more than a rose's purpose is to be pretty. I'm being me."

"How about you, Niru? What is your purpose in life?" Adam was genuinely curious, now that the subject had arisen.

"In my younger days, I often wondered about my purpose. Was kind of driven by it. But with new awareness of the self, that question has become irrelevant. Now it is just being. Or becoming."

"How did you get there? What changed?"

"It was a slow, slow process. But vital at a soul level, in its various incarnations from life to life."

"I am so grateful I met you when I emerged from sleep. With you as my guru – and I hope I do credit to your teaching when I express this – I've learned that the soul, at its level of essence, is immortal, one with spirit. But the limiting duality of life on Earth poses the constant drama of dual and non-dual, humans and gods." Adam spoke with ease with his lately acquired, ever-pleasant smile. "But," he continued, "knowing truth does not mean instant transformation. How does one get from point A to point B?"

"From doing to being." For Niru, it seemed as easy as changing one's clothes.

Adam's roaring laugh broke through the tightly shut windows. "No kidding, Niru! Be serious, this is important for me."

"It was a magic moment in my life. I had not consciously experienced the power of such a moment, nor had I thought of it, since my early life was left-brained, academic, science-oriented. But on arriving in Sedona, touching those energy ley lines in the red rocks, totally unaware, I acted on what today I call 'inner guidance', but back then it was just 'impulsive, irrational behavior' – quite uncharacteristic of me, as my friends and relatives were fond of saying. I bought a piece of land in Sedona, without knowing I could afford it, on the fourth day after arrival. The original plan was to visit the Grand Canyon and Sedona for three days each and return to New York. Besides, I wasn't sure if I could afford a retirement! Or when I could retire. That piece of land – only a quarter acre – turned out to be the miracle of my life. Land infused with sacred energy activated my 'rebirth' so to speak."

"Sedona," Adam said in a low slow voice. "You said Sedona?"

"I was going to ask why you ask, and now I sense that you have roots there yourself, Adam."

"We can go into that when the weather clears and we can go on another walk. At the moment, I want to complete this thought we started."

Niru's face became pensive, musing. "And yet you've brought up another important topic. We've never talked about my going back to Sedona, as I do for part of each year. Or spending time in DC with my students." She watched confusion flicker across Adam's face. "You know how to fly now, Adam," she winked, "and you are of course welcome to visit both places and let me show you around, make new friends. Of course I'll always come back here to be with my grandchildren, for months at a time."

Something deep in Adam comforted him that all these changes in physical location would mean next to nothing. He breathed into the new knowledge and sighed. "It'll be different, yet I feel ready for more adventures, believe it or not. Especially to land infused with sacred energies. I'll share my history later. At the moment, I want to hear more about your rebirth there. Soooo … you allowed your heart to supersede your rational mind?"

"Listen, all that is hindsight analysis. At the time, it just felt right." After a short silence, looking out the window at snow-covered trees, she continued, "Today, I can say that some inner force was guiding me, and I surrendered to it. But as I said, at the time it was an unconscious act that felt right, despite its stark irrationality. Adam, I'm grateful to the universe for letting me trust that knowingness. From a logical point of view, it could've been the greatest mistake of my life, as many of my friends and colleagues had feared. I call it karmic. We're not always aware of our other lives, past or future. But such continuity is real. Surrendering to that larger energy force is a choice. Rational interference destroys it. Surrendering to it, consciously, allows it to manifest and speed up our growth."

"How did you arrive at that awareness, by what means?"

Niru answered slowly, staring at the glistening snow. "Meditation, total surrender to the Force, is a natural flow of living. I know you've become accustomed to my invoking the terms of my ancestry, and this seems to be a good time to do that. You may even remember Satchidananda – Sat, which is truth, Chit, which is consciousness, and Ananda, bliss. When you hold these in union, as I've said, they reflect the ultimate truth."

"But it's hard to make a huge shift like that. It's scary." Adam sounded a bit helpless but somehow hopeful.

"Especially for us older people. Practice and constant vigilance are vital. But for younger generations it's easier, natural, I should say. You know there are many high-tech helpers for making the shift, and even some 'energizing elixirs'. I remember mentioning these to you in other contexts. One can enhance the Force by guided use of such techniques."

Adam was listening, still gazing out the window.

The deep snowy silence had enveloped Niru.

A raven flew across the window view and perched on a snowy branch. Both heard the wave of wind, in that silence.

Adam and Niru kept contemplating the falling flakes that danced in the breeze.

41 Adam's Dream

Now, after a few months, the avalanche of new information had become easier to handle. The initial shock, upon arrival back to the real world from deep sleep in Mongolia, was now under control – or so Adam thought.

After hearing a silent reprise of Soham's account of his telepathically advanced students, Adam was lost deep in thought. His archeologist mind was clearing what seemed to be eons of dust off his own awareness, not clearing dust off a newly unearthed fossil. Or was *he* a new-found fossil? Adam chuckled at the image as he walked along, having become habituated, in his long walks with Niru, to letting the big questions arise while he was in motion. Still, he was surprised at the totality of the next questions floating to the surface: What is the purpose of this ongoing saga of life? All life – not just human, or only earthly, but of *all* living organisms in the entire universe?

"Why are you here, my old friend?" Adam touched the head of the neighbor's dog, Megh, who was waiting for him at the cottage door, as usual. Happy to have completed his daily service and received his pat of thanks, Megh went home.

Still lost in thought, a bit woozy from the array of exotic dishes at dinner, Adam went through the rituals of preparation for sleep. He noticed how comfortable he'd become in his cottage, in this bed, as he pulled open the covers, but he still knew to expect vivid visions through the night, as his mind and body continued their adaptation to so many unprecedented stimuli. He thought kindly of his new friends, visitors from Mt. Uluru, who'd shared with him some dream techniques, ways to be more fully alive and awake within the dreamtime. He remembered his didgeridoo from childhood, reached over to turn out the bedside lamp, rolled over on his side in the dark, and pulled up the covers. Instantly he blacked out.

⁓⌇⁓

"What's your graduation project, Adam?" Ragini asked as the students wandered and chatted before class.

With mischievous eyes, Adam Smith, a thirteen-year-old graduating hopeful in Soham's class, challenged her: "Why don't you telepath?"

Irritated, Ragini taunted back, "Why do I need to waste my energy on an idle issue?"

"Ho ho ho … Aren't we touchy, this morning?" Adam burst into laughter.

The "Stay Awake" call sounded. It silenced the class and sent them to their meditation cushions to begin.

Pa Soham entered, sat on his own cushion, and sounded the gentle bell.

Larger-than-usual inhalations and exhalations whispered through the room as they settled in to meditate, eyes closed.

Adam saw the CERN research center outside Geneva on the French-Swiss border, its Large Hadron Collider campus blanketed with snow that was streaked with sunset colors. In the twilight, he magically drifted toward the main building, where a statue of Shiva Nataraj – now a little weathered after sixty-plus years – seemed to vibrate, to magnetize. Young Adam approached it, hearing his boots crunching in the snow, wondering why Shiva the Hindu cosmic dancer was on the CERN campus. He walked around the statue, feeling the oddness of his head being at the level just above the dancer's feet, the strange sense that Shiva, with bent knees, a raised extended leg and four extended arms, was moving, arms waving, wild hair fanning out in all directions, as perspective changed. He admired the ring of fire around the dancer, with flames that flickered with palpable heat. He felt the power of the great god stomping on the demon of ignorance, letting a cobra uncoil from one arm, the hand of that arm in the "fear not" mudra. He felt the blessing flowing from another hand's mudra, the tick-tock of the universe in the drum held by another hand. And there was fire in one hand – not just surrounding the dancer, but within the grasp of the god. Young dream-Adam felt glad he'd allowed his own senses to tell him the story, round and round, before stopping to read the inscription: physicists using the most advanced technology to portray the patterns of the cosmic dance – a perfect unity of mythology, art, and science, which he felt was the intuitive movement of the multifold spirit, in all its parts, all its singularity.

Circling the statue again, feeling his feet within warm boots, smelling the freshness of the snow-covered evening, he sensed the faint image of a horse and rider emerging from the surrounding darkness, circling the statue in a wider arc, thirty feet away, moving as he moved. As the image intensified, becoming more solid and more bright, Adam noticed – as two witnesses, one that marveled and one that saw nothing out of the ordinary – one that slept and dreamed and one that meditated within the dream – he noticed in all these ways that the horse was in fact a unicorn with astounding powers in his horn, the rider a young woman in a gown of pastels of all colors, a startling expression of spring amid the snow. The image vibrated back and forth between two versions: in one display the unicorn and spring-gowned damsel, alternating with another display, where the sword-power was a gleaming blade in the right hand of the young woman, leaving the horse to be a horse, white as the snow, shimmering and changing as they circled Shiva.

The bell rang to end the meditation. Young dream-Adam opened his eyes.

"Let's start with graduation project proposals. Who will go first?" Soham asked.

"Could we go alphabetically, Pa Soham?" Ragini quickly suggested, adding, with vigorous enthusiasm: "*Adam*, supposedly the first *man*, perhaps can go first?"

Adam looked at her, with an understanding smile on his lips, and said gently, "Pa Soham, my project is about our future. In the beginning of our twenty-first century, with great difficulty Anthropocene finally started a new journey – connecting science and spirituality. In my meditation today I saw the Hindu god Shiva's statue at CERN, the center of ultimate science in those days. It further confirms my project."

Ragini didn't want to disengage: "Adam, that's still the past. Where are you going? Where is the future?"

Adam wondered if she was still mad about their argument – the one about the Anthropocene attitude – on their last date a week ago. "I'm focusing on Kalki, he said, "the future Avatar from ancient Hindu texts, trying to connect our technological future with spirituality."

Pa Soham, as dream-Adam expected, urged him to be specific. "What's new in your project, Adam?"

"My specifics will focus on the image. The sword-like instrument in Kalki's hand is the array of devices and techniques we've developed, to sharpen our insight, our whole existence, through artificial intelligence. Kalki rides a horse…." With Ragini fixated on him today, Adam decided not to mention unicorns. "The birthplace of the Avatar is indicated in the Indian Ocean, meaning that it's our Maldives Island, Mani Dweep. The timing is related to ancient Hindu scriptures that mention 432.000 years for Kali Yuga, the Iron Age...."

Once again, he was rudely interrupted. Ragini's slightly shrill voice called out: "I don't understand why you're still hung up on old religious prophecies."

"Let him finish, Ragini," Soham insisted.

Adam sighed, smiled gratefully at the teacher, and continued. "I researched *many* traditions, and the Kalki in Hindu tradition seems to combine science, mathematics and religion fairly accurately. I modified it with current research and technologies, using machine-learning algorithms, 7G-2 connectivity, FGE-6 genetics, 20G robotics. My project has a female Kalki, ready to raise the consciousness level of Anthropocenes to include all creation." Young dream-Adam, and sleeping-Adam, could both feel but not see, behind them, Ragini's raised eyebrows and slightly dropped jaw.

-ᴗⅮᴗ-

Tuck ... tuck ... tuck .... Adam woke up. Somebody was knocking at the door.

It was Soham. He called out through a partially open window: "You said you wanted to come with me, when I go pick up Lizzy from the Satellite Rocket Station."

Adam rolled out of the bed to a standing position, put on a robe, and moved foggily to the door, opening it while he answered. "Oh, yes, good morning, I guess I overslept," he said, looking at Soham meaningfully, almost quizzically, since Adam was floating in dreamspace where Soham was his elder teacher, and looking at him in the flesh, as his friend Niru's grandson. "I'll be ready in a jiffy. Can you wait?"

"Sure I can," said the wise teacher, long comfortable with his role of calm anticipation, waiting for all the world to wake up, completely.

Epilogue Kalki Avatar

The year was 2100. Anton, Ella and Samir's son, was nineteen years old. As an FGE child of the eighties, his genetically enhanced cells made him grow into an exceptionally advanced young man.

His intuitive grasp of technology, gene enhancement, and telepathic communication, especially in Space research, earned him fond titles from friends, teachers, and extended family. His older brother Kumar, himself a protégé, teasingly addressed Anton as "Savior," with a loving twinkle.

Although impressed and hopeful professors did not elevate Anton to savior status, they were sure he was bound to push humanity a notch higher in its march to supramental consciousness, a watchword used often in conversations since the 2060s.

Now nearly thirty, Zainab, Kumar's consort – "husband" and "wife" were outdated terms – was Anton's guide in a number of her specialties.

"How would you explain heightened awareness to an average human, Anton?"

"There's nothing to explain. With deep awareness, every human knows, is conscious of it. They may not be able to 'explain' it, any more than they can explain why they breathe. Or a mother can explain how and why she feels the pain of her child. All these can be measured, recorded, by devices etched in our bodies." Anton was intrigued by Zainab's question.

"That's true," she said. "But is there no difference between a digitized record, an instinctive motherly feeling, and awareness of higher consciousness?" Zainab's probing was part of their shared practice.

"Perhaps back in the first two dark decades of the twenty-first century, such a question was relevant – when people were unaware. Not now, with all our chips, FGEs, and embedded tools and biotech, in our bodies and in our surroundings. In a way they *are* our bodies, not apart from, but a part *of* our bodies." Anton was not sure of the source of Zainab's question. He continued, "Then there are our robotic stewards, constant companions with fully expanded awareness. Why would you ask?" Anton wondered why Zainab, herself a prodigy as a teenager, would ask such a basic question. Was she testing him?

"Sure, youngest Pundit, you pass my test. You win my heart." Zainab's face was glowing. Passing the scrutiny of his brilliant sister-friend was certainly reassuring for Anton, whose imaginary backpack was full of laudatory comments from superiors and equals.

"Did you and Kumar decide about FGE-6 for the baby?" Anton had been paying special attention to the potential of the newest genetic advancements, notably the SuperCon Genes to enhance fetal supramental consciousness. It was new, still experimental, beyond what he'd received in his mother's womb.

"Well, I'm not yet sure." Her eyes seared through Anton telepathically as she reclined on the sofa and fell asleep.

~\'/~

Zainab walked along a rocky path by a gurgling stream, sheltered under a verdant canopy of ancient banyan trees.

Multicolored wildflowers grew in brilliant clusters.

Clad in a creamy soft gown trimmed in dark magenta silk, a scarf with golden lines hanging from her right shoulder to her knees, she walked with fortitude. Her feet knew the way. Her sparkling eyes gazed intently at her upturned palms that were nearly touching, holding a bright flame that gently waved in the breeze. The flame began quivering, turning, spinning, becoming a round globe of blue and green hue, with lines etched on it. Her eyes, teary with joy, were riveted on the Mother Earth born of the magic flame in her palms!

⁓ˈʲⁱ⸝

Anton sat musing by the window. Then, in a deeper meditative state, he rose to open it and lean out, to feel the fullness of nature. A branch of the huge chestnut tree near the house almost rubbed his shoulder as he leaned out. He watched the Sun gently descending on the horizon, giving him visions of new dawns in faraway parts of the globe.

Against the setting Sun he saw a spider gliding, building its web. Sunrays brightened the strands of the spider's body fluid, with a shine Anton had never seen before. His piercing gaze extended from the web into the ever-expanding infinite universes for a fraction of a moment. Within the energetic field he saw a flickering, shining wave. Whatever it was morphed, like the spider's web, into a distinct shape. A female figure was riding a graceful unicorn. Holding a long spear ready to pierce adamantine obstacles or subtle contenders, she rushed toward him from a distant horizon, ferocious, formidable. Anton saw a beatific smile on the face of the woman, who was now resting on the unicorn under the chestnut tree, two feet beyond the windowsill. Their eyes interlocked. It was a magical moment. A brilliant flash illuminated the scene. Anton *felt* the entire experience in his body as a mathematical formula, coalescing in his ability to feel the ancient mystical geometries of multidimensional numbers and the resonant humming of the subtle filaments of relationship among them – all generating the Reality he perceived.

⚜

When she opened her eyes, Zainab saw Anton standing by the window. Telepathically she knew he was in another reality. With a slow firm voice, she said, "Kumar will be happy to know I'm finally agreeing with him on FGE-6 for our baby. You're the forerunner in this family, Anton. How can a Pundit, Khan, and Smith descendent not have the new groundbreaking FGE-6?" She kept looking at Anton with tender love and admiration.

Then slowly, still with measured cadence, she said, "You helped me make up my mind, little brother!" Zainab smiled teasingly and gave him a big hug.

Anton in turn was overjoyed and hugged Zainab repeatedly. "I cannot *wait* to tell Ma and Pa."

⚜

When Ella returned home, she was greeted by Anton cheerily announcing, "Ma, we'll have a new star in the family. Zainab and Kumar are going to have FGE-6 for the baby!"

Ella was quick to light up. "Really, she decided! I'm so relieved, and excited, of course. I can understand her dilemma, having faced that myself, nearly twenty years ago!" She looked at Anton meaningfully, the proud product of her decision. "But watch out. You'll have to be on your toes! A Super-FGE in the family!"

"Ho ho ho! Trying to scare me, Ma?" Anton burst into affectionate laughter.

"What fun am I missing here?" Samir inquired as he joined them. The day's challenges were etched on his weary face. As Ella told him of Zainab's decision, his wrinkled forehead relaxed. For Samir, news of his granddaughter-to-be was exhilarating, far beyond his usual fascination with the continuity of cultural history and family heritage of exceptional women in all the family lines. He sank into the sofa happy, tears of joy shining in his eyes. Tenderly caressing his head, Ella sat by him. After a few moments of silence, she asked Anton, who was peering out the window at the deep red and violet sunset sky, apparently lost in thought, "What is *your* next assignment, babe?"

"Next Friday I leave for Venus, the crystal planet," Anton replied briefly, still staring out the window. His relative quietness intrigued his mother. She didn't understand his casual, evasive reference to a very important and decisive venture to Venus.

"That's your favorite planet! You don't seem excited."

"Oh, I am. I am," he said, walking away from the window toward his parents. Thinking about something else, deeper, staring at the deep violet amethyst on the coffee table, the stone's natural facets catching the rays of the setting sun, he spoke gently, tenderly. "Ma, intuitively I know the baby will help humans on their next evolutionary ascent. I *feel* it, know it."

Samir and Ella stared eagerly at him. They *knew* something deep was brewing in Anton's intuitive state.

Still gazing into the glowing amethyst, Anton responded, smiling, but with an uncanny strength starting to vibrate in his voice, "The human evolutionary process has brought us to a level where old concepts need a new language, new interpretations. You taught me that when I was thirteen. I guess." His eyes dreamy, he shifted his gaze back to the window, toward the setting Sun's rays. "When Zainab told me of her decision, I *knew* their daughter is Kalki, that the new human evolutionary moment has arrived. That she is the incarnation all ancient traditions have been waiting for: Maitreya, the Messiah, the second coming of Christ, Mahdi and so on. *These names represented a deeper and higher reality than humanity had fully personally experienced or expressed in those times. In these times, at last we have words for the ultimate, shared by all:* Kumar's daughter is our Energy Essence."

At this last sentence, *Samir and Ella felt a powerful unearthly infusion of energy in Anton's words, which resumed from its innermost depth.* "Pa," he said, turning toward them, "you always said one day we will reach superconsciousness." Evidently Anton's super-enhanced FGE neuron chips were on fire. "A little while back, watching the setting Sun, I envisioned a magical mathematical formula that described Kalki riding on the unicorn of technology, carrying a transformational sword with the power to awaken humanity." Samir, transfixed into that rarest of conditions – at a loss for words – kept staring at his son with fatherly pride, joy, and contentment.

Ella was shaking: she *felt* Anton's enlivened spirit. Looking into his eyes, she said, "You've intuited something profound, son. And it is validated by mathematical formula. Stay with it. Let it be absorbed within you. Your words come from a *deep knowingness* of the non-dual ultimate One."

Anton briefly returned her gaze, smiling, and abruptly shifted the moment: "When is Kumar coming home? I wonder how *he'll* respond to these vagaries of my mind!" No matter how advanced, how transcendent Anton became in life, he was always aware of Kumar's big-brother attitude, at once critical and protective.

They heard a drone land on the roof. Ella, still reeling a little from the power of the communal moment with Anton, and his sudden energetic departure from it, said dizzily, "Check it yourself, here he is."

Kumar strode into the room and glanced around at everyone, expecting to have to interrupt a conversation to be included in it. "It's unusually quiet in here, considering Anton's in the room. What's happening?"

"Ask Zainab," Anton suggested "Here she is."

Zainab rushed into the room to meet Kumar with open arms. "You've arrived at an important moment. "I had a dream, dear, and I've reached a decision, with assistance from someone you know well" – she turned her smiling eyes toward Anton. "We will have FGE-6 for our baby." Now grinning uncontrollably, Zainab Khan was lost in overjoyed Kuman Pundit's loving arms.

⁓ᐟ⁄⁓

Each in the family was savoring the magic moment in a unique way.

Anton was thrilled that the future Kalki in his vision was riding a unicorn, not only the emblem of technological strength and genius, but an emanation of the quantum-mathematical descriptors of existence.

Ella saw the culmination of her FGE project blooming into the next generation, continuing the family saga of feminine power.

Samir broke his silence. "I know in my bones that Kumar's daughter is Sri Aurobindo's Savitri reborn, embodying superconsciousness. Savitri rescued her dead husband from the god of death. She will lead our green Earth to the new galactic Force, capturing the ultimate Energy Essence, TattvaShakti."

Kumar listened intently to his father's words, then paused a moment before responding. "That I see clearly," he said. "She will indeed have the genetic capability to lead humankind to its next evolutionary step."

"That's a heavy weight to carry, Kumar," Zainab said, laughing merrily holding her belly. She had shifted the energy, again, and smiles, hugs, and good cheer filled the room.

"Stay Awake" floated mingling in the surround.

About the Author

Born and raised in India, Jayana Clerk was educated in three major regions of the world, specializing in English Literature, World Literature, and World Religions. With a BA from the University of London and a MA from Gujarat University in India, she went on to earn a PhD and MPhil from Columbia University in New York. Her literary teaching career soon included the World Literature of Asia, Africa, and South America as well as Native American Literature, leading to a Presidential Award for Distinguished Teaching and a commission from HarperCollins to publish a textbook of Non-Western Literature.

In 1996, being struck by Sedona's red rocks, she retired early yet continues to share her extraordinary insights. Her focus continues to be the paradigm shift for global harmony, awakening consciousness through understanding and inclusion of the "other." Her extensive travels around the world are as much travels within, an integration of inner and outer realities.

45410351R00151

Made in the USA
Middletown, DE
17 May 2019